Suzann Ledbetter

DELIVERANCE DRIVE

A SIGNET BOOK

SIGNET
Published by the Penguin Group
Penguin Books USA Inc., 375 Hudson Street,
New York, New York 10014, U.S.A.
Penguin Books Ltd, 27 Wrights Lane,
London W8 5TZ, England
Penguin Books Australia Ltd, Ringwood,
Victoria, Australia
Penguin Books Canada Ltd, 10 Alcorn Avenue,
Toronto, Ontario, Canada M4V 3B2
Penguin Books (N.Z.) Ltd, 182–190 Wairau Road,
Auckland 10, New Zealand

Penguin Books Ltd, Registered Offices:
Harmondsworth, Middlesex, England

First published by Signet, an imprint of Dutton Signet,
a division of Penguin Books USA Inc.

First Printing, September, 1996
10 9 8 7 6 5 4 3 2 1

Dedicated to Fred Bean
and in memory of Andy Adams

Chapter One

Jenna Wade French stretched on tiptoes to take her husband's photograph from the whipsawed mantel. She peered at Guthrie's goateed countenance; how the flash of phosphorus had blanched his blue eyes to a ghostly pewter.

Her fingertips traced his features, boyish even at twenty-six. A face too innocent to inspire distrust was key to Guthrie's dubious success.

Laying the oval frame on the cabin's floor, she planted a heel squarely at the bridge of his nose. The glass snapped like a pistol shot. Spiderweb cracks darted at myriad angles.

"You were a scoundrel, head to heels, Guthrie French," she said. "I'm sorry you're dead, but not an jot sorry you're gone."

She gripped the hearth brush in one hand and ash shovel in the other. Kneeling to clear away the jagged shards and glittery bits, she recalled their whirlwind courtship.

"It's a whole new world I'm bound for, Jenna," he'd proclaimed a few days after they'd

met. His horse had thrown a shoe, and he'd
happened upon the Wade farm, hoping for a
replacement. "For all the newspapers and books
boasting of the West's wide-open spaces, can
you imagine glaciers reaching their icy noses to
the sky? Millions of acres of primeval forests
too glorious for artists to capture in oil?

"Come with me to Canada, darling. We'll be
the Adam and Eve of the wilderness."

It had all sounded so romantic to an eighteen-year-old farmgirl destined to marry a local
boy and raise chickens, hogs, crops, and children on a plat of stark, midwestern prairie.

On August ninth, eighteen-and-seventy-one,
no sooner than a circuit-riding preacher declared them man and wife, they'd headed
northwest on horseback. Their union was con-
summated on a grimy blanket, the act witnessed by the pair of ear-twitching mares
tethered nearby.

Guthrie had rolled off her and onto his side.
Within minutes, his ghastly snores competed
with coyotes yipping at the sliver of a moon.
Jenna lay awake a long time, wondering what
inspired all those songwriters' and poets' passionately romantic notions.

"Adam and Eve?" She chuckled mirthlessly,
edging the shovel's lip over a crack in the
floorboards. "For three miserable years we
scrapped like Cain and Abel. And Guthrie's fascination with Canada lasted only until snow

swirled to ten-foot drifts and chilblains numbed our faces and feet."

Despite the murderous weather, her affection for the land had evolved into an abiding quality. There was more than simply twenty-two hundred miles separating the rugged Cassiar District from Hay Springs, Nebraska.

British Columbia's savagely beautiful terrain was as awe-inspiring as it was treacherous. Mere words couldn't describe how dawn bathed cloud-derbied mountain peaks and glaciers in salmon pink light, deepening to majestic blues and purples. She'd seen river canyons so steep their rims seemed to graze the sky, and vast, wildflowered meadows that magically emerged from beneath winter's heavy blanket of snow.

Glass tinkled merrily as Jenna dumped it in the ash bin. "We could have been happy here, if you'd only loved me back. Needed me for something besides a shill for your schemes, a bedwarmer, and—"

Knuckles rapped sharply on the cabin door. After smoothing her hair from her forehead and the wrinkles from her cheap wool skirt, Jenna opened the door just enough to recognize "Cayuse" Mike Duncan's wind-burned cheeks appled above his sandy beard.

"May I come in, Missus French? It's a sad day to be sure, and a blustery one here on the stoop."

Good manners overcame the clenching sensation in her belly. She motioned him inside, then shut the door against the frigid wind, leaving the thong latch dangling.

The region's most successful entrepreneur smiled kindly at her while he removed his mittens, malmot hat, and turka. He stood only an inch or two taller than her five-foot-five and likely outweighed her by no more than a stone, but his presence filled the chilly, dark room.

He took stock of the narrow bunk draped by a tattered quilt; the upended barrel that served as a table with two crates for chairs. A whomperjawed oak safe near the fireplace held tin plates, mugs, a fork, two spoons, a carving knife, a scoured iron skillet, and a dented bucket.

If it's high tea you're expecting, there's not enough food in that cupboard for mice to trouble themselves, Jenna mused. Especially for one whose breath smells of fruit brandy and two-bit cigars.

"You've made a cozy nest from this breezy, old shack," he said, rubbing his palms together.

"What do you want, Mister Duncan?"

His slate eyes widened innocently. "To offer condolence at your husband's passing, of course. Why else would I be here?"

She hugged her arms at her chest. "Let's see, there's rent money overdue, Guthrie's gambling debts to collect . . ."

"Do you think me so flint-hearted as that?" He settled cautiously on a crate. "It's hardly my fault that your husband preferred fleecing others out of their hard-earned cash to working for an honest dollar."

Ah, and the pot does call the kettle black, she thought, silently. Her uninvited visitor and his henchmen plundered the Cassiar's riches as ruthlessly as pirates once controlled the seas.

Aloud, she replied, "Guthrie left little more than a gold-plated watch and a pair of sterling cufflinks, but you'll get what's owed you. Somehow."

Duncan flicked a splot of mud from his custom-tailored, pinstriped trousers. The dapper scoundrel always wore suits, silk ties, and boiled shirts more appropriate to a Stateside banker.

"I take it, Guthrie didn't tell you of his latest project?"

An ominous shiver ricked Jenna's spine. She'd never been able to decide which was worse: knowing what skullduggery her husband was perpetrating and on whom, or remaining ignorant until his outraged victims accosted her on the street.

A chuckle rumbled from Duncan's throat. "You're far too pretty to wear such a grim expression, my dear. It's good news I've brought you, not bad."

"Oh? And what might that be?"

"Several months ago, Guthrie borrowed seven hundred dollars to buy a herd of cattle and have it shipped by steamer to Glenora—"

"Wha-at!" Her heart plummeted to her boot tops.

Duncan raised a manicured hand. "Hear me out, Missus French. The animals are due to arrive tomorrow morning. I'm prepared to buy them for three thousand dollars, minus the amount your husband already owed."

Jenna mentally calculated the difference. "Ye gods, that leaves twenty-three hundred dollars."

"Actually, twenty-one," he corrected. "Lady Luck abandoned your beloved a while back during a hotly contested hand of poker. I covered his losses."

Jenna winced, remembering all too vividly Guthrie's lurching into the cabin, raving at being cheated by a card sharp named Quincy Trent. Questioning why he'd challenged a professional in the first place was answered with the back of his hand.

Duncan rose to his feet. "There'll be a bank draft made out to you at the River Queen by noon tomorrow. That is, if you don't mind being seen entering a gaming house."

Jenna hesitated, a warning rattling in her mind. "Might I have a little time to consider your offer?"

Duncan's eyes narrowed to a feral squint.

Hastily, she added, "Not that it isn't generous. But so much has happened the last few days, what with Guthrie's passing and all, why, I simply can't think straight."

He squeezed her forearm gently. "Though I

realize no amount of money can relieve your grief, such a sum will ease your circumstances. It's the future you must think of, Missus French."

Don't try to con a con man's widow, Mister Duncan, Jenna thought, lowering her gaze demurely. If Guthrie taught me anything, it's that deals that seem too good to be true always are.

"I will, sir," she assured. "I can promise you that."

Chapter Two

Dan Brannum knocked the soles of his size twelve boots against the outer wall of the trading post. With each thud a goodly heap of Glenora's main street splattered on the boardwalk.

April was half over, but the wind slithering down his collar traced his backbone like a doxy's fingernails. "The Cassiar's only got two seasons," he grumbled. "Froze solid nine months a year. Mucky as a hog waller the other three."

Inside the post, Twyford Chaney was bent over a ledger, scowling at its ruled pages. Dan maneuvered around crates, barrels, and tow sacks to reach the counter. "Jaysus, Twyford. Looks like a grizzly ruckused through here in the wee hours."

The trader snorted and slapped the ledger shut. "The Stikine finally broke up enough for a supply steamer to make it upriver. Been too busy cogitating how to pay for all this stuff to get it stowed proper."

Dan grinned, his mouth watering at the heady aroma of fresh oranges, tobacco, coffee beans, and cured meat. "Well, this is your lucky day, amigo. It'll be my pleasure to take a fair load of it off your hands."

"You lighting out for the Clearwater River diggings?"

"Yep. Had a powerful feeling all winter that my third year'll be a charm. Can't count the nights I've dreamed of gold dust winking at me from those sluice riffles."

"Uh-huh. You and about a thousand other flat-poked prospectors."

Dan scratched his heavy black beard. "Maybe so, but there's a difference between me and them. When the snow starts flyin' again, they'll still be dreaming."

He reached into his pocket and drew out a creased scrap of paper. "That's the provisions I'll need. If I forgot something, just toss it on the pile."

Twyford's eyes flicked over the list and back at Dan. "How're you going to finance it?"

"Same as always, I reckon."

The trader shook his head slowly. "I can't carry you on tick this year, Dan. That big company over on the Tahltan stiffed me for a couple of thousand dollars worth of goods." He jabbed a thumb at the center of the room. "It'll take pert-near every nickel I've got to pay the freight on that shipment."

A flush blazed up Dan's neck. "I'm good for it, Chaney. You damn well know I am."

The storekeep crossed his arms atop a paunch that Buddha would have envied. "If I didn't, it wouldn't bother me to tell you no. Fact is, I'd stake you before anybody in the District, if I could."

Dan nodded. "Yeah, I know you would. Sorry I got a tad snorty."

"Can't say as I blame you. There's something about spring that makes a man feel like a cat locked in a cupboard."

Striding toward the door, Dan replied over his shoulder, "Well, this old tom's gonna scat for the hills, one way or t'other."

Hunching his shoulders nearly to his ear-lobes, he clomped along the boardwalk, feeling almost as sorry for Chaney as he did for himself. Almost, but not quite.

"Claim or no claim, a prospector without a grubstake's like a cowhand without a horse," he muttered. "Maybe I'll give it up. Wander down Dakota-way. If that don't pan, they say Nevada Territory's flat crawling with silver ore."

He slapped a post with the flat of his hand. A slab of snow the size of a springwagon's bed groaned off the overhang and exploded in the street.

"Hardly ever saw snow before I came to this godforsaken country. Sure as hell won't fret me none to never see it again."

Hours later, with a sociable amount of the

Kingchauch Saloon's cheapest whiskey smoldering in his belly, Dan was cheating himself at a hand of patience when a sultry voice declared, "I'm told you're from Texas."

He looked up at a dark-eyed, heart-shaped face pretty enough to bring harp music and hosannas to mind. Her willowy, hourglass figure inspired less pious speculations.

"That's right. Born and raised in the San Antonio Valley, if it's particulars you're after."

"Then you know the cattle trade."

He curried his mustaches between a thumb and forefinger. "Think so, eh? Where do you hail from, little lady?"

"Uh . . . Nebraska, but—"

"I reckon that makes you a sodbuster, then don't it?"

The woman dug her fists into her hips. "Mister Brannum, I didn't come here to match wits. As we speak, sixty-five cows are being unloaded at the dock. I need them and the freight they'll carry taken to the gold fields at Dease Lake, immediately."

Nicolai Petrove, the barkeep, chuckled like a beaver gnawing pine bark. Dan aimed a withering glance in his direction. To the cattle baroness he said, "Appears you've got the drop on me. You're wise to my handle, but I don't know you from Adam's off-ox."

She hesitated. Her high cheekbones glowed crimson. "Jenna French. Missus Jenna French."

Guthrie French's widow, he thought. Figured

as much. White women were as scarce as
prickly pears in northern British Columbia.
Dan had run on to only one fire-and-brimstone
missionary and a couple of crow-baity whores
since he arrived in seventy-one.

"Pull up a seat, Miz French."

"I'd rather not."

He eyed the stubborn set of her chin, the
mended rents in her gray jersey dress, the
cameo choker banding her long neck. "Suit
yourself. I won't talk down to you, but damned
if I'm gonna talk *up* to you, either."

Grudgingly, she dragged a chair from beneath the table edge and settled in its seat.

"All right, let's start the race over from the
gate, little lady. How'd you come into this passel of beeves?"

"My late husband had them shipped from
Washington Territory. I knew nothing about it
until last night."

"Got a bill of sale?"

She chuckled, but there was no humor in it.
"It appears that Guthrie's last deal was cut
square, Mister Brannum."

First time for everything, Dan thought wryly.
French had bilked greenhorns on everything
from crooked shell games to worthless "Aurum
Detecting Devices"—dousing rods designed to
quiver when gold deposits were detected.

His scheming caught up with him three days
earlier when a company of prospectors discovered that the claim he'd sold them was not only

salted, the conniver had never even owned it. French was doing his best to trade the blood-eyed argonauts for an "absolutely guaranteed bonanza" when one put a bullet through his head, then jerked him to Jesus for good measure.

"Seeing as how everything's nice and legal, wouldn't it be a helluva lot simpler to sell your herd here in Glenora?"

"Believe it or not, that solution already occurred to me. Cayuse Mike Duncan's offered twenty-one hundred dollars—"

"That's all Mike'd go? Jaysus, a coupla sled-dog rigs'd bring that much."

"True," she replied, "but it's a far-sight more money than anyone else in the District has stashed under a mattress."

Damn straight on that, Dan agreed silently. If I had anything besides dust and mouse turds under mine, I'd be five miles closer to my claim by now.

"Reckon that does leave you between a rock, a hard place, and cow-poor," he said aloud. "I know the feeling. When I was a kid, Pa gauged how bad off we were by how many longhorns we had grazing."

He paused for her response, but received only the merest hint of a smile. "No disrespect intended, but I'd bet your dearly departed couldn't tell a dewclaw from a single-tree. Do you know what kind of, uh, cows he bought?"

She leaned forward on one elbow, furrows

tined between her brows. "Mostly red ones, Mister Brannum," she said, her voice as grave as a schoolmaster's. "Big, husky, red ones."

Strangling noises, like a barrow rooting fresh slops, burbled in Dan's throat. He averted his gaze to the caribou head mounted above the bar, the raftered ceiling, the yellow-keyed upright piano, everywhere but at Jenna French's stone-serious expression.

He coughed into his fist a few times to compose himself. "I don't mean to be indelicate, ma'am, but are you sure they're cows?"

A weary sigh whistled through her lips. "To be honest, I'm not real sure of anything right now."

Whoa, Dan, he cautioned himself. Don't let those sad, doe eyes churn you like butter. You've got troubles enough without borrowing a swindler's widow's.

"I wish I could help you, but I'm heading out in the morning. Got a claim that was showing glitter-dust before Old Man Winter put the kibosh to it."

"I'll pay you five hundred dollars to trail-boss the herd north, Mister Brannum."

"You don't have five hundred dollars, Miz French."

"I will, when they're sold in Laketon and the freight fees are collected."

Amusement and admiration collided in his mind. She was gambling with the iron nerve that comes from nothing left to lose. In poker,

DELIVERANCE DRIVE   **21**

that kind of grit drags the pot as often as paired aces.

Aloud, he itemized the complications involved in the venture. "A hundred-and-twenty miles of gut-bustin' mountain lay between here and there. If you used that new trail, the tolls'd gobble the profit.

"Mules don't take the climb easy—never heard of anyone even trying it with cattle. And I ain't too sure about using bovines for pack animals, neither."

"All of which is why I need someone with experience," she shot back. "It's worth six-fifty to me to get it."

Dan flipped the row of playing cards face-down. He bowed the trey of diamonds like a shovel blade, scooped them into a neat stack, and shuffled them expertly.

"Yeah, and that'd make it late June, more likely, mid-July before I could start sluicin' up at the Clearwater."

"Seven hundred, Mister Brannum."

He considered his long supply list and the four dollars and change in his pocket. His thumb whipsawed the edge of the deck.

"For heaven's sake, Mister Brannum." Jenna French's strident tone abruptly ended Dan's reverie. "Has that rotgut addled your brain?"

"No, ma'am. Leastways, not enough to take a job driving a herd by myself. Much less, afoot."

Her full lips curved ever so slightly upward. "Four horses and tack were shipped with the cattle. A cook and two additional hands will be ready to leave at dawn."

"Provisions?"

"I traded Mister Chaney two of the animals for a month's supplies. I believe I've thought of everything, Mister Brannum."

"Not quite, Miz French."

"Oh?"

"Have you thought about what you're gonna do when I turn you down flat?"

"You won't."

"What makes you so damn sure I won't?"

She stood and splayed her fingers on the table. Faint traces of lemon verbena flirted with his nose. In a voice hardly louder than a whisper, she said, "Because, Mister Brannum, you're a stubborn, surly, arrogant son of a bitch, but I don't think you're stupid enough to turn down a thousand dollars hard cash for a month's work."

Dan grinned up at her. Jenna French was prettier than an April morning—positively breathtaking with a burr under her saddle. At that moment he'd have gladly carried those beeves all the way to Laketon.

"No, ma'am, I reckon I ain't. I suspect you've done bought yourself a cowboy."

Chapter Three

Delmonico's Restaurant was doing a land office business when Dan sauntered in for supper. The musky odor of buckskin, fur-lined parkas, and unwashed bodies competed with the aroma of fresh-baked bread, boiled coffee, and moose stew.

Francois LaDue, the eating house's owner, was a devout believer in simplicity. The night's menu consisted of whatever he'd felt like cooking that morning, and plenty of it.

No sooner than a customer found an opening along one of the three ten-foot sawbucks, one of LaDue's Chinese waiters filled the elbow space with clean tableware, a bread basket, and a steaming platter of food. Bowls of tallow butter and crocks of applesauce marched down the center of the table inviting a boardinghouse reach.

Dan eased his long legs into an empty slot at the far side of the room. Nodding at the adjacent diners, he grinned when he spied Milo Woolley hunkered catawampus across the table, dredging pot liquor from his plate with a fat chunk of sourdough.

"Surprised to see you're still around, Milo. Figured you'd be rocking a long tom on Sheep Creek by now."

"Naw, we ain't found a scrap of color up there in two blessed years. Me and a couple of the boys is aimin' to follow the Stikine east into the high country."

"Who's staking you?"

Milo leaned back to allow a waiter to ladle another helping of stew. He grunted his thanks, then said, "Good ol' Cayuse Mike."

Dan shook his head. It seemed like sooner or later, everyone in the Cassiar got themselves in hock to the wily Scotsman. Legend had it that a nubile Indian maiden he used to warm his sheets originated the Cayuse nickname. But those who crossed him found out fast and usually fatally, that like an outlaw bronc, Duncan was a cold-eyed man-killer.

"That ain't Robin Hood you're hooked up with," Dan remarked. "What percentage'll you boys have to pay if you strike?"

"Seventy-five," Milo grunted. " 'Cept seventy-five percent of nothin's nothin', too. Least we'll eat good while we're goin' broke."

The burly prospector wiped his lips with his sleeve. "Why don't you throw in with us? Won't cost nothin' but your life if the bastard decides we shorted him an ounce or three."

Dan washed a mouthful of stew down his

gullet with a swig of coffee. A swipe of his tongue cleared some of the bitter grounds from his teeth. "Appreciate the offer, but I've got an ace in the hole playing. Say, you've drifted more territory than I have up here. What can you tell me about Guthrie French?"

Milo's watery hazel eyes narrowed at the mention. "That he's deader'n Abe Lincoln, mostly. Good goddamn riddance."

"He put the cozen to you?"

"Naw, but he sure monkeyshined a passel of greenhorns. Come up here a couple of years ago with his bride—pretty gal. Musta been plumb lolly-eyed over that grifter to trail him from one camp to another. They departed most of 'em a few hours ahead of a peacemaker."

"I heard French had a straight sure thing working when he got rope-burned."

"Uh-huh. Heard a feller could gather gold nuggets like hens' eggs in this District, too. Guess them pullets quit layin' afore I got here."

"How about his wife? She's a sidewinder, too?"

Milo shoveled up a huge measure of applesauce and dumped it on his plate. "I figure she got screwed—no joke meant—the worst of anyone. Guthrie could sell a canoe to an Injun easier'n I could sell branch water in the desert. He must've painted her a sweet picture to get her up here, then kept her so broke and beholden she couldn't leave."

Interesting, Dan mused. That's how Chaney

spells it, too. Aloud, he said, "Ain't that the way of it? The bad actors always waltz away with the fairest gals at the dance."

"Yeah, but"—Milo winked at him slyly—"them buck-toothed, ox-butted homelies huggin' the wall shore can get grateful for the attention."

Dan laughed as he stood to drag a few coins out of his pocket. They chinked on the table in front of his plate. "Godspeed and good luck to you, Milo."

Outside, moonlight glistened off the street's mucky puddles and silvered the melting snowbanks. The faint, off-key conspiracy of banjo and Jew's harp belting "Camptown Races" drifted from the Kingchautch Saloon.

Glenora's boardwalks were all but deserted. Those who lacked for funds warmed themselves beneath blankets; flusher nomads polished barlips with their belt buckles.

Near the river landing Dan smelled the earthy scent of cowhide before he saw the cattle. The herd was crammed into a livery corral built for half that number of pack mules. A man could step off the top rail and walk across their backs to the other side without ever touching heel to ground.

Accustomed to snorty, stampede-happy longhorns, Dan hummed a tune as he approached. Several pairs of glassy, bovine eyes angled in his direction, their dark depths holding more hope of rescue than wild defiance.

"Well, you're a pretty tame bunch, ain't ya?"

He noted their barreled torsos and the sleekness of their mottled hides. "Reckon that long boat ride didn't hurt you none. Somebody must've grained you good all the way."

He reached to scratch the nearest animal's poll. The feel of that coarse tuft brought the well-remembered taste of Texas dust billowing up from a struggling calf's haunches on branding day.

The spring before he died, his father was getting ready to copyright a hefty yearling with the Rocking B brand when he paused, squinted at Dan, and handed him the hot iron.

"Been breathin' singed hair for a quarter century, boy. Time you got a snootful."

Micah Brannum wasn't prone to pretty words, Dan thought. *Settling that iron into my glove was the closest my father ever came to telling me he loved me.*

As if the freak accident that cost Micah Brannun his life weren't enough, Dan lost everything else he'd ever cared about the afternoon of the funeral.

For as long as he could remember, his older brother, Darrin, had hated him with a fierceness Dan never understood and was powerless to rectify. Though they resembled each other physically, their personalities and abilities were as opposite as day and night.

Hard as he tried, Darrin simply wasn't cut out for ranch work and resented Dan's easy, "born to the saddle" abilities and the close relationship he forged with Micah because of it, although their father went out of his way not to show favoritism—at times, hurting Dan in the process.

After Preacher Bill expressed his final condolences came Darrin's chance to exact revenge on the brother he despised. Pouring a tumbler of whiskey, he raised the glass and sneered. "Congratulations are in order, Danny boy. It seems that Father's will has left the Rocking B to me, alone."

"You wall-eyed bastard!" Dan snarled. "I was still in knee pants when Pa had those paper drawn up. You know full well he meant for both of us—"

"Too bad he didn't put those intentions in writing, baby brother. Now, move your gear to the bunkhouse with the rest of the hands or get off *my* land. The choice is yours."

Dan's blood had turned to ice. Within arm's reach, a rack of rifles, oiled barrels gleaming deadly blue, had taunted him.

The desk's center drawer slid open. Darrin cocked the hammer on their father's Navy Colt. "Go ahead, Danny boy. Try it. Pa'd appreciate the company."

The Regulator's brass pendulum ticked off several seconds before Dan trusted his voice not to tremble. "Three years, four on the outside is all it'll take for you to destroy what Pa worked half his life to build. I'll be back to buy you out. You'd best keep an eye on your shadow while you're waitin'."

"The Rocking B's mine, Danny boy. You'll never own an acre of it. I'll see to that."

Spinning on one heel, Dan strode toward the door, teeth grinding at Darrin's mocking, triumphant laughter.

The tightly packed herd's mournful bawling brought Dan's mind back to the present.

I wonder who's scabbing hides with Pa's branding iron, now, he thought. Not Darrin, for sure. Ever since that mossy-horned bull put the prod to his backside, he's been scared shitless of cattle.

Dan gave the steer a final pat and turned back toward town. "Damned if it won't be good to have horseflesh under me and a herd behind me again. Driving these beeves'll be easy as leading Baptists to a foot-washin'."

He recalled Milo's earlier remark. "And when I ride in with my saddlebags full of sale money, Lordy, there's just no tellin' how beholden the lovely Widow French is gonna be."

Chapter Four

As Homer Goodacre, the livery owner, cinched a tarp down on a pack-loaded steer, Jenna caught a glimpse of her newly clean-shaven trail boss.

Slouched against a building's corner post, Brannum's lean, broad-shouldered frame dwarfed Mike Duncan's fur-draped profile. Neither man glanced in her direction, but she sensed she was the topic of discussion.

"I'm surprised at your ambitiousness," Duncan had said the day before when she'd told him her plans. Strangely, he hadn't argued or tried to discourage her; only reminded her of Guthrie's outstanding debt before wishing her a safe journey.

I wish Granny Detheridge had taught me to read lips, Jenna thought. The wizened crone had become deaf as a stump, but was quite eagle-eyed. She not only out-gossiped every matron in Hay Springs; they were forced to come to her for the juiciest bits she translated from distant whisperings. That social stew stirring undoubtedly kept her alive long after the customary three score and ten.

Goodacre cursed as heartily as the animal bawled. With its nose snubbed tight against the corral rail, vapor streamed from the animal's flared nostrils. Several dozen other freight-corseted cattle shifted restlessly nearby.

As deftly as a dancer, Goodacre capered with the skittish steer, avoiding its stamping hooves. The animal's tail crooked upward. Steamy, greenish clumps of manure oozed forth and splattered the man's Wellingtons. Jenna chortled and buried her face in the bend of her elbow.

"Mornin', ma'am," Brannum greeted from behind her. He tossed his knapsack and bedroll in a dry trough. "Didn't expect you to see us off."

"It's a fine-looking herd, don't you think?" she said evasively.

"Well, now, I'm partial to longhorns. Only breed I've wrassled with. I suppose these'll swallow all right, if there's any meat left on them when we get there."

"It's your job to see that there is."

"I'll do my best, but like I told you, I'm not convinced these bossies are built for a pack train."

Jenna tipped her slouch hat back on her head. "I don't know why not. Oxen have freighted goods for centuries—"

"Give him what-for, honey," came a voice like hail on a tin roof. "By God, there's more to havin' balls than being born with 'em."

Jenna couldn't help laughing, though she felt her face flush hot. At six-foot-three and nigh three hundred pounds, Yolanda Diamond wasn't the only prostitute in the Cassiar, but was certainly the biggest.

Despite her occupation, Jenna had liked her instantly when they'd bumped into each other, literally, during a blinding blizzard. Yolanda wrapped a beefy arm around her shoulders and all but carried her home to her cabin. After a pot of weak tea and several hilariously bawdy stories, Jenna knew she'd found her first woman friend.

She had no idea how Yolanda heard about the cattle drive, but when she'd begged to join up, Jenna couldn't think of a good reason to refuse.

Twyford Chaney had introduced her to the scowling, eye-patched codger standing in Yolanda's considerable shadow. Known only as "Soupbone," the grizzled, veteran prospector was short on words and social graces, but willing to work cheap.

"Me an' Soupbone's rarin' to go," Yolanda boomed. "Point me toward the stoutest horse you got, and I'll start putting the bow in its backbone."

"In the livery"—Jenna started before an obviously furious Dan Brannum interrupted.

"Sashay over by that tree, Miz French. Now. We've got some talkin' to do."

Jenna opened her mouth to argue, then

thought better of it. Once out of earshot, he growled, "What in God's name are you trying to pull, lady?"

"I'm not trying to *pull* anything. I told you I had a cook and two hands hired. Yolanda, Soupbone, and I are going with you."

"The hell you are."

"The hell we're not. We made a deal yesterday."

Dan stuck his face so close to hers, Jenna could smell the castile soap he'd washed up with. "Where I come from, two drovers and a cook don't savvy into two skirts and Grampa Moses."

She backed away a step, flicking her shoulder-length hair from her face. "I did the best I could. Gold fever's got everyone hightailing it to their claims. Finding any willing, able-bodied help ought to count for something."

"Able-bodied, my a . . ." His voice trailed off, eyes riveted over her head.

A stable boy was leading a cadre of horses from the barn: a pair of grays, a chestnut, and a supple, white-socked black.

"That spikes it," Dan wheezed. "I might be persuaded that a rusty, sunk-cheeked scarecrow can cook something besides kindling. I might even be persuaded to nursemaid you and that whale of a whore cross-country. But I'll be damned if I'll fork a McClellan saddle for a month whilst I'm doing it. If that tack ain't Civil War cavalry surplus, I'll eat it for dinner!"

Through gritted teeth she snarled, "Then you're nothing but a low-down, double-dealin' welsher," and whirled to walk away.

He grabbed her, spinning her around again. "If you weren't a woman, I'd belt you for that."

"If I—"

"Oh, shut the hell up and listen for once. You hired me to trail-boss, except you don't have the slightest idea what that means. I'm telling you for true, it ain't just moseying along with the lead bull's snout poking your horse in the butt."

Like a parson reciting the commandments, he droned, "Battle-dressed ponies aren't rigged for a high-country droving. It's gonna be tough on them and tougher on their riders.

"Steers with a couple hundred pounds of freight on their backs are gonna get snorty, and snorty steers are apt to do anything, any time, day or night. Hands without a lick of cow sense won't be worth two bits for stopping them, either.

"That being the case, it's still the trail boss's job to make sure everyone—man and beast alike—gets across the mountains in one piece. And no one but the trail boss'll be faulted if they don't."

"They're my cattle, and herding them north is my bailiwick," Jenna replied evenly. "I certainly won't blame you if anything goes wrong."

Dan released his hold on her, letting his arms drop to his sides. "Maybe not. But I will."

She stared at him for a long moment, then

glanced over her shoulder. Goodacre was almost finished securing the freight. The stable hand was patiently showing Yolanda how to tie her belongings behind the saddle's cantle. Soupbone's mules brayed and do-si-doed as he hitched clanking camp equipment over their pack trees.

We'll never make it without Brannum, Jenna thought. And I'm in far too deep to back out now. Maybe that's why Duncan was so agreeable. He's betting I'll give up and sell out dirt cheap.

Anger flared like the heat from stirred embers. Maybe that's what Duncan was talking to Dan about: bribing him to quit so I'd have to sell, then driving them to Dease Lake on Duncan's flusher payroll.

With barely controlled fury, she asked, "While I realize the risks involved, would it make any difference if we were partners?"

Dan's eyebrows peaked to his Stetson's brim. "What, like fifty-fifty?"

"More like seventy-thirty."

Grinning for the first time that morning, he drawled, "Sixty-forty's got a nice ring to it."

Jenna nodded curtly and stuck out a hand. "Done."

The touch of his callused fingers closing over hers set off a delicious, unexpected tingle. She jerked from his grasp as if bee-stung.

"You coulda gotten off a lot cheaper, little lady."

"I was prepared to split the take with you yesterday, if need be."

"Oh, you were, huh? Well, seeing as how we're in this together now, what do you suspect those beeves'll go for at Laketon?"

She smiled, recalling the estimate Chaney ciphered on a piece of butcher paper. "Freight fees and slaughter price together should bring in the neighborhood of thirty thousand dollars. Minus expenses, of course."

Brannum let loose a low whistle. "That's a right fine neighborhood we're in, partner."

"All we've got to do is get them to it, trail boss."

"Yeah," he grunted. "It ain't gonna be easy."

Jenna smiled ruefully. "I don't know the meaning of the word 'easy,' but I plan to learn with the proceeds."

Rocking back on his heels, he asked, "Mind if I ask a couple more questions before we light out?"

"Such as?"

"Can you shoot?"

Relieved that his inquiry wasn't of a personal nature as she feared, Jenna replied jauntily, "Better than that, I generally plug what I'm aiming for and surely will with the Sharps I bartered out of Mister Chaney. In case you're curious, I can't embroider worth a hoot, though."

He reared back and belly-laughed. "Fair

enough. How about forking a saddle? Most ladies are kinda tetchy about that."

"Most ladies wouldn't hie off into the wilderness in the company of a man they weren't married to, either," she countered. "How I get there's the least of my worries."

"That's the other thing I aimed to ask you about," he said, studying the slushy ground. "You're already standing in Guthrie's shade. Folks are bound to talk about your going off with me . . . even Soupbone, if they're bored enough."

Jenna shrugged her shoulders. "Let 'em."

"You really won't be hurt if that happens?"

"No, but what about you? Heavenly days, consorting with the notorious Missus Guthrie might prove your ruination."

Dan looked at her as straight as a banker ruminating a hefty loan. "I'll risk it. Any time."

Tipping his hat, he ambled away toward the livery. She paused, oddly confused, wary, and elated by his remark, depending upon its myriad interpretations.

Turning to follow, she saw a figure watching from one of the River Queen's second-story windows. Cayuse Mike, without a doubt. Suddenly, she felt like a pawn in a game she didn't know how to play, much less, win.

"The foolishness of fools is folly," she muttered. "Keep your head, Jenna French, or that ornery Texan'll make a fool of you, too."

Chapter Five

The McClellan saddle's center slot and wooden seat fit Jenna's anatomy like rail fence fit a high-straddled dog. She squirmed, wishing for the first time in her life that her rump had the Wade side of the family's two-shoats-in-a-sack proportions.

Cracks in the rawhide sidebars left rents as sharp as sawteeth. They nipped the insides of her thighs through sturdy canvas Levi's and the itchy drawers she wore beneath them.

Her chestnut gelding seemed unmindful of the saddle's weight and her own. Neck bowed, it nuzzled the chartreuse sprigs of grass that braved the diminishing snow cover.

Dan sidled his supple black mount among the scattered, obviously unhappy steers. Several rubbed against tree trunks, their packs scraping the bark with raspy groans.

"Je-hosophat," Yolanda bellowed, hopping sideward with one boot planted in the wooden stirrup. Her awkward capering strained the seams in her dungarees to the limit.

"Stand still, you rat-ugly grulla, or I'll make you a true mare."

Soupbone grabbed its halter to steady the animal. "Ain't rid many hosses, eh, Yolanda?"

Her face was purely deadpan. "The opportunity don't arise very often, bub."

"Saddle up, snappy," Dan ordered. "A few words need saying before we move out."

An excited flutter, like hummingbird wings, commenced in Jenna's belly. *Am I a lunatic to even attempt such a dangerous venture?* A timid voice at the back of her mind answered a resounding yes. With a snorty chuckle Jenna squeezed the stiff leather fenders with her knees, guiding her horse toward the waiting trail boss.

Dan slumped against the cantle, hands crossed atop the wishbone pommel. "First day or three, we won't tarry for cooking noon victuals. There's a parcel of bacon biscuits yonder, so keep your pockets full or go hungry."

"How about resting the horses?" Soupbone inquired slyly. "We run these glue makers into the ground, and we'll be riding shoe leather from there on out."

"We'll rest regularly and no faster'n we'll be traveling, they'll go it all right. Main thing is, I want the steers plenty tuckered so's they'll forget those packs and bed down nice as lambs."

Jenna surveyed the milling, heavy-laden herd. "I guess the faster we get to Laketon, the easier it'll be on them, too."

Yolanda fairly cackled. "Save some of that frettin' for us, honey. We'll be wearing our butts for earbobs before the week's out."

"Flapdoodlin' females," Soupbone growled. "Hush up and let the boy speak his peace."

Judging by his expression, Jenna could tell Dan wasn't fond of being called a boy, but he continued as if he hadn't heard. "The secret to getting beeves to head how you want them to is letting them think it's their idea."

He pointed at a shaggy, brockled steer. "That there's General Sherman. He's gonna lead the rest of these troops on the trail. Soupbone, you'll ride point and keep the General on the straight and narrow."

The cook gawked at the massive, one-horned beast. "Now boy, I hear tell that the pot-rustler's usually brings up the rear."

Dan glared at him from beneath his hat brim. "You heard wrong, old-timer, and there ain't much usual about this enterprise anyhow. Unless you're heart's set on breathing cowshit, I'm riding drag. Ya'll are too shiny to turn my back on up front."

Soupbone grunted an inaudible reply, then geed his mottled gray and the two mules tethered to it in the direction of the riverbank.

"Jenna, you're swing and Yolanda, the flanker. Let the steers string out if they've a mind to, but don't let them mosey too far afield. Put about twenty between you gals and ride

amongst them if you want, long as you keep a
sharp watch for stragglers."

From the corner of her eye, Jenna glimpsed
Yolanda's sober expression. Topped by a bizarre,
tri-cornered hat, a mass of kinky, bottle-blonde
hair tumbled to her shoulder blades. Her ruddy,
pocked complexion appeared puffy, rather than
just amply fleshed.

Yolanda's as nervous as I am and as hellbent
not to show it, Jenna thought. Surely, she has
her reasons, good ones, for signing on with this
outfit, but I can't feature what they are.

"Hullo, Miz French," Dan called sarcasti-
cally. "If you're through woolgathering, we've
got a ton of steak to deliver up north."

"Sorry, boss."

He stroked his mustaches to hide a sly smile.
"Sweet talking won't get you nowhere with me,
missy. Put your heels to that cayuse and start
cowboying proper."

A smart flick of a rope to General Sherman's
haunch sent him and dozens of his brethren
lumbering toward Soupbone. He casually adjusted his eyepatch, reached to scratch a nit
near his privates, then spit a stream of tobacco
at a fir stump. His way, Jenna guessed, of showing Dan that straw-bossing thousands of
pounds of muscle-bound bovines was no sweat
for a old salt like himself.

Boys to men, the sons of Adam simply never
outgrow the need to be king of the hill, she
mused. It'll be fascinating to see the elder stag

and the young buck tussle for sway. If I were
a betting woman, I'd give a slight edge to Soupbone. After all, a smart man doesn't trifle with
the fellow in charge of the ladle.

Yolanda's banshee whoops startled the animals that had drifted into the trees. Bawling
and craning their necks to glower at the packs
juddering on their backbones, the steers trotted
straight for the river.

Then, as if divinely inspired, they suddenly
veered from the rest of the herd.

"Swing 'em," Dan yelled.

Jenna wheeled her chestnut, its hooves
churning the soft earth. Leaning into the pommel, she maneuvered alongside their white-
faced leader. Snouts held high, neck muscles
straining, the animals hardly wavered an inch
from their preferred course.

Angling slightly ahead of them, she used her
mount's massive body to divert them into a lazy,
leftward crescent. With the Stikine River on the
south and Yolanda denying them a northerly
break, the cattle lurched between the trees, re-
joining their kin like yearlings down a chute.

A huge sigh of relief gusted past Jenna's lips.
She peered over her shoulder at Dan, expecting
approval for a job well done.

"Jaysus, a whole twenty yards behind us already and only one nigh stampede. Ya'll are
born cowhands, and that's a fact."

Jenna about-faced. "Smart-mouthed . . .
Texan." Cantering past Yolanda to take her po-

sition in the sluggish bovine parade, she heard the calico queen stage-whisper, "Kinda strains the notion that God made them in His own image, don't it?"

The chestnut's porch-glider gait and the herd's surprisingly docile cooperation let Jenna's knotted muscles slacken and allowed eyes to wander beyond the tick-tock swagger of twenty-seven lumps of diamond-hitched canvas.

She realized that labeling the sparse, ice-patched swale meandering between the Stikine and the dense forest a "trail" would be the kind of embroidery Guthrie was famous for.

The steers stumbled like drunkards over deadfalls and stobs lurking beneath the clinging snow cover. A slurping concerto of cloven hooves trampling manure into the permafrost competed with Soupbone's horrific, tuneless wails of "Nobody Knows the Trouble I've Seen."

Jenna chuckled. *No wonder I've hardly glimpsed a bird overhead. That sourdough's rusty-hinge screeches would send hungry bears loping for their dens.*

She reached into her mackinaw pocket and pulled out a biscuit with bacon wedged in the split. Left too long in the Delmonico's oven and now half-frozen, the crust snapped when she bit down. Grimacing at the taste of clabbered grease and bitter soda dust, she chewed quickly and lofted her chin like a baby robin, an art well practiced during childhood due to her mother's abiding belief in castor oil's curative properties.

By the shadows' gnarled, spidery fingers reaching out from the trees, she reckoned it to be around two o'clock. A world away, Mama's probably scouring skillets and pots left from dinner, pausing only to brush gray, tickling strands of hair from her brow.

For a moment she longed for that drafty lean-to kitchen and the aloof, puritanical woman who reigned there almost as passionately as Jenna wanted shed of them when Guthrie proposed the means.

Naturally, Drucilla Detheridge Wade despised Jenna's suitor at first sight, whereas Hank Wade, her twinkle-eyed imp of a father, had been enthralled by Guthrie's adventures on Mississippi riverboats and in exotic ports like Baton Rouge and Cairo, Illinois.

Maybe I am as flighty as Pa, she mused. Selfish and ungrateful for those sacrifices Mama was forever telling us she'd made. But was it truly so wrong to want more from life than just enduring it?

Granny Detheridge certainly hadn't hidden her lights under bushel baskets to keep their shine from being seen. Though she'd exceeded her biblical allotment by several years—even Mama wasn't sure how many since Granny altered her birthdate with impunity—that cotton-haired sprite told anyone who'd listen how she'd buried five husbands run off a sixth with a scattergun, and retained the last name of the original just because she'd liked it best.

Jenna's neck wrenched painfully when the chestnut shied from a steer's pole-axing hind legs. Heart pounding, she grabbed for the sloped pommel to keep her seat.

"They're balled too tight, Jenna," Dan hollered from his drag position. "String them out like I told you."

"Yes, boss," she muttered, reining in to comply. "Whatever you say, boss."

The grade steadily inclined. Across the river icicles toothed the rocky precipice like giant, upended organ pipes.

The steers' and her horse's breathing became more labored. Jenna's own lungs begged a little as altitude thinned the frigid air. When Soupbone's ungodly yowling ceased, the cadenced thwok of hooves and chuffy pants replaced it.

Every nerve ending warned that a misstep along the silty bank would send horse and rider splashing into the Stikine. If its deceptively placid current didn't shag them, immersion in its icy depths would surely prove fatal.

Countless gallops over tabletop Nebraska prairie hadn't prepared Jenna for this kind of exhilarating terror.

Again, the herd clustered nose-to-tail before lumbering to a dead stop. The trail had curled inland. Jenna couldn't see the cook riding point or Yolanda behind her. Had something happened to Soupbone?

She could hear Dan's husky baritone, but distance and the slushing river garbled his words.

Hands sweat-slick inside her mittens, she gripped the reins and eased past the steers' jostling hindquarters. Her gut clenched when one beast commenced a butting contest with his follower.

The chestnut stutter-stepped. A hunk of bank tore free. The horse faulted, Jenna lurching to the right. The water's fishy smell and lapping, Lorelei melody enveloped her senses.

Whinnying and surging forward, the chestnut regained purchase on slippery but solid ground. Sweat poured the length of Jenna's body. She closed her eyes and patted the horse's neck, thanking God and Homer Goodacre for buckling the wide leather girth extra tight.

The chestnut's instincts proved keener than his rider's. Using his superior height and broad chest like a battering ram, the horse urged the steers back into an orderly line.

Regaining her own wits, Jenna warned, "Flanker, ease in from the riverbank. It's too soft at the edge."

Yolanda snapped a pert salute at her tricorn's upturned brim.

"Had Napoleon the First had her size," the swing rider noted wryly, "Lord knows what worlds he'd have conquered."

Soupbone's snarling curses were audible for a hundred yards before she spotted his mangy fur cap. His grulla contentedly grazed above him along the edge of a knoll while the skinny argonaut was trying to jerk his pack mules up the slope. Worrying their halters and nigh squatted on their haunches, the knobheads flatly refused to budge.

"Sumbitchin' devil's lap dogs. Hie up that sumbitchin' hill or I'll stick my hog-leg in yer sumbitchin' ears and blow what brains you got to Billy Thunder."

Jenna hefted her leg to swing it over the pommel. Muscles she didn't know she had felt as if they were tearing from her bones. She dropped to the ground, knees as wobbly as a newborn fawn's.

Noticing Soupbone's puckered amusement, she sucked in a deep breath and gritted her teeth. "Be ready to jump when those jennies do," she said, sloggy through fidgety cowhide and muck.

"Aw, sure. What's a woman know 'bout giddapin' a mule?"

More'n you do, you old grissel-heel, Jenna countered silently. Twisting the first mule's tail like a taffy string persuaded it into an upright stance. Settling her shoulder against its rump, she ricked its tail as tight as coiled hemp with one hand, landing a solid haymaker to its upper thigh with the other.

With an ear-piercing bray, the mule scrambled up the rise to escape its tormentor, its wide-eyed cousin close at its hocks.

"Well, I'll be damned," Soupbone wheezed,

staring at Jenna as if she were one of Salem's witches. "Where'd you learn that mischief, gal?"

"You'd be surprised how much I know about jackasses, just from being around one kind or another most of my life."

"What's the trouble up there?" Yolanda shouted.

Jenna grinned at the cook, then yelled back, "No trouble. I took care of it."

"Atta girl, honey lamb. Trail boss says, find a patch of level ground. Reckon these beeves need their beauty sleep."

Soupbone half turned, shading his eyes with his hand. Looking down at Jenna, he said, "Best knot them steers' fly-swatters and bring 'em on, Head Heifer. We got us a fine stretch of meadow over yonder."

"I'd be delighted to show you how it's done," she replied slyly.

Crow's-feet wrinkles splayed from the corner of his good eye. "If I bow-tie my apron instead, there'll be coffee boiled by the time you're done."

The mere thought of that hot, invigorating brew fluming down her throat made Jenna's mouth water in anticipation. "Get crackin' then, cookie."

As it happened, a snail's pace would have sufficed. The sun hadn't set, yet hours passed before Jenna shuffled into the copper circle painted on the snow by the campfire's flames. The north country's lengthy days and short nights totally skewed the human internal clock. In theory, Hank Wade would welcome eighteen- or twenty-hour days, assuming that darkness would never catch him with chores left undone.

The spirit might be willing, Jenna reasoned, but the body's too frail to keep pace. Haunch-dragging weariness won't bring sleep either, without night giving my eyelids cause to close.

Soupbone's comfortable situation canted against a pile of supplies could have brought his demise if she'd had enough strength left to strangle him.

"I suppose you knew we'd have to sweep the field with fir boughs before the cattle'd graze," she moaned, sinking onto a heap of dry wood. Instantly, she cocked up on a hip, her rump as sore as a boil.

"I suspected as much. Cattle is poor foragers."

"Sloshing buckets of water on their backs wasn't much fun, either."

"Mebbe not, but if it keeps 'em from galling, it'll be worth the trouble."

"Seems you're kind of strutty about not helping us bed down the herd . . ." Jenna said, sneering.

He sat forward, glowering. "Listen here, my heinie's just as flagged as yours. I unhitched them kitchen mules, bucketed their worthless hide, chopped firewood, ground a fresh batch of coffee makings, slopped up the supper vittles, and'll clean up after you're snoring and'll be banging breakfast together before you stop."

"Oh. Uh, sorry. No insult intended," she stammered meekly, feeling like a bratty child.

"Don't cozen your elders, Miz French." Soupbone's tone was snarly, but Jenna glimpsed a grin hiding behind his thatch of salt-peppered whiskers.

The aroma of beans, fatback, Arbuckle's Best, and biscuits invaded her nostrils. Over the crunch of the other hands' approaching footfalls, her long-empty belly rumbled like thunder.

"What're you waiting for, gal? Grab a plate and chow down afore that she-ox finds the trough."

"I heard that," Yolanda howled. "Them jug ears of yours is gonna make fine bootjacks, bub."

Soupbone adopted an expression of bewildered innocence. "Wimmen. Ain't known but one with the sense of humor God gave a cougra."

Chapter Six

"All hands, boots and saddles."

The drawled, gruff delivery identified the speaker. Obviously, a simple "Time to get up" was too bland for a Texan, Jenna thought.

Groggy and chilled to the bone, she curled tighter under the blankets. Layered spruce boughs, or Irish feathers as Soupbone had called them, may have kept some of the chill from seeping through the canvas fly under her bedroll, but not nearly enough for comfort.

She also felt a kinship with parlor rugs dragged outdoors come spring and fall and draped over clotheslines for a good beating. Near as she could tell, the only body parts that didn't ache were her pinkie fingers and earlobes. Not much comfort in that, either.

Maybe if she just laid possum-still, the others'd forget about her. As Granny'd often said, let the saints march right on in those pearly gates. She figured Peter would rouse her with a nudge when her time came for harp lessons.

The sharp odor of scorched oatmeal mingled

with campfire smoke. Cracking one eyelid, Jenna peered at the rumpled cook bent over a cast iron pot like one of the *Macbeth* witches.

If supper had been any indication, Soupbone knew only two ways to prepare food: raw and burnt. She gazed lovingly at the tin cup with steam blasting from its rim that Dan was greedily refilling.

A hellacious yowl split the quietude. Startled bawls rose from the herd's bed ground. Jenna gasped and scrambled to her feet, head whirling to find the source of the blood-curdling bellow. Yolanda's mountainous form loomed nearby, arms up and reaching for the clabbered sky.

"Good God, woman," Dan spluttered above the hiss of coffee-doused embers, "your yawnin's enough to set off a stampede."

With a flip of her yellow hair she replied, "I'll try to be more dainty in the future, boss."

Soupbone banged the wooden spoon against the pot's thick lip. "That'll be a stretch, for damn sure."

Shivering, Jenna tugged on the mackinaw that'd served as her pillow. Following Yolanda's example, she knelt to straighten her mussed quilt and blankets, folding the canvas fly over them.

Jenna stowed the twine-tied gunnysack holding her meager personals at one end and rolled her bed into a compact bundle, securing it with short lengths of rope to keep it that way.

Noting that their still-hobbled, four-horse remuda was already saddled, she massaged her tender hindquarters.

During one of his campfire tales, Dan said it took anywhere from a day to the Twelfth of Never to saddle-break a horse, depending on the personality and attitude of the trainer and the animal. Jenna wondered how long it would take to break her own behind to that unforgiving McClelland. Too bad riders don't get saddle blankets for padding, same as horses do. She shrugged and turned to join the others.

"I don't expect we'll get much past Telegraph Creek today," Dan said. "Probably won't break camp until after dinner."

"Why?" Jenna asked.

Dan hooked a thumb in his gun belt. "Are you fixing to argue or just curious?"

"I suppose it depends on your answer."

Yolanda snickered through a mouthful of grub. Jenna winked at her, then took the wooden bowl of grayish, lumpy goo that Soupbone proffered. The spoon was mired in the middle like a flagpole. She extracted it, tentatively licking its edge. To her surprise, the sweet, grainy stuff didn't taste nearly as bad as it looked.

"In case you forgot, little lady, we got sixty-five head of steers to pack, and they're not gonna stand around chewing cuds while we do it."

Jenna nodded, more concerned with filling

her empty stomach than with Dan's explanation.

"Soupbone, you're an old hand at cinching canvas and tying diamond hitches. It's your job to make an expert out of Yolanda."

"Like I ain't got enough to do hauling firewood, cooking, and washing up? Not to mention packing them mules, too."

Dan's eyes creased at the corners. "Well, now, maybe if you talk real nice to her, she'll help you with your other chores."

"And maybe if he don't," Yolanda shot back, "I'll pound his knot head like a tent stake."

Oatmeal gobbets flew from the wooden spoon as the cook shook it at her. "You may be bigger'n a goddamned musk ox, but I ain't afraid of no female, nohow."

She took a huge step forward. Soupbone chucked the spoon into the pot and darted behind a pile of supplies.

Dan chuckled. "That's enough, you two."

"Why, I was just going after seconds, boss," Yolanda simpered. "A gal's gotta keep up her strength."

He pointed at Jenna. "You and me're gonna rope and snub steers so's her and Soupbone can load the pack trees. Think you can make a cow pony out of that chestnut?"

She thought back to watching Homer Goodacre out-maneuver the herd's more reluctant members. Such confident handling was a sure sign of decades of experience, whereas tossing wobbly loops over her father's milch cow's horns when she was a kid didn't count for much.

"Probably a lot easier than you can make a roper out of me," she said.

A lazy smile split the space beneath his mustaches. "If I didn't think you could do it, I'd have cut the teams different."

Hours later, Jenna was wishing he had. Thus far, sitting astride Cariboo—the name she'd decided to affix to her horse—and keeping a steer's hemp necktie pulled taut at the pommel was the extent of her duties.

Dan was having all the fun, sending those loops singing through the air, collaring the intended, then heel-catching the animal with a second loop. Once securely garroted and with only three hooves touching ground, they accepted the burdens Soupbone and Yolanda stacked on their backs with resigned indifference.

Smudgy clouds tumbling in the sky seemed in danger of snagging on the spiky, pine-clad mountain peaks. Jenna turned up her collar against the shrill breeze. The smell of rain was in the air.

Thirty-two unencumbered head still fanned across the meadow, grazing and drinking from Dodjatin Creek. Dan's throwing arm stiff at his side and his weight shifted to the balls of his stirruped feet, he charged at a mottled roan steer. In one fluid motion, his arm came up and the rope bloomed into a wide halo.

The animal's blocky head reared, green shoots sprouting from its jaw like misplaced whiskers. It feinted right, left, then right again and broke into a halfhearted lope.

Poised in the saddle as if his body was a natural part of it, his features graven with concentration, Dan's eyes locked on the bucking steer. His wrist snapped. The loop sailed at a slight angle, hovered a scant instant, and dropped over the roan's horns.

At a slight shortening of the reins, Dan's horse bowed its neck and stopped squarely on both hind feet, forelegs tattooing a few walk steps. The rope stretched its limit and yanked the bawling steer off-balance.

Jenna geed Cariboo out to take charge of the beast. Just before she and the balky animal reached Soupbone and Yolanda, Dan's heel-catch would ensure good behavior.

Except this barrel-torsoed brute wasn't quite ready to surrender. Saddle leather squawked and creaked with each yank on the dallied rope. Cariboo whinnied and stamped a hoof. He didn't appreciate the jerking sensation any more than Jenna did.

"I'll teach him some manners," Dan called. He leaned against the cantle, cuing his sweat-sleek gelding to back up a step.

The steer's manacled leg scissored wide from its mate. Sides heaving, it sucked in great lungfuls of air and bellowed like a steam locomotive.

A fifty-pound sack of beans slid from a startled Yolanda's grasp. Eyebrows canted above a menacing glare, she stomped over and slapped the steer right on the nose.

"Stand still and shut the hell up."

Jenna tensed, fearing the animal would fight for all he was worth. When the steer's head seemed to retract into his shoulders like a turtle's, she giggled with relief.

Once the pack was in place, Yolanda scratched it behind the ears and whispered something, presumably something kind, in his twitching ear.

She removed the neck rope as Dan dropped the other line. Given their freedom, the steers usually shot away like awkward cannonballs. This reformed bully didn't budge.

"Acts like he's dead and forgot to fall down," Dan drawled. "Either goose him or gut him, Yolanda. Jenna'll catch another one for you to hammer on, directly."

"I'll what?"

"You heard me. Go drop a loop over . . . General Sherman, yonder." He ran his tongue over his teeth and clucked. "Unless you're too 'fraidied to try."

I'll show you, Mister Highfalutin, she thought. Ignoring the moisture glistening on her palms, she coiled the line just as Dan had, with her little finger holding its end separate from the others strands, the hondo dangling some distance from her fist.

Cariboo's steady, sure-footed gait beneath

her was a confidence booster. He ambled toward the drowsy steer as if he'd understood the trail boss's dare.

Other animals milling nearby lumbered away as they approached. General Sherman held his ground.

Jenna raised up in the stirrups. Cariboo broke to a canter. He flinched slightly, catching a glimpse of the rope whisking past his ear. Jenna's wrist rotated the coiled hemp as if born to it.

Beyond a glazy stare, the General paid them no mind.

"Easier'n Daddy's milch cow," she muttered, grinning.

A crisp, snap motion sent the loop flying from her splayed fingers.

"Oh, no!"

Jenna lunged for the loose tail end her pinkie forgot to hold on to. Still coiled, the rope thumped the steer square between the eyes.

She drew back on the reins, thoroughly humiliated. Cariboo juddered to a halt, and she dismounted to retrieve the rope. General Sherman favored her with a wet snort, as if saying he was as disgusted as she was with her performance.

Yolanda, bless her heart, let out a hale, "Pretty good, for your first try," as Jenna approached. Soupbone busied himself wrapping Dan's black gelding's reins around a snag.

Expecting an immediate and merciless ribbing, Jenna thought, by cracky, maybe I didn't do so bad after all. Even Dan's not doubled over hee-hawing like I figured he'd be.

The trail boss's back was turned, checking the girth on one of the grays. On closer examination she noticed that his entire body was trembling like a fat crow on a telegraph wire.

He glanced at her, chortled once, and broke into a side-splitting fit. "Gawd almighty, girl . . . can still hear . . . that rope go . . . *clunk.*"

Gasping, he wrapped his arms around his belly. "Steer looked at ya . . . like you was . . . plumb loco."

Soupbone buried his face in the black's flank, trying to muffle his own cackles. It didn't work.

"C-l-u-n-n-k," Dan howled. Tears streamed down his flushed face.

Valiantly, Yolanda clapped a hand over her mouth. Chuckles percolated up her throat like bubbles in a coffeepot.

Jenna couldn't contain herself any longer. She burst out laughing, which set Cariboo into a nervous stutter-step. Her ribs were aching before she regained enough control to say with a sneer, "Blubbering fools. Least I tried."

"Gotta tell you, I've seen worse," Dan said, swiping an arm across his damp cheeks. "My brother, Darrin, forgot to let go of the rope, peeled sideways, and fell off his danged horse."

Thank you, Lord, for sparing me that, she thought. Had I gone truckling ass over elbows across that bunch grass, Dan would have surely choked to death.

"I'll get the hang of it. Eventually."

"Just takes practice. But in the meantime, how about if I catch the rest of them beeves so we can hit the trail?"

"Fine by me."

"Better let that chestnut—"

"His name's Cariboo."

His eyes swept the length of the gelding. "Well . . . I reckon he's your horse. Hitch him next to Blackie and let 'im blow—"

"Blackie? Lawsy, you must have pondered for hours before you came up with that handle."

Swinging up into the saddle, he wheeled the gray and started for the meadow. "That's enough outta you, caballero. Get a fresh mount and get back to work."

A cold drizzle was falling by the time they'd outfitted the herd, broken camp, and urged the animals onto the trail. The sun was a pale butter pat, all but lost in the thick cloud cover and well west of midpoint.

"Keep 'em close and moving," Dan called from drag. "Rain'll put the balk to them if they string too far."

Jenna waved, signaling that she'd heard. Moisture seeped through her denim-clad thighs at an astonishing rate. That the rain was rapidly melting the snow was its lone, saving grace.

She glanced at the bawling, wall-eyed steer beside her. Blinking against the rivulets that trickled from his tufted poll, he looked as miserable as she felt. Dry cattle hardly smelled like honeysuckle in bloom. Wet hides exuded a stench strong enough to chew but too rank to swallow.

To take her mind off her troubles, Jenna reviewed the catch-rope procedure, mostly what she'd done wrong. She didn't need Dan to tell her how much two ropers would speed the packing process. At this rate they'd be lucky to make Laketon by Christmas.

She patted Cariboo's soggy mane. "We'll loop us a steer or three tomorrow, won't we, fella?"

A gouge in the dense, fir- and pine-covered foothills revealed a shantied homestead more humble than Jenna's Glenora cabin. Tattered wool socks and grubby drawers hung from a twine clothesline strung between two trees.

The tantalizing aroma of drying jerky wafted from a canvas, tipilike affair, its smoke rising to meet a feeble tendril curling above the cabin's whomper-jawed chimney. But if the owner was at home, a bovine parade obviously didn't rate a curious peek out the door.

Curving around a bend, the rutty trail sloped downward and widened to a proper road. Jenna startled when Dan cantered past.

"Coming into Telegraph Creek," he informed without breaking Blackie's stride. "Bunch 'em up, then fall back to drag."

Dan must have slowed Soupbone to a plod, for the herd almost immediately spread five

abreast and nose to hindquarters. Jenna reined
in to let Yolanda by.

The bedraggled Cyprian sat regally astride
her straining gray, yet her weariness showed in
her slack, pallid features.

Earlier, Soupbone had almost complimented
her on how quickly she'd learned to distribute
pack weight and cinch it properly. Yolanda
acted as if it was no mean accomplishment, but
Jenna could tell she was proud of herself, and
deservedly so.

Along the mucky trail that was the main
street, most of Telegraph Creek's log cabins and
commercial regards crouched in a sloping vee
between the Stikine and the ravaged, stump-
littered hogback.

Clustered and single structures, a majority
constructed of wood frames and canvas, stair-
stepped upward wherever whimsy and a convenient stand of trees had deemed it appropriate.
From the town's ramshackle, willy-nilly appearance, not many Stateside carpenters or survey-
ors had plied their trades en route to the gold
fields.

An assortment of bearded, scruffy townsmen
coveyed under a dripping, shake awning to jeer
at the cattle drivers. Jenna couldn't help smiling
at their wisecracks.

"Bless my soul, lookit. There's another female follering behind."

"Must be that big un's runt pup."

"Dadblastedest sight ever come to this country. Steers trussed up with trade goods, a young buck, a one-eyed pioneer, and two gals aherdin' em? Why, I couldn't conjure sech a thang with a snoot fulla hootch."

Jenna pulled up near the last speaker. The moose that provided his mangy coat and breeches must have been skinned years before she was born. By her downwind position, she figured he hadn't bathed much since he'd acquired it, either.

"Afternoon, gents."

Moose Suit's Adam's apple bobbed in his throat. "Uh, howdy, ma'am," he stammered, his bluster giving way to embarrassment. Lightning quick, he snatched off a matted fur hat and clutched it to his chest.

Leaning casually on her pommel, a breezy load of bushwah Granny Detheridge and Guthrie would've been hard pressed to top proceeded to ramble from Jenna's lips.

"Just so you'll know, this is the . . . the Cassiar Cattle Company strolling through your fair city. History in the making, fellows. I suspect you'll tell your grandchildren about it someday."

Moose Suit and the winter-gaunt cronies surrounding him adopted such somber, reverent expressions, she almost laughed aloud.

"Gloryoski zero," one wheezed. "How many head you got there, ma'am?"

"Sixty-five and about twenty thousand pounds of freight."

"Where you bound for?" another asked in a

hushed tone. "It gets right grim, much north o' here. Ain't no better, east."

"Come the Fourth of July, those miners up at Laketon ought to be plum foundered on prime, juicy beefsteak," she replied.

Giving Cariboo's flanks a gentle squeeze, Jenna eased the chestnut forward. She tipped her slouch hat courteously at her wide-eyed audience. "Kind of gets your mouth watering just thinking about it, now doesn't it?"

Chapter Seven

The next day, Dan made an announcement that caused Jenna almost to choke on her biscuit. The syrupy Arbuckle's scalded her tongue as she washed it down.

"What do you mean we're short nine head? You said they'd be too foot-sore to wander very far."

Dan glanced at Yolanda and Soupbone, clearly wishing they were out of earshot. "It's not the first time I've been wrong," he mumbled. "Won't be the last."

Her lips parted, then pressed shut. Giving him what-for wouldn't find those strays. But trail boss, Jenna vowed silently, we're going to have us a serious parley, later.

"Humble don't become you, boy," Soupbone replied drolly. "If I was you—"

The toe of Dan's boot chucked a rock like a gunshot. "Coosie, if I was *you*, I'd get my butt in the saddle."

"Don'tcha want me to start hitching packs?"

Yolanda clamped a hand over Soupbone's

shoulder. "C'mon, old fool, before he wraps a line around your scrawny neck."

"Angle away from the river, then circle back," Dan instructed curtly. "Squeeze off a shot if you need help."

"Uh, boss?" Yolanda's baleful expression resembled a child in need of an outhouse, but too embarrassed to say so. "I've never fired a gun before. Truth is, they scare the bejabbers outta me."

Dan waved a hand dismissively. "Nothing to it. Just point the barrel at the sky and pull the trigger back easy."

She sighed and plopped her hat over her tangled curls. "All right, but you'd best hope I don't hit a vital on accident. In case you ain't noticed, I'm the only one in this bunch that don't argue with everything you say."

Her remark was surely aimed at Soupbone, who glowered meaner with one eye than most could with two, but Jenna felt a slight sting, too.

But blast it all, she rationalized, *I wouldn't balk so often if Dan ever bothered to explain things.*

The wooden stirrups and vintage leather creaked beneath her weight as she swung into the saddle. Astride Blackie, Dan was already disappearing into the willows and cottonwoods.

Because the British Columbia government had chartered steamboat captain William Moore's plans to collect hefty fees for using his newly constructed trail, Dan decided they'd pioneer their own route, gratis.

At Telegraph Creek they'd skirted Moore's tollway, veering steadily northeast. They'd spent two days lugging freight up a forested hogback that stretched from the Stikine's bank into the distance as far as the eye could see.

"It ain't billy goats we're herding, boy," Soupbone had said, shaking his head. "Gonna take a helluva lot more'n tail twisting to get them beeves from here to up yonder."

"Steers climb better than you give them credit for," Dan argued. "It's Miz French's General Mercantile, Hardware, Miner's Supply, and Dry Goods Emporium they're hauling that's the problem. Appears we'll be toting it up ourselves."

Yolanda's idea of bundling the goods in the canvas tarps and mule-powering them uphill with ropes was nothing less than brilliant, but the four sweated buckets and strained muscles to the maximum before the chore was complete.

The terrain blessedly flattened beyond the bluff. Dan thought the herd would be satisfied with stripping the new-furled leaves from their branches until they were ready to move on.

The morning count, however, showed that while the exhausted drovers slept, a few adventuresome bovines had decided to seek out those infamous, greener pastures.

Like drowsy dogs that rise, turn around, and

resettle, steers have similar habits, except a flash of appetite or thirstiness often resulted in wee-hour foraging.

Since Yolanda and Soupbone rambled eastward, and Dan, due north, Jenna peeled off to the west. It worried her that they were abandoning the balance of the herd, but Dan said they'd graze contentedly without nursemaids.

"Of course, he said much the same thing when we set camp," she muttered, "and here we are, fanning out through the forest, looking for his errors in judgment."

Swiveling her head, she peered into the haze. Slanting, feeble shafts of sunlight tricked the eye. At first glance, boulders and bramble thickets closely resembled bedded steers.

Muscles corded in Cariboo's bowed neck as he picked his way down the slope. Considering the grade, she wasn't at all sure the nine nomads would backtrack. Then again, water was more accessible this direction and the fodder equally as tender.

Chattering squirrels and birds darting and chirping above warned friend and foe alike of the intruders in their midst. Such rambunctious harbingers of spring brightened Jenna's mood. She scanned the terrain with the same diligence, but let her senses absorb the wonders of a land renewing itself.

The earth's sweet pungency reminded her of line-dried muslin sheets. Burying her nose in their crisp folds was ample reward for hours bent over a washboard, scrubbing them clean with harsh lye soap.

A brushy wall of downed trees, collapsed atop each other like matchsticks, bounded a scrape where an avalanche had plowed through. A glint near the deadfall caught Jenna's attention. She turned the chestnut toward it.

A pile of airtights, their ragged tops punched open and curled back, indicating that the way-farers had feasted on tomatoes and beans. Puddled dregs would identify the tins' contents even without their labels.

Hairs prickled on the back of Jenna's neck. She dismounted, leaving Cariboo's reins dragging on the scarred dirt.

Like a nest of bleached cockroaches, the tamped butts of numerous hand-rolled smokes neighbored the tins. Adjacent, overlapping hoofprints and fresh horse apples showed that the cold camp was occupied for at least two days—and by only one person.

Foreboding wrapped her like a cloak. Tired as they'd been, Soupbone had kept the drovers' fire well stoked, the flames visible for a goodly distance. That welcoming beacon should've attracted any traveler like a bear to combed honey.

"And if he was that unsociable, why didn't he build his own fire?" she pondered. "Why spoon beans straight from the can for that long? They're far from lip-smacking even after they're heated."

The implications brought gooseflesh rippling up Jenna's arms. In her scramble to safety aboard Cariboo's back, her foot slipped from the stirrup. She fell, landing spread-eagled on a carpet of pine needles.

Sitting up on her haunches, she brushed off her clothes and chuckled. "That's what you get for letting your imagination run away with you. Next thing, you'll see boogeymen lurking under your bedroll."

Her second attempt was not only more dignified, but successful. She moseyed the chestnut around the camp's perimeter, but couldn't find any clear tracks revealing which direction the rider had gone, much less come from.

He could just as well have been heading away from the herd, she reasoned. "He's probably at Telegraph Creek, hunkered over a stack of flapjacks and jawin' with Moose Suit by now, eh, Cariboo?"

The horse craned his neck, favoring her with a skeptical gaze.

"Yeah, I know. And maybe I'm George Washington's great-granddaughter." She dug her heels into his flanks. "Set your sights on the sun, boy. We're lighting for home, cross-country."

At their elevation the water-loving cottonwoods and willows had long given way to stands of firs and pines. Snarled undergrowth and humped roots challenged Cariboo's surefootedness.

The gritty smell of lathered horse filled Jenna's nostrils. Her pulse skipped when he whickered and drew up short. His ears pivoted, then froze, canted forward.

She leaned into the pommel, straining to hear what had put the chestnut on point. Her fingertips slid down her rifle's smooth stock.

A faint bawl whispered through the trees.

"Giddap, old fella," she cried, snapping the reins. "We've got us an outlaw bovine to catch."

Minutes later, her joy at finding the steer plummeted to despair. Trapped by a cruel tangle of briars, bloody slashes crisscrossed the animals legs and hide. Its sides heaved like hearth bellows and foamy slaver dripped from its mouth.

Cariboo almost bolted when Jenna's Sharps boomed a call for help. She tied him securely to a branch, but stayed well back from the steer. Enmeshed as it was and lacking a stout knife to cut it free, she was powerless to help it.

It seemed like an eternity before Dan, Yolanda, and Soupbone crashed into sight.

"What's the trouble?" Dan hollered.

"Steer's caught in the deadfall."

He dismounted and hastily toggled Blackie without averting his eyes from the trapped animal. Whipping a bowie knife from its belt scabbard, Dan set to work hacking away at the undergrowth.

"We was roundin' up the others when we heard the shot," Soupbone said as he came up behind Jenna. "This 'un brings us up to a full cadre again."

The trail boss backpedalled when the steer bellowed and lurched from the brush. Stumbling, it trumpeted in agony. He knelt beside it and ran a hand along a front hock.

"Shit. Leg's busted."

Shaking his head as he stood, he hurled the bowie to the ground in disgust. His fist closed around the handle of his Colt.

Jenna whirled. "Oh, Soupbone, isn't there something—"

"You know damn well there ain't."

Dan inserted the barrel into the steer's ear. The animal's eye, gleaming more white than black, followed the movement.

Cr-a-a-ck.

The sharp report ricocheted off the tree trunks. Jenna felt the reverberations in her chest.

Dan snatched up the bowie, turned, and strode past, holstering his revolver. "It oughta take more'n two cents worth of lead to kill a six-hundred-dollar profit."

She despised him for saying that, without knowing exactly why. Clenched teeth sent her jaw muscles into spasm. She stared at the still, white-faced corpse. Inexplicably, it took on Guthrie's waistcoated proportions. Jenna's throat closed, battling the tears threatening to choke her.

Was that how Guthrie died? Terror laced

with hope suffusing his features? Did his lifeless body crumple to the cold ground with that
same, sickening thud?

Her index finger traced the skin where a wed-
ding band would rest, had Guthrie not
pawned it.

She'd accepted the fact her husband was
dead, but watching that steer being put out of
its misery brutally portrayed the calm resignation Guthrie must have felt an instant before a
bullet shattered his skull.

She remembered what her mother said when
she announced her betrothal. "I can't stop you
and won't try, but I wouldn't give two cents for
that fancy man, Jenna. No-sir-ree, not two,
shiny, copper pennies."

The irony twisted Jenna's heart.

An arm curled around her shoulders. She
looked up at Yolanda's jowly face, then into a
pair of knowing blue eyes.

"I've seen your kind of haunty-blanch before," she said. "You were too angry with
Guthrie to grieve, weren't you, honey? The son
of a bitch spirited you away from all you'd ever
known, then left you in a strange place
amongst strangers."

Jenna's mouth fell open. "You knew
Guthrie?"

"Only by name. I don't need to know a feller's
shoe size to know the kind of man that's wearing 'em."

Jenna's lips quivered. "But he did bring me

flowers, once. A whole derby full of arctic lupine. And when I lost the baby, he gathered me in his lap and rocked me for hours, promising me there'd be another, someday. Six, if that's what I wanted."

Yolanda's callused, clubby fingers peeled damp strands of hair from Jenna's cheek. "Nothin's pure black nor white. Even newspapers has got yellow mixed in, they say."

Jenna smiled wanly. "I know. It's just that hating Guthrie didn't hurt nearly so much . . . as this."

"Ain't got time for no funeral, ladies," Soupbone hollered. "Steers don't have souls to save, anyhow."

"Aw, git on with you. We'll catch up directly."

Yolanda gave Jenna a bone-crushing hug. "I got a peace to speak, and I'm gonna speak it. Now, I don't claim the sense God gave a goose, but a long time ago, a man told me something about hate that stuck between my ears."

"Oh, don't pay me any mind," Jenna said, shaking her head. "I never truly hated Guthrie—"

"Sure you did, and you had a right to. Trouble is, like ol' Zachary told me, hate's a door you slam and bolt to keep out your enemies. Seems pretty smart, till you realize that your friends get locked out, too."

Instinctively, Jenna knew "ol' Zachary" was merely a figment Yolanda conjured to lend credence to her words. After all, a whore wasn't supposed to be wise, just willing.

The men were disappearing from sight. Wrestling demons would have to wait. She had cattle to drive and a future to secure.

"Thanks, Yolanda, for listening and all," Jenna said softly. "I couldn't have explained how I was spinning inside and didn't have to, to you."

"Well, I've been around the barn more times'n you, lamb." She winked slyly. "Been behind it kinda regular, too."

Chapter Eight

Dan sighed in frustration. "I know that ain't right," he mumbled. "But how the hell do you spell it?"

He glared at the penciled p-r-o-f-f-i-t-t scrawled on the sheet of foolscap. Licking a fingertip, he tried rubbing out the offense, but the smudge it left only compounded the error.

"Guess I should have listened to old Horseface Schwartzentrub a mite closer." He chuckled, adding, "Except it was kinda hard to concentrate on the chalkboard with such pure, unadulterated meanness crouched between it and me."

Settling for p-r-o-f-i-t-t and declaring it good enough, he finished the letter, signing his name with a flourish.

Turns out, it's just as well the horses were too winded after that bovine posse to move on today, he thought. I'll hightail it back to Telegraph Creek in the morning, shove this at a postal clerk, and be back before anybody knows I'm gone.

had more practice at hearts-and-flowers speechifying. "My pa worked his life away building our ranch—the Rocking B—into one of the finest cow-calf operations in the San Antonio Valley. I was raised up believing it'd someday belong to me and my brother, Darrin.

"Except Pa neglected to add my name to the will. After he died, my beloved, Janus-faced brother gave me two choices: stay on as a hired hand or find leather."

Reopening old wounds hurt more than Dan expected. His gut clenched tight as a miser's purse. Jenna's obvious indignance soothed him somewhat.

"Couldn't you have hired a lawyer to contest your brother's claim?"

"With what? My good looks? Darrin took over, lock, stock, and strongbox." His chuckle held more venom than humor. "I'll admit, I did consider killing him. Considered it real strong. Would have, if it'd gained me the deed to the Rocking B."

"So . . . what? You came here to put as much distance between him and you as you could?"

"That, and to wash enough placer gold to buy back my land. Darrin's sure to milk it for all it's worth, then sell out the day his greed costs him a half dime. Trouble is, that's about the sum total I've prospected in three years of trying."

Jenna grinned mischievously. "And did *you*

have a gold digger's guidebook in your rucksack when you got here?"

Dan picked up a pebble and flipped it at her. "Okay, smarty-pants, what if I did? That still don't make you a cowhand."

"Yeah, well, a flat poke doesn't make you much of a prospector, either, Texas Dan Brannum."

Yawning hugely, she stood and stretched. Those languid, sensuous movements gave a new and dizzying perspective to her ample charms.

Incredibly, the woman seemed oblivious to how desirable she was. There wasn't an ounce of coquette in her, which made her all the more attractive to him.

"Sorry," she said, patting her lips. "I hear my pillow calling."

"I'm kinda tuckered myself. Glad you came to visit, though, even if we did start off a mite rocky."

She nodded, turned away, then reversed herself. "Think your share of the drive will be enough to buy back the Rocking B?"

Dan looked at her as stone-serious as he knew how, fingers tattooing his pocket. "That ranch is as good as mine, Miz French. I can feel it in my bones."

Chapter Nine

Dan jerked his kerchief down, exposing his face to swarms of bloodthirsty mosquitoes. "Good God, that sumbitch must be seventy-five feet long."

Soupbone made a choking sound in his throat. "Every bit of it. And the whole kit and kaboodle's lashed together with nothing but cedar withes. Injuns ain't never heard of nails."

The snow-melt swollen North Fork River roared beneath the native-built pole bridge that spanned its high banks. To Jenna's horror, the swift current carried with it a moose carcass, its enormous body whisking past as effortlessly as a leaf.

"Makes me light-headed just lookin' at it," Yolanda wheezed.

Soupbone eyes traveled the length of her. "I'll wager there's more'n a-plenty elsewhere to anchor you sufficient."

Jenna half expected to see the cook go sailing over the bank for his remark, but Yolanda merely stared into the distance.

It wasn't the first of Soupbone's insults that had gone unanswered of late. Yolanda's pensiveness was not only uncustomary, it was downright peculiar.

Jenna couldn't be certain, but earlier she thought she caught a glimpse of a flask raised to Yolanda's lips. Whatever she'd clutched in her hand disappeared behind her back in an instant.

"Once we get to Laketon, we'll cut our wolves loose till we can't hit the ground with our hats," Dan had said before they'd departed Glenora, "but I'll not abide any drinking on the trail. Don't bother swearing it's for medicinal purposes either. Only thing whiskey ever cured was a hangover."

Jenna knew the warning was aimed at Soupbone, who, at the time, could have ruined a teetotaler's reputation just by breathing on him. But Yolanda'd certainly heard it and the threat of an immediate firing if it wasn't obeyed.

Jenna's worried woolgathering ended abruptly when Dan ordered, "Since you got General Sherman's attention the other day with that roping exhibition, go drop a loop over him and see if you can sweet-talk him across to the other side."

Jenna started to snap back a reply, then realized by his expression that Dan wasn't joking. He truly did expect her to sashay across that crude bridge with their lead steer in tow like a puppy on a string.

"Uh-uh. You're the trail boss, Mister Brannum. Showing us how to ford rivers is your job, not mine. I'm just swing rider."

"I s'pose that means you're partial to prodding the other sixty-odd head across behind him? Fine and dandy with me." Dan tipped his hat and started away.

"Now, wait a minute," Jenna cried. "I never said I wouldn't do it. I just . . . well, what if that bridge doesn't hold?"

He took a long gander at the span, then regarded Jenna, a wicked grin on his face. "I reckon if it tears loose, some lucky jasper downstream'll have steaks for supper, whilst we survivors'll be scouting for another place to cross."

A stream of tobacco splatted against a nearby tree. "Rest assured, we'll sing a couple hymns to your memory afore supper," Soupbone drawled. "Mebbe even composit a poem about how you was a brave woman whose light got snuffed in her prime."

Jenna stifled a laugh. The prospect of dragging that fourteen-hundred-pound pot roast across a bunch of poles no thicker than her wrist was just as terrifying, but if she made it, oh, how the men would suffer long and often for their tomfoolishness. If she didn't, she vowed to haunt them for the rest of their natural lives.

As she approached, General Sherman eyed her as warily as she did him. Taking the precaution of snubbing him to a tree, she loosened the pack ropes, spread the canvas on the ground, and piled the plunder on it.

"Are we fixin' to tote all that stuff across the bridge, too?" Yolanda moaned. "I'm tellin' you right now, once I'm on t'other side, ain't nothin' gonna make me cross back."

Above the raging North Fork, Jenna heard Dan answer, "Naw, she's only making that bait-steer feel nice and comfortable. Give him one less reason to balk."

A smug smile hardly tipped up Jenna's lips when he added, "Kinda surprised that sodbuster's daughter didn't need to be told to do that, actually."

Jenna didn't bother favoring him with a scathing look. As Granny'd opined on numerous occasions, the only thing worse than letting an idiot get your riled was letting the idiot know he had.

Jenna laid a loop atop General Sherman's neck and to his nose before untying the snub line. He veered sharply left, breaking away from her.

The second rope dropped into place like a collar. Knowing she'd lose a tug-of-war with the beast, Jenna quickly looped the line's loose end around the tree and let it do the strong-arming for her.

His pride clearly wounded, General Sherman snorted and pawed the ground a while, then proceeded to nibble at the uprooted grass clumps as if that was his intention from the outset.

"Why, that's nasty ol' thistle next to what's waiting for you across the river," Jenna crooned, tugging on the rope. "Ugly brute, c'mon—c'mon now."

One foreleg, then the other minced toward her reluctantly. Bawling, his head hitching like a rooster's with each step, he plodded along in Jenna's wake. From the corner of her eye she saw the other hands circle around to coax the rest of the herd to fall in behind the General.

Anchored by a pair of burly, cedar support posts, the bridge's width was generous—six feet or better, Jenna gauged, and the side walls almost waist high. It appeared as stout as a train trestle. Then again, Guthrie had appeared as prosperous as a banker.

She strode onto the slatted floor, willing herself not to look through the cracks at the rollicking white torrent churning below. Like a hammock, the span swayed languidly, its floor rippling as gently as Old Glory in a breeze.

The lead rope pulled taut. Jenna's boots skidded on the slick timbers. Lurching sideward, the bridge rail cuffed her beneath the ribs, the bar and the wall lashed to it bowing outward on impact. She gripped the banister so tightly that splinters gouged the tender skin under her fingernails.

On wobbly legs she turned and glared at General Sherman. The animal stared at her from solid ground, as immovable as a bronze statue.

Taking on a streetfighter's stance, Jenna yanked hard on the rope. The General reared back, bringing his flyweight captor with him.

"Give it another tug," Dan shouted as he and Yolanda drove their shoulders into the steer's hindquarters. Nose lowered ominously, eyes squinted shut, General Sherman bellowed and charged straight at Jenna.

She whirled and sprinted for the far side. Babam, ba-bam, the steer's hooves pounded the slats. The bridge groaned and gamboled up, down, side to side.

Jenna's arms and knees pumped harder . . . faster. She sensed the enraged steer closing the gap between them. Three steps to the anchor posts . . . two . . . her heel slammed into the muddy bank, jarring her clear to her skull. Jenna swerved left, vaulted a deadfall, and crashed into a thatch of chaparral.

Bent double, her lungs burning like fire, she sucked in great gulps of air, caring little that several mosquitoes whooshed down her windpipe as well. Sweat poured off her brow, stinging her eyes. She lacked the energy to stanch it with her sleeve.

"Hy-eep! Get along there, bossies," Dan hollered.

A rumbling noise, like a train rolling across the prairie, resounded in Jenna's ears. Palms climbing her thighs to force herself upright, she parted her sanctuary's lush, fan-shaped plumes.

"Well, I'll be damned."

One by one, their progress supervised by the other drovers, the herd was crossing the bridge as stoically as monks answering the call to morning prayers. Fifty yards down the riverbank, General Sherman, their fleet-footed leader, munched blissfully on a clump of bunch grass.

"I did it!" Jenna crowed, punching a weak haymaker through the foliage. Stumbling out into the open, she spied Dan waving his hat and returned the greeting to signal she was all right.

"Sodbuster's daughter, my sweet Astrid. You may be able to outrope, outride, and outsmart me, trail boss, but sure as I'm on this side of the river, you damn sure can't outrun me."

With cattle and drivers reunited on the far bank, Dan called for a rest break and told Soupbone to prepare a hearty, albeit cold dinner. "Letting those beeves graze a while should shake the spooks out of them. They may've cooperated, but they didn't like it one iota."

I wasn't particularly fond of it myself, Jenna mused wryly. She'd recovered enough gumption to slap at the mosquitoes hectoring her face, but not enough to abandon her sun-washed stone perch.

For all the stores Mister Chaney commissioned me to haul, there's not a yard of netting to be found. Bad enough forking a saddle all day and sleeping on the ground. Now there's gallnippers by the thousands to contend with.

Gingerly, she fingered a welt rising above one eyebrow. Strange country, British Columbia. One week her toes were frozen together like cordwood, and the next the mosquitoes are draining you dry. Such privations are supposed to build character, she thought. Lord knows, by the time we reach Laketon, I should have enough to sell the excess by the pound.

"You scared the bejesus outta me this mornin', lady."

Startled, Jenna's head wrenched sideward. Dan's voice held a husky timbre she hadn't heard before. "Scared? I presumed you'd laughed yourself breathless watching General Sherman roaring at my heels."

He held out his hands to bring her to her feet. "I've seen a steer's hooves and horns bust every bone in a man's body."

His face took on an ashen, grief-stricken cast. "A longhorn bull tossed my pa around like a scarecrow before stomping him as easy as he would a prairie dog." Dan's eyes bored into hers. "If that'd happened to you . . ."

Jenna felt as wobbly-kneed as she had when the bridge rail buckled. She was acutely aware of the sensual intimacy of her hands cradled gently in Dan's larger, rougher ones; mesmerized by and wary of the desires and emotions his touch awakened.

His warm, full lips claimed hers. Losing herself in his kiss was like falling, weightless, into a bottomless chasm. The splendor of it frightened her.

She broke away, completely discomfited. "I, uh . . . lawsy, I don't know what to say."

"I reckon I shouldn't have done that," Dan said, a chilly edge to his tone.

"Oh, no. I mean, yes"—Jenna giggled nervously. "I'll bet you've never kissed a cowhand before."

He adjusted his Stetson, an angry glint in his eyes. "Never kissed a woman against her will before, either. I won't make that mistake twice, Miz French." Striding toward the herd, he all but snarled, "Yolanda, Soupbone, saddle up."

Jenna folded her arms across her chest and glowered at his broad back. *Well, pardon me for not swooning, you . . . you barrel-legged Lothario. If you'll think I'll shrivel up and die for the lack of your kisses, you've got another think comin'.*

An hour later, she was extolling the male gender's myriad faults in general, and Dan's, specifically, in Cariboo's twitching ear when she thought she heard coyotes barking . . . no, it sounded more like a pack of dogs.

The snaky line of steers ambled to a halt. Jenna heeled Cariboo through the crowded aspens and spruces toward Soupbone's position. Dan trotted by as if she were invisible.

She questioned whether she should backtrack to ride drag in his absence as she usually did. Impulsively, she kneed the chestnut into a cautious lope.

Beyond General Sherman and the mules, Soupbone sat rigid aboard his grulla, invariably addressed as "Jugheaded Damned Gluepot." Dan eased from his saddle with the deliberation of a man leery of making a move that could be misinterpreted. Yapping mongrels wearing hide saddlebags harried Blackie's hind legs.

At a guttural command from an unseen source, the dogs cowered and slunk away.

Cariboo's head came up, nostrils flared. Whuffing the air, he shortened his gait without a like-sign from his apprehensive rider. Jenna sidled the chestnut between the black gelding and Soupbone's gray.

"Don't even sneeze," the cook warned from the corner of his mouth.

A tall Indian, whose expansive chest and shoulders were disproportionate to his short, skinny legs, gestured wildly at Dan. Jenna guessed him to be the leader of the band, for the other men flanking him merely watched the one-sided exchange.

Copper-skinned women with oddly Oriental features carried loads of furs on their backs, while several black-eyed, inquisitive children pointed and giggled at their visitors. One young lad gazed rapturously at Blackie.

Wouldn't it be wondrous if I could swing him up on the saddle and let him stroke that geld-

ing's silkly mane? Jenna mused. A little child shall lead us, so says the Good Book, and far better off we all might be if one did.

Judging by his scowl, the chief held no fascination for the drovers or their remuda. What he wanted, as nearly as Jenna could tell, was for them to skedaddle back from whence they'd come.

A high-pitched whinny and a muttered obscenity warned of Yolanda's arrival on the scene. Soupbone and Jenna exchanged anxious glances; she waggled a hand behind her back, praying the flanker understood its meaning.

Circling quietly to Blackie's starboard side, Yolanda winked at Jenna, then turned her attention to the parley.

Dan's head shook so continually that Jenna was surprised he didn't lose his balance. The chief's native tongue was an unintelligible series of grunts and cobbled vowels, but there was no mistaking that he was not going to allow them passage.

Grim-faced, Dan wheeled and stalked to his mount. Jerking his rifle from its scabbard, he ordered, "Fill your hands. Load 'em so's Geronimo there can see you do it."

Reluctantly, Jenna obeyed. The clack of her Sharps's brass side-bolt met the other three weapons' metallic snaps.

The chief and his underlings were startled. The native women swooped down upon the children, pushing and shoving them into the underbrush.

Dan strode toward the assembly, his rifle barrel aimed skyward, yet only a pulse beat away from a point-blank position.

Clearly alarmed, the chief motioned frantically toward the women and children huddled in the thicket. Dan jerked a thumb at his chest, over his shoulder at his motley army, then indicated that no harm would come if the cattle drive continued on.

After turning to palaver with the other men, the chief adopted a wily demeanor. Kneeling in the dirt, he scattered pebbles on the ground. One by one, he picked them up, scrutinizing each intently.

He's pantomiming a prospector examining gold nuggets, Jenna determined, but why? He must know we're not gold hunters.

Unknotting a tattered rag, the chief spread it wide in the palm of his hand, exposing the cache of gold dust it contained. He grinned, waggling a finger between it and the pebbles.

"Damned aborigines expect us to pay a toll for using their trail like they charged them argonauts," Soupbone growled. "The way they're actin', you'd think they own the whole dad-blamed country."

The chief drew four lines in the dust. Dan squatted on his heels, wiped the lines out, and etched one. Grunting and shaking the rag under the trail boss's nose, the chief added two more furrows.

Dan regarded them for a long moment, studied the party's treasure, then brushed away all but his original mark. The chief hunkered as motionless as a cat watching a robin hop across the grass.

Jenna thought she'd scream from the tension. Knowing she couldn't have opened fire on the natives, she'd palmed the cartridge rather than chambering it, and now was doubly glad of it. *The way I'm trembling, I could wind up shooting my own foot off.*

Catching Soupbone's eye, she murmured, "Why doesn't he just pay the man his four dollars and be done with it?"

Cocking an eyebrow, he stared at her as if she'd suggested he stroll down Main Street naked.

The chief's finger hovered for a moment, then plowed a deep trough beside Dan's fainter hash. The trail boss hesitated, then nodded curtly. As both men rose to their feet, Jenna let out a whooshing sigh of relief and returned her rifle to its scabbard.

Dan struck out toward the herd, four tribesman following closely behind. Pairing up to grab two steers by the horns, the Indians cut the animals from their milling brethren and all but carried them to their chief. Dan raised a hand in salute and strode toward his horse.

"Wait a minute, Brannum," Jenna said. "I

didn't know you were haggling with my steers. I thought you were offering them money."

"Might have, if I had any." A hand reached for the pommel as his boot breached the stirrup's quadrangular opening.

"Don't you dare mount up and ride away until we settle this."

Swinging a leg gracefully over the cantle, Dan slid onto the curved seat. Head semibowed, he spoke softly through gritted teeth. "Got three things to tell you, partner. Number one, if you don't think your life's worth a coupla beeves, then get off your butt and go take 'em away from Geronimo over yonder.

"Two, unless you want to donate another head or three, I'd suggest we vamoose before the chief decides he let us off too cheap.

"Lastly, if you don't like the way I'm running things, fire me. Otherwise, shut your mouth and find your place in line."

Chapter Ten

Jenna's eyes watered from the smoke as she waved the bundle of fern-leaved tansy over the campfire.

"What's them weeds supposed to do?" Soup-bone said, sneering, "Stuff-o-cate the skeeters?"

"They smell a far-sight better downwind than you do," Yolanda retorted.

"My grandmother rubbed tansy on raw meat to ward off flies," Jenna explained. "I can't swear it'll work for mosquitoes, but it's worth a try. Like she'd say, doing something to relieve misery's better than just sitting and grousing about it."

"Hmmph. Nothing's better for curing what ails you than a swig of Perry Davis's Pain-Killer. Up on the Yukon River diggin's, it made a right-fine thermometer, too."

"Yeah, I've heard that one before," Yolanda scoffed. "Whiskey freezes at fifty-five below, kerosene at sixty-five, but when Perry's pizen gets hard, you know it's more'n seventy-five below and high time to double the dosage."

"Yep, a man can't do nothing about the weather, but the right kind of medicine does wonders for his disposition."

Chuckling, Jenna crushed the wilted leaves into the gold pan Soupbone donated to the cause. "Seen gallnippers drive a man plumb loco," he said, "but you're not gonna witch doctor with my cooking utensils, no how."

Yolanda scooted nearer to help. "By golly, give me a clump of those whatchamacallits. First time in days I don't feel varmints nibblin' at me."

The cook jabbed a stick down his shirt collar, working it like a churn dasher. "Well, there ain't no lack of 'em over here."

"Maybe you're defaming the wrong critters, Coosie. One thing trappers, prospectors, and savages got in common: They're all lousier'n bull buffaloes."

Before Soupbone could retaliate, Jenna asked, "Is there any lard to spare? I want to mix the tansy into it for a salve."

"Got plenty of pork renderings . . ."

Her nose crinkled at the thought of basting her skin in bacon grease. With a shrug she said, "If that's all you've got, I suppose it'll have to do."

He spooned a hefty dollop of the speckled, congealed drippings into the pan. "Say when."

"Whoa, that's plenty."

Mashing the flakes into the whitish lump quickly created a bilious, slimy mass. Yolanda

canted closer to investigate. "Ugh. Looks like
something a dog'd hawk up."

Jenna favored her with a wry glance.

"No insult intended, lamb. Got in the habit
of calling things as I see's 'em and—" Her face
screwed into an expression of pure agony. She
sucked her lower lip between her teeth, biting
it so hard the skin blanched.

"What's wrong?" Jenna laid a hand on the
older woman's forearm. "Are you ill?"

"Naw ... too many years of ... misbehav-
ing's catching up with me." Color washed her
cheeks as quickly as they'd paled. "Been a while
since I was in pantalettes, you know."

" 'Twas afore Columbus set sail, I'd suspicion," Soupbone drawled, yet there was concern in his voice.

Yolanda eyed him malevolently before reassuring Jenna, "Don'tcha fret over my puny
spells, child. I surely don't. Get that bug grease
whupped together so's you can take a dab to
Dan. I'll wager the mosquitoes is eatin' him
alive."

Jenna recommenced stirring without argu-
ment. She had no intention of delivering the
concoction to that sulky, mean-mouthed Texan,
but saying so would raise questions she didn't
care to answer.

Absently shaving a twig's soft bark with his
knife, Soupbone mused, "You know, I can't get
a handle on that boy. Moody cuss. For my
money that spells a man with more under his

hat than his hair or something gnawing fierce at his innards. Mayhaps, both."

"Aw, just because that tall, handsome trail boss'd druther talk to them cows than us don't mean he's troubled."

Chin tucked nigh to her chest, Jenna's only comments came from her wooden spoon thunking against the wide metal pan's angled sides.

"The boy ain't no prospector at heart, that's for sure. His claim had to be paying—a body can't winter in town every year on pocket lint and promises. Don't make sense that he's traipsing north with us."

"Does too, and lots of it," Yolanda argued. "Dan'll collect wages from the drive, then placer all the dust he can before his sluices freeze over."

"Horse apples. Miner's law's a bit hazy in these parts, but a man's gotta work a claim to keep it. If Dan's don't get jumped, it'll be a damned miracle."

"He mentioned going back to Texas after we're done," Jenna blurted. "His, uh, family has a ranch—"

"See, ol' buzzard? That explains it."

"It don't, neither. If Dan's quitting the country, why didn't he sell his claim instead of same as giving it away?"

The Cyprian sighed like a mother whose patience with a child's questions was waning. "And how do you know he didn't?"

" 'Cause I asked Cayuse Mike."

Jenna's head snapped up at the mention of Duncan's name. "Why him? What's his connection to Dan?"

Soupbone hesitated, regarding her oddly. "Don't recollect saying there was any. But since a cow moose don't drop a calf in this District without Mike knowing about it, he's the first to find out when claims change hands."

He flipped the mangled twig into the fire. "Shoot, when Twyford Chaney told me Dan'd joined up as trail boss, I was sorely tempted to jump his diggin's myself. Would have, if I'd had the price of a sack of beans for a grubstake."

Why would Dan give up a paying claim? The question nagged at Jenna. Guthrie'd sold heaven knows how many that hadn't shown a speck of ore; abandoning one that was producing, regardless of how much, was downright stupid. And Dan's a lot of things—cocky and temperamental among them—but not stupid.

Uneasiness crept over her like a draft; the eerie chorus of prowling wolves abetted the mood. At the same time her conscience admonished her for not squelching the speculation when it started; that unanswerable "why" rekindled the distrust she'd felt at the outset.

As much to herself as Soupbone, she asked, "If you're so curious, why don't you just ask Dan about it?"

He puffed up like a tomcat spoiling for a fight. "Ain't none of my affair what that boy does nor don't do." His joints popped like tinder as he gained his feet. "You wimmen can gossip all night if you're a mind to. I'm hitting the hay."

Yolanda chuckled with more sarcasm than amusement. "There's not a man alive that doesn't prattle more'n any woman I've ever known and nary a one'll admit to it."

Jenna tamped her fingers in the slimy green mixture. "Wel-l-l, my father's on the quiet side. Told me stories and such, but didn't clish-maclaver just to hear himself talk."

"That place you're from—Hay Springs? Wide spot in the road, I suppose."

Jenna nodded.

"Bet it's got a general store, though."

Patting the "salve" on her neck, Jenna replied, "The Farmer's Exchange. Why?"

Yolanda scooped a generous measure from the pan. "Maybe your pa kept his lips buttoned at home, but if he didn't pull up a chair, rest his heels on the rim of the cracker barrel and start palaverin' with his neighbors about politics, the war, crop yields and worthless kinfolk, I'll eat this bug grease for breakfast."

She sniffed at her palm. "Danged if it don't smell halfway larrupin' at that." Smearing it on with gusto, bacon grit and bits of leaf freckled her glistening nose and cheeks. "It's kinda soothing on my windburned hide, too."

Jenna laughed, knowing she must look just as comical. "I think I should've crushed the leaves a little finer."

Groaning as she stretched her legs out straight, Yolanda clambered awkwardly to her feet. "Honey lamb, I don't care if I wake up green as a grass widow's skirt, long as it keeps the skeeters off me whilst I'm snoring."

After scraping the potion into an empty airtight, Jenna plopped the gold pan and spoon beside the wash bucket. Soupbone was certain to complain about cleaning up after her, but dishwashing was part of his job. Besides, he'd grumble if his mules ate milkweed and gave pure eggnog.

"Uh . . . Jenna?"

Thinking Yolanda had already found her blankets, she was startled at the soft-spoken query. "You're not feeling poorly again, are you?"

"Naw, I'm weary as sin, but prime-fettled. I just wanted to tell you, don't let Soupbone muddy your opinion of Dan Brannum."

Jenna wiped her hands on her shirttail, favoring her with a rueful grin. "Oh, I won't. But that opinion does tend to change faster than the wind direction."

"Dan'll stand by you when you need him," Yolanda murmured, as if thinking aloud.

She then turned and walked away, leaving a befuddled Jenna staring after her.

Chapter Eleven

"Lord, if I'd known it would've been *this* hard . . ."

As she had dozens of times over the last week, Jenna shook off that thought without finishing it. There was a vast difference between listening to, believing, and sympathizing with others' tales of hardship, and personally experiencing such travail.

The day after their barter with the Indians, the undergrowth became almost impregnable, and the steers' packs started catching between tree trunks.

Taking turns, the drovers slashed and hacked through stunted, slender spruces as dense as wheat stalks and a treacherous, thorny ground cover with tentacles that snared trespassers like manacles.

One steer became so entangled in the vines, it fell to its knees atop a granite slab, the impact shattering the cartilage in both the animal's knees.

Within minutes, another carcass and mound of freight marked the herd's passage.

"Seems a helluva waste," Soupbone said. "I could try my hand at butchering him—"

"No sense in it," Dan countered. "Time's awasting, too, and we've got more weight than we can carry already."

Raised by a mother who knotted tiny bits of twine for later use, leaving hundreds of pounds of fresh meat to rot bothered Jenna, too. But, like its unfortunate predecessor, she doubted whether she could have swallowed a bite of it.

At the Tahltan River they found another native bridge. Its span was less than half that of the one General Sherman chased Jenna across, but this one was as rickety as a bummer's shack.

"What are you cogitatin', boss?" Yolanda asked Dan, an expression of sheer terror on her face. "That current sure is rollicksome."

Most likely to tease her, Dan sauntered over and wobbled an anchor post. The bridge brayed like a sick mule, tipping drunkenly at the near side.

"Well, it's a shade doddery, but I reckon it's stood here for quite a spell."

Soupbone slapped his knee with his hat. A cloud of beaver hair and dust billowed up. "Hell, boy. Moses was still alookin' for them tablets when the aborigines trussed that pile of sticks together."

"Ya'll reckon there might be a better place upstream?"

Three heads bobbed in unison.

"All right then, saddle up."

They'd followed the Tahltan's western bank for ten miles before finding a site where the current slackened and there was plenty of stout timber available to build their own bridge.

For four days, they'd felled trees, lopped off limbs, and cut the logs to uniform lengths. Even after the day's labors ended, Jenna's raw, blistered hands tended to curl like claws around an invisible axe handle. Splaying them stung like fire and brought a tugging sensation, as if the skin had shrunk.

Only the day before, the bridge's foundation timbers, stacked like cordwood on the river's rocky bottom, rose high enough to crest the water's surface. The structure was not only beginning to take shape; it promised a sturdiness that would last several lifetimes.

Jenna had said as much to Dan that morning while the cowhands-turned-lumberjacks wolfed down their breakfasts.

"Nope. Won't last a year," he'd mumbled around a mouthful of frying-pan bannock. "Come the first flood, she'll wash away easy as matchsticks."

She ruminated that disheartening opinion along with her own portion of greasy oatmeal bread. North toward the river's birthplace, dawn was bathing the snowcapped mountains and glaciers in breathtaking pink hues that deepened to salmon and glorious violet. Combined with the high-country tributaries swollen with snowmelt, the seasonal runoff would roar through this peaceful river valley with devastating force.

With that realization came a greater understanding of why the Indains suspended their bridges between the banks. Frightening as they were to cross, the structures were built to give when the river reached flood stage, rather than fight against the current—and invariably lose.

"But doesn't it bother you that in a few months there'll be nothing left of all our hard work besides a bunch of tree stumps?" she'd asked, her tone as mournful as a hound's.

A grin had rambled across Dan's haggard features. "Long as we get those beeves across safe and sound before it falls apart is all that matters to me." He'd chuckled, adding, "Never set out to build a damned monument."

Jenna's mind jolted back to the present when her axe glanced off the pine log, missing her ankle by a wink. The blade's whetstoned edge curved like a wicked smile as if daring another haphazard stroke.

Cold sweat prickled her forehead. She peered out from under her lashes, hoping her carelessness had gone unnoticed. Yolanda was using a sapling for a lever to roll a log Jenna'd already stripped of its branches.

Kneeling on the stacked foundation, Soupbone's hammer whanged rhythmically as he
toe-nailed a shoring log that would support the
bridge's floor. Heels braced and back straining,
Dan was pulling another rope-shackled log
into place.

Jenna paused and sucked in the spicy, pine-
scented air, rationalizing the need for a moment to recollect her wits. Ambling into the
clearing, she stopped short, ogling Dan's bare-
chested, muscle-bound physique.

Though it was quite unseemly for a man to
expose himself in such a fashion in a lady's
presence, Dan obviously didn't include Yolanda
in that category or expect Jenna to lurk in the
bushes, staring like a child through a privy's
knothole.

"But a girl can't help being curious, can she?"
she murmured, fascinated by how his sweat and
spray-drenched skin gleamed like bronze
marble.

The vee-shaped thatch of dark hair matting
his chest tapered to a thin track down his flat
belly, then disappeared, quite intriguingly, at
his belt line.

She'd never seen her father or Guthrie un-
dressed beyond their dingy woolen undershirts
and matching drawers. In fact, during childhood, she was convinced her father slept in his
baggy, cotton-drill overalls, which seemed an
ingenious time-saver for a man who started his
chores long before the sun rose.

Later, when she'd asked her husband about his unrelenting modesty, Guthrie's vehemence had astonished her more than his hateful reply. "A gentleman who respects his wife has the decency not to remove his unmentionables. And for a woman to desire such a thing . . . why, it's beyond harlotry, Jenna. It's—it's a *perversion*."

Gripping the axe handle, she sneered, "In a pig's eye, it is, Guthrie French." She swung hard, the blade slicing off a host of fingerling branches like a hinged knife through hoop cheese. "Something tells me if you'd had Dan's formidable frame, you'd have strutted down Main Street naked as a plucked rooster."

Soupbone hadn't finished scorching the kettle of rice and beans he was preparing for supper when a more formally dressed Dan proudly pronounced the bridge, "Bull strong, pig tight, and goose proof."

Considering its lack of side rails, Jenna started to correct the latter two claims, but hesitated, not wanting to dampen his prideful enthusiasm.

"Uh, boss?" Yolanda asked quietly. "You mean you're gonna leave it, well, open like that?"

He scratched his stubbled cheek and drawled, "I kinda figured if steers are smart enough to keep the straight and narrow, the rest of us oughta be."

She motioned toward several saplings stacked

near the bank. "I suspicioned you'd had us cut those for railings. Guess not, huh?"

"Uh-uh. After supper I'll fashion a chute from them. Cattle are like people—the worse the memory, the clearer they'll recollect it. With that last crossing still festering betwixt their horns, we'd best connive them into making this one."

A visible shudder rippled through the skitterish woman. "But . . . I can't swim. Fact is, my pa shoved me out of a skiff into the Mississippi when I was little, thinking that'd teach me how in a hurry.

"Oh, I learned something, all right—learned an abiding, monstracious fear of water deeper than a hip bath."

She sighed and turned plaintive eyes on him. "Make sport of me if you want, Dan, but I'm getting the heebie-jeebies real bad just looking at that thing."

Squaring her shoulders, Jenna was primed and ready to give him what-for the second he started teasing the distraught Yolanda.

Dan nodded solemnly. "I suppose everyone's scared of something. Nothing to be ashamed of." His own gaze locked on his boot toe. The heel pivoted in a clump of pine needles. "Never admitted this to a living soul, but it's spiders that sets this tough, old son of Texas's hair at attention."

And it's me that's ashamed for thinking the worst of you, Dan Brannum, Jenna confessed silently. I do believe there's a soft heart beneath that leather-bound hide. If only you'd show it a little more often.

"I'll need a hand waiting on the other side before we drive the herd," he said. "You think if I sorta strolled you across on foot . . . ?"

"Why, I may be a coward, but I ain't fool enough to decline a promenade in the moonlight with a handsome feller." Crooking a finger, Yolanda beckoned him closer. "And you can count on me to trounce any six-legged crawlers we meet."

Rather than having an evening's relaxation and tale swapping around the campfire, Yolanda and Soupbone packed the steers, and Jenna scrubbed up the mucky kettle, frying pan, and dishes while Dan hastily rigged the chute.

No sooner had Jenna finished her camp chores than Dan called, "Gather up those limbs you whacked off and heap 'em against these rails."

"For once, I think I know why," she said smugly between trips to the brush pile.

"Oh, yeah? Well, if some dude by the name of Cimarron Slim pulled the same trick in one of your dime novels, I truly don't want to hear about it."

Planting her hands on her hips, she stuck her tongue out at him. "Believe it or not, trail boss, women are born with brains same as men. Mine says you're hoping that with the light fad-

ing, the herd'll lope through the chute and be
on the bridge before they realize what's happened. They won't have much choice but to
keep going."

"Yep. That's the plan."

"Think it'll work?"

"It better. Don't have another in my hip
pocket."

The three drovers saddled up to cut General
Sherman and a half dozen others from the
herd. Drowsy and likely confused by the change
in routine, the animals bawled irritably, but
sauntered toward the bank.

As Dan had instructed, when the cattle were
within spitting distance of the chute's angled
wings, Soupbone and Jenna spurred their
mounts, whooping and waving their hats like
lunatics.

Built like a funnel, the structure's narrow
neck forced the steers into a single-file forma-
tion. Running was not a natural bovine gait, yet
if any got the notion to stampede, their heavy,
tight-cinched packs would provide sufficient
discouragement.

A third of the way across, the General faltered, but his followers goaded him forward to
where Yolanda waited, ready to relieve them of
their burdens and bed them down for the night.

Grinning triumphantly, Jenna wheeled Cariboo to round up another batch.

The fording continued at a smart pace,
though increasing cloud cover brought darkness

earlier than they anticipated. If not for their ghostly, canvas-covered humps, the remaining twenty steers would all but have disappeared into the forest's deepening gloom.

Giving the horses and themselves a short rest, Dan cocked his Stetson on the back of his head. As if thinking aloud he said, "Gone plumb smooth, so far. I suspect we could divide this last bunch in half without any trouble."

"I dunno, boy," Soupbone replied. "Seen many a fella push his luck at the faro table and go home broke as the day he was born."

Jenna sided with the cook, but decided to keep it to herself. She hadn't forgotten Dan's fury when she'd questioned the trade he made with the Indians. It'd taken a couple of days before things got friendly between them again. She surely didn't want to rekindle his steel-eyed, silent wrath.

Those good intentions evaporated when Dan asked, "Hey, Cimarron Slim, what's your pleasure? Two groups or three?"

Soupbone's grunt relieved her of a response. "Might as well ask the wind as a woman for an opinion. 'Bout the time you get it, another one'll blow by from a different direction."

"Coosie, you're just not real fond of females, now are you?" Dan asked, chuckling.

"Hmmph." The cook glanced at Jenna and cleared his throat. "I ain't saying this just 'cause she's sitting close enough to cosh me upside the head, but it's a damn shame there ain't

more gals like her. Most of 'em's closer akin to
visiting kinfolk.

"For a day or three, they'll tell you the food's
the best they ever et, how your place is just
finer'n a frog's ass, and that you're 'bout the
best thing the world's seen since Mary and
the manger.

" 'Bout the time you get to believing it, they'll
dash pepper in the stew, put the catawampous
to your house goods, and advise which church
you oughta go to, who to vote for, and which
dad-blamed boot to mule ear first."

Dan laughed heartily. "Well, then, Miz
French, seeing as how Soupbone holds you in
such high regard, you decide how to move the
rest of these bossies."

"Me? I—but . . . All right, in two bunches."

"You heard the lady. Let's head 'em up."

A huge sigh of relief whistled through Jenna's
lips as the first ten clattered across the bridge
without incident. As she maneuvered Cariboo
to collect the last of the herd, Soupbone sa-
luted, and trotted away to fetch his mules.

He'd muttered all afternoon about the stupid-
ity of deserting a perfectly good campfire only
to stoke up another on the east side of the river,
but Dan had been adamant.

"For all we know, it's raining Billy Thunder
in those mountains right now. The one rule a
top hand never breaks is putting water betwixt
the chuck and the herd."

Jenna circled behind and clucked the animals

into motion. She counted packs, coming up with only nine.

"Dan? One's strayed off. I'm going after him."

"Naw, it's darker'n a cat's womb, gal. Come up and hold these beeves—"

"You're already there with 'em. You hold 'em."

"Damn it, Jenna, I don't want you traipsing the back-forty alone."

The crunch of Cariboo's hoof falls served as her reply. Holding the reins slack, she let the chestnut determine the safest, meandering course between the trees.

In spite of her bluster, the scuttling night creatures and unseen branches tickling across her cheeks were downright spooky. Even Cariboo whickered and stutter-stepped when an owl commenced hooting right above their heads.

She was puzzled how one steer could wander so far, so quickly. If the dumb beast passed the night all trussed up, it'd serve him right. Much as she hated to double-back, the risk of Cariboo misstepping was a greater concern.

"C'mon, fella," she murmured, easing him into a lazy crescent. "Not a lot of night left, anyway."

As the horse complied, a light-colored patch sidled beside a tree trunk about fifteen feet away. "Whoa—"

The object leaped at them. Cariboo whinnied in terror and reared on his hind legs. Jenna screamed, hurtling backward off the saddle.

She landed spread-eagled, the impact flattening her lungs.

Struggling to breathe, she heard footsteps running one direction and the ka-thump of Cariboo's hooves heading the other.

Chapter Twelve

Jenna groaned as she rolled to one side. Amber flickers, like tiny fireflies, danced in her eyes.

She knew she should get up; the chill from the loamy, ever-shaded ground was seeping through her clothing. But verily, such effort seemed nothing short of herculean.

"Jen-na?"

Dan's voice sounded two octaves higher than normal. He was near enough for Blackie's hoof-beats to reverberate in her bones.

"Over here, knight in shining armor."

Struggling into a sitting position set the world spinning. She closed her eyes but the yellow lights capered merrily on behind her lids.

A horse snorted, presumably Dan's. Saddle leather creaked. Seconds later, a hand laid easy on her shoulder.

"Jaysus, you're taking ten years' growth off me pretty regular, fair maiden."

She smiled wanly at him. "I reckon you're tall enough already."

"That smarty mouth's working fine. I guess

that's as good a sign as any. What the hell happened?"

The seconds preceding Cariboo's hieing up and clawing frantically at the air flashed through Jenna's mind along with an odd hesitancy to disclose what had occurred.

It had definitely been a man cowering against that tree. For an instant, she'd thought it was Dan. Yet, it couldn't have been—could it? And why would he or anyone intentionally spook her horse?

"I'm not really sure," she stammered, staring at his red flannel shirt. "I thought I'd found the steer ... saw something whitish over there in the trees. Whatever it was, it scared the liver out of Cariboo. Next thing I knew, I was fourteen hands closer to the ground."

He pivoted on his toes toward the spot she'd indicated. "Nothing there now."

"Did he make it back to camp all right?"

Dan whipped around. "Who?"

"What do you mean *who*? My horse."

Massaging his brow, he said, "Oh, yeah, sure. That empty saddle's what sent me after you."

"I'm sorry I didn't find that stray," she said, then chuckled. "And my backside's awful sorry I tried."

Expecting a lecture for not obeying him earlier, his silence intimated that a missing steer wasn't his main concern.

Drawing his legs up Indian-style, he anchored elbows on knees and chin on knuckles.

"I got some good news and some bad news to tell you. Might as well fire both barrels. You musta miscounted, because shortly after you trotted off, I had a full ten rounded up and ready to send down the chute."

"That's—"

"Only the half of it," he broke in. "Them beeves were parading across like cavalry troopers until one in the middle dug his heels in and balked. Either the two behind didn't see him or tried to cut around. They keeled over into the river."

A hollowness spread from the pit of her stomach. "I don't suppose they could've swum out."

"Not packed, they couldn't. Sank like rocks."

Jenna was grateful she hadn't witnessed their demise, and at the same time, wished he hadn't described it quite so fully. Dreading his answer, she asked, "What about the others? Did they make it across?"

"Thanks to Yolanda, they did." He laughed, waggling his head in disbelief. "That big ol' she-bear marched out on the bridge, cussing a blue streak. She whapped that balky steer on the nose just like she did that one a while back, yanking his stubborn hide by the horns all the way to the bank. I don't know how she does it, but them steers is cowered as lap dogs when she gets the rile up."

"Yolanda did that? The same woman who was so affrighted this afternoon that her teeth were chattering?"

"Yep, and I'm button-busting proud of her, too. Even Soupbone gave her proper due, right to her face."

Jenna would certainly add her own praise and thanks first thing in the morning. Still, two more steers were dead, and another three-hundred-dollars worth of freight, lost.

"Without her, there'd be no silver lining," she said with a sigh.

"Could've been moving fifty-one head tomorrow, as easy as fifty-nine," he reminded.

"You're right, trail boss. I guess I'm a tad too weary to think on the bright side."

He rapped on her boot sole. "Feel like climbing aboard Blackie and moseying home?"

Jenna nodded and eased to her knees. Dan quickly gained his feet, holding his hands out to help her. She pulled herself up, pleasantly surprised that her muscles and joints didn't scream in protest.

Dan's arms slid around her waist, drawing her close. His warm breath bathed her face while her breasts burrowed deliciously into his chest.

"Are you going to kiss me again?"

"Do you want me to?"

Jenna looked into his eyes and asked herself, are you a Judas, Dan Brannum, or are you simply the most desirable man I've ever met?

"Yes, I want you to," she whispered. "Very much."

Chapter Thirteen

"Eeeeyahh . . . shit . . . yowww!"

The blanket exploded as Jenna bolted upright, blinking owlishly, her heart thumping.

Near the campfire, Soupbone, high-stepping and thrashing his arms madly, let out another bloodcurdling shriek before throwing himself bodily into the Tahltan, the splash swallowed by a mighty clap of thunder.

Trees swayed and twisted, their branches crackling as gale force winds howled through the river valley. A volley of red-orange embers whipped from the fire, fanning scattergun fashion toward Soupbone's tousled bedroll.

Jenna sat stupefied, her mind unable to grasp the hellacious scene unfolding before her eyes. A lightning bolt rifled from the sky. The earth shuddered with its impact. An acrid, metallic odor like a fresh-forged horseshoe rent the air.

"All hands," Dan bellowed from somewhere behind her.

"They're tryin' to run."

Rolling onto all fours, Jenna crawled, then

staggered upright. Yolanda rushed past. Seconds later, a dripping, gasping Soupbone appeared.

Above the wind's roar the cattle bellowed in terror. Bunched tightly, they feinted side to side en masse. If one broke rank, a stampede would ensue.

Dan was astride Blackie, riding bareback along the flimsy rope corral. Fingers interlaced like a stirrup, Yolanda catapulted Soupbone onto Jughead.

"Need a leg up?" she shouted to Jenna.

"What about you?"

Despite the chaos, Yolanda cut loose with a booming laugh. "I'll climb a tree and ambush my cayuse if I hafta."

Legs splayed wide over Cariboo's barreled flanks, Jenna wriggled around, her tailbone grinding into the chestnut's spine. Skitterish, ears pricked and swiveling, he was clearly as hesitant as she was to abandon the trees' shelter.

Dan's voice blew away with the wind. By his gestures Jenna gauged that like the other hands, she was to lap the herd and keep them huddled.

Lightning flared, and thunder rumbled almost simultaneously. The storm cell hovered directly overhead. Jenna's hair whipped her cheeks and neck, leaving strands plastered across her eyes, blinding her. Dragging a forearm over her face to clear her vision, she gawked, almost losing a single-handed hold on the reins.

A faint blue-white glow outlined the tips of Cariboo's ears. Beyond that, the eerie specter flared from several steers' horn points.

"God in heaven," she wheezed, "St. Elmo's fire. Pa swore lightning could do such a thing, but I never believed him."

The ethereal marvel vanished in a pulse beat. With another quaking thunderclap, rain pelted from the sky, drenching Jenna to the skin in seconds. Silvery sheets slashed this way and that, the torrent's fury threatening to drown her on dry land.

The hard-packed earth softened to muck. Cariboo and the steers bowed their heads, shielding their eyes from the downpour. Chin tucked and neck craned to maintain some semblance of vigilance, Jenna's temples throbbed from lack of sleep, the rude awakening, and fraying nerves.

The clouds rumbled, but less fearsomely. "Five Mississippi . . . six Mississippi . . ." She counted the seconds elapsing between it and the next lightening flash. By her reckoning, the storm had already traveled east, nearly seven miles.

Dan rode up and paused beside her. "You doing okay?" he shouted.

"Been better." She attempted a smile, but knew it likely resembled a grimace. "I think the herd's lost their rowdy."

He nodded, a stream of water pouring from his hat brim's channel. Jenna envied him the good sense to wear one.

"Wiser to play it safe, though. Let's keep nursemaiding 'em until the sun tops the mountains."

"Whatever you say, boss."

A positively leering grin broke below his mustaches. "Watch out, Miz French. A man might be tempted to take that for an invite."

By late morning the bedraggled herd and cowhands were slogging due north. The terrain had leveled, but the ground was mushy and growing softer.

"Kee-kee, kee-kee." Home from the hunt, a kestral falcon gloated his capture of a redback vole. The blue-winged, compact raptor perched on a soggy branch, clutching the mouse in his dainty beak like a trophy.

Though the bird might have disagreed, the clear, sunny skies proved more curse than blessing for the herd and its drovers. The cloying humidity made Jenna feel as if she were breathing through a goose-down pillow. She squirmed in the saddle, about as miserable as a human could be. There'd been no time to change clothes, which hardly mattered since Mother Nature had laundered everything Jenna owned in rank, muddy water.

Furtively, she reached down to tug at her jeans' crotch seams. "Bad enough, I've got to *wear* the damn things dry. I swear, they're drawing up six sizes smaller in the process."

Like her pants, the herd was shrinking, too, and not just in number. In spite of almost a week's rest and passable forage, ribs staved where the hide once curved smoothly over their bulging torsos.

The steers were keeping a steady pace and didn't appear to be laboring, but as Yolanda had remarked that morning, "The pack ropes is gettin' longer every day." As was the dangle-end of Cariboo's cinch, Jenna noted silently.

During the next rest break she joined Dan as he meandered among the grazing steers, tugging pack ropes and checking whether any of the animals were favoring a limb.

"Mind some company?" she asked.

"Nope." He hunkered to inspect a festering sore.

"That's got to be painful."

"Hurts like hell, I'd reckon. Most all of them's getting galled pretty bad. It'd be worse, though, if we didn't slosh them down every evening."

Jenna turned to examine a brockled steer. Raw, ulcerated wounds gleamed scarlet in contrast to its creamy, liver-spotted hide.

"I don't understand why they didn't heal more while we were laid up so long at the river."

Dan stood, anchoring his hands on his hips. "Combination of things, I suspect. These aren't range cattle. They're accustomed to rich pasture grass and grain. The fodder they're getting ain't the kind they need."

"Don't think I haven't noticed how much weight they've dropped. It worries me, too, and not just because they'll sell by the pound."

Striding toward another group lowing nearby, he continued as if he hadn't heard her. "Those packs joggling back and forth is the real villain. Shoot, rub a feather across the back of your hand long enough and it'll bust the skin open."

"And there's nothing that can be done about it," Jenna stated rather than asked.

Dan reached under the next animal's belly for the lash rope. "Other'n leaving all them goods for the next pilgrims that pass through. We can't afford that."

With the pack battened down to his satisfaction, he retied the end into the lash cinch's ring. "You ready to ride, partner? I want to put some long country behind us this afternoon."

She rocked on her heels, eyes pegged on a cropped clump of grass. Dan slid a fingertip beneath her chin and raised it gently.

"Yolanda's crouping like a beagle hound. You're not coming down puny on me, too, are you?"

Jenna shook her head and forced a smile to reassure him. "Let's just say I'm not at my prime after getting the starch knocked out of me last night, and only two, maybe three hours rest."

"Well, you look plumb fetching to me," he said, chuckling lecherously.

She felt a warm blush flare up her neck. "Uh-huh, like something half dead that the cat fetched home."

Studying her intently, he asked, "Is something wrong?"

"Not wrong, exactly. . . . All right, if you get snorty, you get snorty. Considering that we left the trail quite a ways back, do you have any idea where we are? How far it is to Laketon?"

His arm fell to his side. "Damn it all, you still don't trust me worth squat."

"I knew you'd get angry."

"Then why'd you ask?"

"Because if you did, I'd know you really don't have a solitary inkling where we are or where we're going."

"Think you're pretty smart, don't you?" His expression was darker than the morning's thunderstorm. He started toward the tethered remuda.

Jenna trotted in front of him, planting herself like a boulder. "No," she said softly, "but, I'm pretty sure I'm right. And as far as trust, I'm also pretty sure you don't trust me enough to be truthful with me."

His eyes bored into hers. Their knowing challenge discomfited Jenna immensely.

"Tell you what, Miz French, sight your pistol straight and I'll do likewise."

"I . . . I don't understand what you mean."

He edged around her, muttering over his shoulder, "We're about fifteen miles north-northeast of the Tahltan, fixing to angle east-northeast. Dease Lake's about fifty miles."

Not another word was exchanged as they climbed aboard their respective mounts. Dan cantered away to start up the front of the line while Jenna joined Yolanda to give the herd their marching orders.

They'd traveled at least a mile when Jenna saw Dan waiting for the string to pass by before taking his position at drag. She reined Cariboo in beside him.

"I'm sorry I doubted you," she said to his graven profile.

"That's all right. Getting kinda accustomed to it."

"Dan, look at me, please."

Expecting the stony mask he was known to adopt, his features reflected the same emotional turmoil she felt churning inside.

"Just because I know where I am doesn't mean I'm not still a little bit lost," she said.

He hesitated, polishing the saddle's broad pommel with the palm of his hand. "Yeah, well, just because I'm a man doesn't make me the same breed as Guthrie, either."

His eyes flitted to her stirrup. "Them boots of his don't fit me any better'n they do you, Jenna. I wish you'd believe that."

Chapter Fourteen

The stinking, gray-brown bog of partially decayed vegetation cankered the landscape to the north and east. Its murky deadness was a sinister contrast to the grassy slough where the pack train waited.

Jenna and Yolanda rode side by side along a strip of solid ground, searching for a safe crossing or a route around the muskeg.

"Kinda reminds you of Soupbone's gravy, don't it?" Yolanda quipped through clenched teeth.

The women's faces were veiled with netting torn from bacon slabs, scant armor against the swirling, black blizzard of mosquitoes.

"Worse," Jenna said, crinkling her nose. "Smells as bad as a backhouse that's set in one place too long." Groaning inwardly, she clamped her lips shut. It was impossible to breathe, much less talk, without sucking insects down her throat or up her nostrils.

Their supply of tansy salve had run out before the bridge was finished, but it would have been powerless against the buzzing, relentless swarm.

Yolanda's eyelashes were matted with the varmints, her cheeks bloody from successful swats. Jenna shuddered, knowing she must look equally gruesome.

They'd trotted in silence for another two miles or more when Yolanda raised up in the saddle like an enormous prairie dog haunched atop its burrow. She pointed at a knoll sloping upward from the dark ooze. At Jenna's nod they spurred their mounts to hasten the investigation.

The rise proved hardly more than a ridged islet bound together by plant roots. The horses sank to their fetlocks with each cautious step, but the elongated strip seemed as sturdy as granite compared to the swampy morass it divided.

Soupbone and Dan were basking in the smoke from a smudge fire when the women arrived back at camp. In ever-increasing numbers, whining clouds of gallnippers had harried drovers and animals alike for two days.

"But boys," Jenna said, yanking the greasy net from beneath her hat brim, "you're in pure-de-paradise next to what's ahead."

Soupbone spit a stream of brown juice into the fire. "Can't be that many skeeters left, seeing as how you two's wearing a coupla million of 'em."

Jenna wiped her face with her shirttail, which

came away smeared by a disgusting array of insect remains.

"Oh, that's an improvement," Dan said. "Now you've got the stuff streaked every which-a-way."

"Neither of you are sights for sore eyes, either." She sniffed, dampening the other shirt flap in the wash bucket.

Yolanda cackled into her crooked elbow. "Damn right, honey lamb. Never knew that whiskers made such bodacious mosquito seines."

Casually running a hand over his scraggly stubble, Dan tried unsuccessfully to hide a flinch. His cheeks and jaw weren't nearly as flecked as Soupbone's tangled beard, but he was far from alluring.

"What say we put the hiatus to the insults and commence with the scouts' report."

"Well, boss, it's like this," Yolanda started. "We found a crossover place, 'cept it's a mite soggy in spots."

"Think it'll hold?"

Fresh-scrubbed and wearing a Southern-belle smile, Jenna simpered, "Why, gracious sakes alive, you know how things fret a woman's little ol' pea brain. I think it'll do jes' fine, but . . ." Gnawing on a knuckle, she sighed. "Then again, it might jes' *tumble* right on down."

Soupbone's merry howl set the cattle to bawling. "She spragged your wheel good with that 'un, boy. Serves you right for tormenting her back at the bridge."

"Me? You're the one that said women—aw, hell. Break camp and find leather." Dan trudged off toward the herd's grazing ground, muttering, "Some days, a man just can't win for losing."

All too soon, the slow-moving pack train was engulfed in the muskeg's warm, sulfur-stinking, mosquito-filled stream. The steers' tails switched continually. They waggled and ducked their heads, trying vainly to clear their nostrils and eyes.

Cariboo and his swatting, slapping rider weren't faring much better. The chestnut plodded resignedly as if convinced he'd never take another breath of clean air.

Lord, if we could only rig a way to drag a smudge fire along with us, Jenna thought. I'd swear we've put ten miles behind us. So help me, if Soupbone blundered past that knoll, he'll learn what hell on earth truly is.

Dan too, by God. I reckon me and Yolanda were good enough to send out for scouts, but ride point to the crossing? Oh, no—a skinny, one-eyed codger's gotta lead us to the Promised Land.

She was so busy blaspheming and savagely flattening bloodsuckers, she didn't realize for a moment that the line of steers was curving gently to the right.

With his chin raised like a conquering warlord, Soupbone juddered side to side with his gray's awkward, wading-through-pudding gait. The kitchen mules and General Sherman followed like bored aides-de-camp.

Jenna eased Cariboo into the bovine parade. She trusted the chestnut's surefootedness above her own, but one falter and both would sink into that god-awful, stinking quagmire. Starting across the islet, the heaving sensation felt like a gallop mystically converted to slow motion. She didn't remember the knoll being nearly as spongy earlier when she and Yolanda had tested several yards of its length.

She turned to look back at the flanker, the steers straggling for nigh half a mile, and the trail boss moseying along at drag.

Jenna couldn't be certain at that distance, but Dan's eyes not only seemed to meet hers, they also expressed emotions and apprehensions neither of them would have admitted aloud.

Facing forward again, she intoned silently: Heavenly Father, I remember Granny telling me that she struck a bargain with You the night I was born—that You'd better give a sign that me and Mama were going to live or she'd sell her soul to the competition to save us.

Yolanda's my friend, she thought, and whether I ever tell him so or not, I care for that man trailing behind her. Like Granny said, faith's gotta be a two-way road. If You won't keep them safe, then devil take me.

Resisting a powerful urge to glance over her shoulder, Jenna sat stiffly astride Cariboo, focusing on the steers straining and churning the mossy surface.

The animals bawled with relief as their hooves struck somewhat firmer ground. They scattered into a bordering stand of willows and high grass, a succulent reward for the effort expended.

Soupbone's mules were tethered to a snowbush, but the cook had disappeared. To afford him the privacy Jenna assumed he'd wandered off in search of, she dismounted to watch the rest of the procession.

Some of the heavier steers sank to their hocks. The marshy land bridge sucked at their hooves, threatening to bog them so deeply they couldn't free themselves. Jenna's breath caught in her throat, as much from the muskeg's horrendous stench as from anxiety.

Head drooping and lathered like a sulky racer, Mouse carried his pale, rock-jawed rider to a clearing beside Jenna's chestnut. Wide, arrowhead-shaped sweat stains darkened Yolanda's shirt clear to her waist. Her knees buckled as she all but fell out of the saddle. "Honey lamb, I'll tell you true, I ain't never been so glad to see anyone in my whole damned live." Lifting her kinky curls off her neck, she added, "Kinda surprised to find I ain't wearing my gizzards for earlobes."

Jenna chuckled, yet her attention was riveted on Dan.

While the dainty-hooved Blackie had proven the best of the lot as a cutting horse, he was also the worst "mudder." Due to the supple gelding's habit of digging his forefeet below him instead of laying them carefully in front of him, they spiked the mire like slender fence posts.

Shoulders seesawing and slouched like a drowsy night-herder, Dan's lips moved as he murmured encouragement to his neighing, clumsy-gaited mount.

"Only ten yards to go," Jenna whispered. "C'mon, Blackie. Don'tcha dare flounder."

"Uh-oh. Lookee yonder. Swamp water's creeping over the edge."

Jenna cupped her hands around her mouth. "Dan, get a move on. The inlet's collapsing behind you."

"Grab a rope," he commanded. "Be ready to use it."

Jenna sprinted to her horse, yanked the coiled hemp line from the pommel, and ran back to the edge of the marsh.

"Why in blue blazes doesn't he just lead that cayuse across?" Yolanda asked. "Dan's a strappin' fella. Lightening the load'd—"

"Blackie'd balk for sure if he did, and dynamite wouldn't get him going again."

Brackish slime lapped at the gelding's hooves. His jaunty white socks vanished under a thick coat of mud. Five yards to go.

Jenna's fingers clenched the rope in a viselike grip.

Four yards . . .

Yolanda yelled, "That-a-way, boss. You're
gaining ground."

Three . . .

Jenna wheeled at what sounded like a moose
crashing through the brush behind her. Soupbone burst into the clearing and gasped, "Ya'll
ain't gonna believe—"

A shrill whinny rent the air. Jenna pivoted as
Blackie plummeted to his chest. Arms flailing,
Dan pitched over the animal's head into the
muskeg.

Slipping the hondo to form a generous loop,
Jenna's wrist popped rhythmically as she raised
the coils. With weeks of practice, she thought
herself as proficient with a rope as Dan was.
The time had come to prove it.

The loop skidded within inches of its target.
With Yolanda and Soupbone pulling with her,
Dan emerged from the swamp, putrid water
streaming from his nose and mouth.

"Gotta help Blackie—" He tossed the rope
aside and curled into a ball, coughing and
retching.

Cautiously, Jenna stepped out on what remained of the span. Wild-eyed and thrashing
against the bog's formidable suction, the gelding was mired stirrup-deep.

"I might as well shoot the poor sumbitch,"
Soupbone said mournfully.

"The *hell* you will," Jenna fairly screamed. "Bring up the mules. Yolanda, get me another rope. Hurry!"

She tied a bowline around Blackie's head and pitched its free end toward the bank, repeating the action with the second line.

"Lash those to the mule's pack saddles."

Soupbone planted his hand on his hips. "Gal, you're gonna break that gelding's neck."

Staggering like a drunken bummer, Dan croaked, "Do what she says."

The ropes stretched between Blackie and the mules. Soupbone waved his hat in the pack animals' faces. "Git. Git back."

The lines pulled taut. Plunging madly, the gelding heaved forward a few feet.

"Back . . . back it up, you lazy jackasses."

Blackie surged a full body length. Jenna leaped for the bank as his front hooves found purchase. Seconds later, the gelding stood with his head down, chest heaving, his lustrous coat and tack dripping stagnant, foul-smelling mud.

Before Jenna could remove the life-saving ropes, Blackie's owner spun her around and captured her in a bone-crushing hug.

"Dan, no—oh, yuck," she cried, wriggling from his embrace. "You're nastier than a hog wallow."

He stepped back and burst out laughing when he saw the damage he'd done. "Sorry, darl . . . er, Jenna. Reckon I got a mite rambunctious."

Glancing ruefully at her grimy shirt, she peeled the soggy fabric away from her skin.

Yolanda and Soupbone sauntered over, the latter dragging the tow lines. "Seeing as how you're mussed anyhow, we got us another brute to pull outta the bog."

Dan peered over him at the milling herd. "What are you talking about? The steers made it across slicker'n goose grease."

The cook hesitated, averting his gaze to an adjacent copse of willows. "A whiles back, I was goin' for a constitutional and—wel-l-l see, there's this . . . now I know you ain't gonna believe . . ."

Yolanda punched him playfully in the arm. "What this half-blind old buzzard's trying to tell you is, there's an Injun squaw what's got some long-necked, blunt-snouted monster stuck in the swamp 'bout a stone-chuck south of here."

Dan and Jenna exchanged perplexed glances.

Finding his own voice, Soupbone blurted, "Dunno what in tarnation that Yahoo is, but the gal acts right fond of it. I couldn't savvy her aborigine, but she's sobbing to beat sixty."

Swiping the neckerchief Yolanda proffered across his forehead, Dan warned, "I won't play out the horses or the mules any further. Think the four of us can muscle that, uh, whatever it is?"

The cook cogitated a moment. "Worth a try, I suspect. 'Cept, judging by its neck, God knows how fer down the rest of it goes."

Jenna started coiling her rope. "Whether we can help the girl or not, this swamp monster's something I've gotta see."

"Want me to stay with the herd, boss?" Yolanda asked, her tone a shade on the plaintive side.

"Naw. They won't get near that reeky muskeg again."

Falling in behind Soupbone, they stomped a path through the elbow-high reeds and tassled grass. As she ducked under a tree limb Dan held aloft, Jenna asked, "Are you really all right? That was a smart tumble you took off Blackie."

He looked less like a minstrel-show performer than he had a few minutes earlier, but mud creased in the lines of his face gave him a gaunt, decades-older appearance.

"My nose has made my spurs' acquaintance more times than I can count. That muskeg's plumb nasty—tastes worse'n it smells, I can tell you—but leastwise, it was soft."

Momentarily, her throat constricted at the thought of swallowing mouthfuls of brackish sludge. "Better than bones getting broken, I guess." She stole a glimpse at the sky. "I'm awfully grateful you weren't hurt."

Dan grinned as slyly as a fox. "Careful, Miz French. You're liable to turn this ol' country boy's head."

Jenna snickered. "Know what my pa'd say to that?"

"Nope. Figure I'm gonna, though."

Lowering her chin to effect a rumbling baritone, she said, "When that feller passes on, if he isn't buried in a rose garden, it'll be a sad waste of prime fertilizer."

From beyond the undergrowth came a rude "b-r-r-up-p-p."

Jenna stopped in mid-stride, then reversed herself a step. Another horrific blat gusted through the foliage, followed by high-pitched chattering.

"Simmer down, lady," Soupbone shouted above the din. "We come to help you."

Jenna and Dan parted a shuck of grass and peered ahead. Dan sucked air, letting it out in a slow, lilting whistle.

The native woman—a girl, actually—with whom Yolanda was trying to communicate with via sign language was several inches shy of five feet and couldn't have weighed over eighty pounds.

Copper-skinned, with enormous doe eyes and glossy, raven hair falling below her waist, she was the most beautiful creature Jenna had ever seen.

And I'll bet if I made Dan turn around and asked him to describe her, he wouldn't know whether she's blond, a carrot top or bald, she grumbled to herself.

Wearing nothing more than calf-high moccasins and a thin, cotton nightdress ripped at the sides almost to her buttocks, the girl might as well have been naked. The wet, once-white fabric clung like a second skin, her lush, full breasts' silver dollar-size aureoles as visible as the dark triangular thatch at her groin.

Dan stood spellbound, breathing more heavily than necessary, considering their walk's short duration.

"For heaven's sake, haven't you ever seen an Indian before?"

"Um-umm, not one like that, I ain't. Jaysus, no wonder Soupbone was hell-bent-for-election to get back here."

Jenna stomped past him, letting the weeds slap him before she took that pleasure upon herself. Pacing as close to the muskeg's edge as he dared, Soupbone was assessing the bogged animal's plight.

More snidely than she intended, Jenna pointed to the beast and said, "Long-necked moose monster, eh? Looks like a camel to me."

"Of course, it's a camel. I was here in sixty-two when Frank Laumeister got the bright idea of buying a couple dozen from the army and reselling 'em for pack animals."

"Well, if you knew that, why didn't you say so?"

" 'Tweren't sure you wet-eared children'd know a camel from a deformed antelope." He crossed his arms and grunted. "This 'un's not sinking anymore, but it's still in a helluva fix."

Jenna didn't acknowledge Dan's appearance on the scene.

"Can't rope him out, that's for sure," he opined. "Might try slipping a log or three between his legs to break the suction, first."

"Could work," Soupbone agreed. "Better than anything I've come up with, anyhow."

Other than emitting occasional, thoroughly disgusting belches, the camel seemed neither concerned nor particularly interested in the men's rescue efforts.

Once its forelegs were spraddling hefty chunks of deadfall and three bowline windlassed around adjacent trees, Dan called, "Ready . . . now . . . heave."

The ungainly animal's neck strained forward, an evil glint in its heavily lashed eyes. Rearing back, it spit rank cuds that splattered the ground not ten feet from the Samaritans.

"That's one reason Laumeister turned them sumbitches loose," Soupbone growled.

Dan shouted, "Give it all you got this time."

Flattened head weaving like a coiled snake's, the camel lurched from the muskeg. Jenna gagged at the choking stench that rose from the beast's matted brown coat.

Soupbone coughed and spat his own brand of cud. "That there's the other. Ain't nothing on earth smells worse'n an A-rab camel."

From the corner of her eye Jenna saw its nubile, beatifically smiling owner circle her humped mount as if it had been magically resurrected. The girl nodded when Yolanda signaled her intentions to join the other drovers.

"What now, boss?" she asked. "We can't just leave the missy to fend for herself. I don't have a parley going too good yet, but she's powerful afraid of something."

"Catching her death, I'd suspect," Jenna shot back.

Yolanda graced her with a withering look. "Don'tcha think if she had something decent, she'd be wearing it? Even Injuns has got pride. Some, more'n white folks."

Jenna blushed to the roots of her hair. "I . . . I have things I could lend her. They'll be miles too big—"

"Whoa now, mother hens. Since nobody's bothered to ask the trail boss's opinion, I'll tell you straight out: The last thing we need on this drive is a foster child tagging along behind us."

"Her name's Lanatk," Yolanda argued. "I'll see that she don't pester you none. Nor any vicee-versee neither, if you know what's good for you."

"Stick to yer guns, boy. One whiff of that A-rab camel and them steers, the mules, and our horses are gonna cut didos like you ain't never seen. Drives 'em crazier'n—"

"Oh, Dan . . ." Jenna wheedled, "me and Yolanda'll watch over Lanatk, and one tiny, little camel isn't going to cause a ruckus."

"Tiny! That she-humper's seven feet tall if she's an inch."

Pointing fingers and waving their arms, Yolanda, Soupbone, and Jenna started jabbering at once, trying to outyell each other.

"Goddamnit," Dan roared. "Stanch the yapping, and I mean *now*. Trot your butts back to the herd and get it moving."

Jenna hung back as the other two turned to comply. "Dan?" she asked meekly, "what about Lanatk?"

Even his whiskers looked peeved as he growled, "She'll ride drag with me so's as not to discompose the steers. Satisfied?"

Nodding, Jenna hastened to catch up with Yolanda and Soupbone, hesitating as a thought occurred. I'll grab Lanatk a change of ... no, Dan'll have a conniption if I tarry to give her my spare dungarees and a shirt.

Yeah, and with that nightgown slashed up to *here* and those big ol' bosoms jiggling like kittens in a tow sack, he'll be so goggle-eyed by the time we make camp, he'll have to sleep with 'em open.

Strangely enough, she didn't find that prospect particularly comforting.

Chapter Fifteen

Dan kicked the blanket off, ran a hand down his boot to scratch a maddening itch, then gained his feet. Three or four of the cattle bawled morosely.

"Aw, shut the hell up."

He flipped the bitter dregs from his tin cup and stalked to the campfire. Assuming the others were abed, he almost turned around when he spied Soupbone. The cook crouched like a shaman, slicing potatoes.

"Can't sleep either, huh?" Dan said quietly.

"Should've gone out like Lottie's eye"—Soupbone chuckled—"or mine, I s'pose."

Dan poured himself a measure of coffee. "Appears you're putting the time to good use. Me, I'm just gonna sit."

"You won't when you get my age, boy, and them birthdays'll slide by faster'n you think." He chucked a handful of spuds into a bucket. "I reckon the more they stack up, the more you realize there ain't as many ahead as done gone. Makes a man get downright industrious."

Dan watched as those knobbed fingers carved a delicate, springy potato skin ringlet. He remembered how graceful his mother made that task appear, too, the long, tapered tools of a former concert pianist begrimed and gnarled from keeping a house and a huge garden for her adoring husband and two sons.

One day, not long before the consumption took her, she was coaxing a Mozart concerto from the wheezy, dust-choked pianoforte when Dan asked, "Why'd you give it all up?"

Sick as she was, her laugh still sounded like silver bells tinkling in the breeze. "I do believe, I've told you a hundred times how your daddy leaned a ladder against my window at the boardin' school, swearin' he'd simply die if I didn't run off with him—"

"That's how, Mama, not why."

The glorious peaches-and-cream beauty that the years, the harsh, south Texas sun, and disease had stolen from Evangeline Brannum returned in an instant. "Oh, I had dreams, Danny, I won't deny it. If I'd listened to my head, I might've filled the world's greatest concert halls with my music. But my heart told me that lovin' Micah, sharin' his dream, and bearin' his children was infinitely more precious than any applause I'd ever hear."

She reached up and caressed his cheek, tears brimming in her bottomless sapphire eyes. "My heart was right, Danny boy. Even through the

hard times, I've never once regretted followin'
it."

Staring into the flames, Dan was startled
when Soupbone growled, "I've had finer conver-
sations with a damned rock."

"What?—oh, sorry." He took a sip of the
grainy Arbuckle's. "Was woolgathering when I
should have been listening."

"Hmmph. Didn't say nothing worthy of pos-
terity, anyhow."

As much to himself as to the cook, Dan
asked, "You think taking Lanatk along's a griev-
ous mistake, don't you?"

Soupbone's lone orb narrowed as he pondered his response. "Put it this way: I raised
chickens onc't. The more hens I had vying for
the rooster's attention, the more they squabbled
amongst themselves. Noisome birds. Caught
myself cheering for the fox that kept slinkin'
through the fence."

Dan chuckled. "I'm neither rooster nor fox,
old—"

"That Injun wench kinda tears a hole in de-
mocracy, too," Soupbone continued as if Dan
hadn't spoken. "Three women and two men?
Ain't real fond of them odds. Hmmph. Weren't
terrible fond of 'em before."

"But Lanatk can't even speak English."

"That's even worse, boy. She's got that she-
ox speakin' for her."

Dan looked past him at the camel's bizarre
silhouette. Resting in a kneeling position, it's

neck curving aloft from its humped back resembled a mammoth teapot with the handle broken off.

Soupbone's prediction had proven correct. When the other animals had caught "A-rab's" scent, they'd bucked, bellowed, brayed, and clambered over each other trying to get away from it.

Draping his filthy shirt over Blackie's nose like a feed bag had settled the gelding some, but he'd still crow-hopped when Dan least expected it. Thirty more miles of that nonsense might make a pedestrian of him—or a cripple.

Dan sighed and shook his head. Too late for much beyond enduring it. The girl couldn't be more'n twelve, thirteen at the most—a scared, half-starved kid with a woman's body.

"Yolanda tells me Lanatk's been roughed up pretty bad, especially where it don't show."

"I'd've guessed as much." Waggling his knife, Soupbone's voice had a brittle edge. "That's what galls me most about the dad-blamed aborigines. They raise up their whelps like they was little gods, but don't think nary a thing about tradin' their daughters for a couple dozen blankets."

"Don't the chiefs know what some of them fellas want 'em for? Not dearly beloved wives, for sure."

"Mebbe they don't. Mebbe they don't give a rat's ass. It don't matter, the result's the same."

Soupbone spat a stream over his shoulder,

then wiped his lips with his sleeve. "Can't hardly stomach it myself, but there's some bucks that thinks takin' virgins every way they can divine puts the kernel on their cobs. Soon as that flower wilts a mite, they chuck her out and barter a new one."

"Think that's why Lanatk won't go back to her tribe? Because she's ashamed of what was done to her?"

"Dunno. That's part of it, I reckon. Probably afraid of being sold again, too. I don't know how such things work, but I figure her being . . . seasoned and all, means she's no prize for one of her own, either."

"Fools come in all colors," Dan muttered. "She's too beautiful to look at very long. Leaves you wondering if she's real or if your eyes are playing tricks."

Soupbone chuckled low in his throat. "First time I saw her, the blood rushed outta my head so fast I thought my ears were gonna meet in the middle."

"Jaysus, don't I know? It ain't easy forkin' a saddle with two pommels to contend with all afternoon. That getup Lanatk had on—"

" 'Tweren't the duds, boy. 'Twas what was rattlin' around in it."

"Yeah, and dangling from it."

Dan groaned as taunting, erotic images of Lanatk astride that camel flashed in his mind. The muscles in her thighs rippled sensuously with its plodding gait, her breasts swaying, threatening to burst free of the gauzy fabric that bound them.

He hadn't lain with a woman since Alyssa Sue Mainwaring decided Darrin's prospects were far greater, and forseeable, than his younger brother's. Bedding a whore had occurred to him on numerous occasions, and he'd dropped a few dollars down milky, willing cleaves before realizing that what he really needed couldn't be bought like a sack of flour.

"I surely wouldn't advise letting Jenna hear you talk rutty like that," Soupbone cautioned. "She's green-eyed as an alley cat over Lanatk already."

Dan stretched and knuckled his spine. "I think you've been paintin' your tonsils on the sly. That filly wouldn't give me the time of day in a pocket watch factory."

"Uh-huh. And what's bothering you most, your pride or your spirit?"

Dan surprised himself by blurting, "Both."

"Then here's a word to the wise, boy." A fist glanced off the cook's kneecap. "Why in thunder-ation does your jaw jam tight ever time I starts benefitin' you with my wisdom?"

"I don't like being called 'boy,' " Dan replied evenly, adding to himself, *because my brother never used anything else, including my name.*

"Well, there's no insult meant to it. Would be, if I called you 'son,' 'cause you ain't. But, 'boy'? That's just what a codger sees, peering

out at a face that's newer than half his boots
and all his notions."

"I'll try to remember that. Now, get to
preaching, codger. I'm fading faster than Yolanda's virtue."

"Me, too. 'Bout lopped my thumb into the
taters a second ago. But what I want you to
take to your blanket and sleep on is this: Jenna's got sand and a heap of it, but she's been
mauled some, too. Enough to leave scars.

"She's falling for you, knows it, fears it, and
fights it because she's afraid she'll get hurt
again."

"I already know all that, but I'm not the one
that treated her rough. I didn't make those
scars. And I damn sure don't aim to add to
them."

"Don't tell me, boy. Show her."

"Think I haven't tried?"

"Takes time to get a spooky horse to trust a
man again, don't it? I suspicion it ain't much
different for a woman."

Dan ran his fingers through his hair and
sighed. "I ain't given up. Just tired of wrestling
ghosts, I guess."

"Hers? Or yours?"

Stetson resettled in its customary position,
Dan tipped the brim and said, "Both."

Chapter Sixteen

Jenna tore a hunk of bannock with her teeth. A previous bite of the coarse bread seemed stuck midway in her craw.

I'm acting like a brat, she thought, watching Soupbone tempt Lanatk with crisp shards of bacon. Sure, he's always saved those bits for me—doesn't mean anything. He's just trying to be kind. Just like Dan, fawning over her last night.

Horse apples.

"I'm telling you, bean wrangler, her kind don't eat food in the morning," Yolanda blustered.

"That's plumb foolishness. How the hell we gonna put meat on her bones if'n she won't eat?"

Jenna swallowed her breakfast along with the sharp retort lurking at the tip of her tongue. Though the shirt she'd lent the girl was several sizes too large, it certainly wasn't Lanatk's ribs that bulged the fabric so provocatively.

Soupbone shrugged and turned toward

Jenna. "If she ain't gonna take 'em, you might as well have these nibblings. No use going to waste."

"No, thank you. I'm not that hungry, either."

He stomped into the brush, upended the frying pan, and banged it on a tree trunk. "Wimmen. Try to be nice to one, and the others'll fluster up and peck you to death."

Yolanda's fists found her ax-handle hips. "Cantankerous old coot, you didn't even ask me if I wanted them."

" 'Fraid you'd swaller the damn pan to get the leavings. Ain't noticed you wasting away none, anyhow."

But she is, Jenna thought. Those dungarees are slacking badly at the seat, and not because Yolanda's worn them for days on end.

"Well, don't just stand there lookin' snarly," Soupbone muttered. "Get to packing up them steers. I'll be there soon as my mules is ready."

Taking that as a cue to get cracking with her roping chores, Jenna flipped her plate and spoon into the wash bucket. "Where's Dan?"

"I dunno. We sat up jawing pretty late last night. Reckon he's catching up on some shut-eye."

"Lazy sidewinder. I'll be delighted to roust him from his blankets."

With no fresh water and scant fodder to satisfy them, the herd had raised from the bed ground before sunup. Unlike them and the remuda, A-rab, tethered as far downwind as possible, was belching and stoically munching anything its flabby lips curled around.

Jenna crinkled her nose. Lawsy, that beast is the nastiest, stinkingest creature God ever breathed life into. Earlier, she'd asked Soupbone how Lanatk could have acquired her strange mount.

"When they ain't harrying each other, tribes trade all manner of things amongst themselves. A north country buck likely came across this 'un and decided it didn't look fit to hang from a spit.

"Or, coulda been big medicine at a potlatch—that's a monstracious wingding the chiefs throw to show the other hoodoos how rich they are. They pile up furs, blankets, baskets, thousands of dollars' worth of plunder, and give every bit of it away to them that shows up."

Jenna chuckled to herself. I'll bet A-rab's passed through more hands than a Liberty copper-nickel.

She strode toward an elongated lump covered by a dirty Hudson's Bay blanket. Drawing back a foot to plant a boot toe on Dan's hindquarters, she paused, then hunkered beside him.

From one end to the other, the brightly striped wool quivered like a hooked bass on a creek bank. Jenna folded back the fabric's upper edge.

Dan's eyes were squinted shut, his features flushed and taut with pain. Fetid, rapid breaths wheezed through his cracked, white-scummed lips.

She laid a palm on his forehead. It was hot and dry as a sheet of foolscap. He fidgeted, pulling his knees closer to his chest.

"Be ar-right. Somethin' I ate."

"I don't think so, Dan. Not something Soup-bone ladled up anyway. Have you vomited?"

"Nope."

She sat back on her heels, pondering how to continue the diagnosis. Chills, fever, dried out as a wrung dishrag—Jenna was almost sure he'd taken dysentery from gulping down that swamp water.

"Dan, uh, have you . . . do you need to . . ." Groaning inwardly, she blurted, "Are your bowels loose?"

"Loose, hell. Left 'em yonder in-na bushes, couple hours ago."

Jenna couldn't help smiling. Poor man hadn't lost his gumption, despite his misery. Patting him on the shoulder, she said, "I'm going for Yolanda and Soupbone to help me move you nearer the fire."

"Meddlin' female. Tol' ya, I'll get mobile, d'rectly."

Jenna jogged to where the packers were working. "Dan's real sick. Dysentery, I'm pretty sure."

"Don't surprise me none, after that dunkin' he got yesterday," Soupbone said.

Yolanda frowned. "If it is, he's gonna need

fresh water and plenty of it, or he'll wither from the inside out."

"She's right, and I used the last we had to make coffee this morning." Soupbone rose on tiptoes, scanning the terrain. "Rocks and more rocks, nary any which way you look."

"It ain't doing the boss any good just standing here praying for rain," Yolanda declared. "If I can scout a crossing over that muskeg—"

Soupbone snapped his fingers. "By God, A-rab'll sniff out water if there's any to be found. Camels are plumb famous for it."

He peered up at Yolanda. "Think you can savvy that to Lanatk?"

"Probably, but I'm not partial to sending her out by herself. I'll go with her."

"No insult intended," Jenna countered, "but with two and four-legged varmints skulking around, maybe I'd better go. I am a little handier with a rifle."

Soupbone spun on his heels. "Consarn it, I can out-shoot you any dad-blamed day of the week. You ain't leaving me here to midwife no cowhand."

"Dan's not giving birth," Jenna said wryly.

"Hmmph. If he's got the dysentery, he damn well feels like he is. So, we're agreed. Me and Jughead'll do the goin'."

Yolanda stepped close enough that her chin parted his eyebrows. "Coosie, you lay a hand to that girl anywhere it don't belong, and I'll pluck you bald to your toenails."

Huffing and backpedaling, he exclaimed, "Well, you best be telling her likewise, by gum." Out of cuffing range, he jutted his chin, adding, "I ain't one to be trifled with either, you know."

"Simmer down, you two," Jenna ordered, laughing. "First thing we've got to do is move Dan into camp."

Within an hour the patient had been made as comfortable as possible and Soupbone and Lanatk were on their way to find water. While Dan slept between bouts of diarrhea, Jenna and Yolanda thought it wise to check the herd and make a count.

"Ain't nothing punier than a big man brought down by the collywobbles," Yolanda said. "Nursed a party of miners through scurvy one winter. Ugly affliction, that one. Them boys was helpless as newborn babies. Too weak to wipe their own noses."

"I wonder why that is? Mama and Granny complained about this paining them or that twinging fierce, but much as they grumbled, the meals got cooked, the scrubbing done, and the chickens and hogs grained and slopped."

"The Lord made us second, honey lamb. I guess He fixed a few things whilst He was at it and put us here to mend the others when they broke down."

Jenna paused, finger jabbing the air to be sure she didn't miscount the morose bunch of steers clustered around a stunted aspen. Her brow furrowed, then smoothed when she spotted another roan hide shadowing its neighbor. "Fifty-nine by my reckoning."

Flexing her huge hands, Yolanda grunted. "Good enough for me. I got sixty-two. Never could cipher worth spit."

She lifted her hat and started wadding her hair into a pinless bun. "Air's thick as sorghum already."

Along the center part and down her temples, a dark stripe contrasted with the rest's straw yellow shade. Jenna caught herself staring at the tonsorial wonder.

"I know, looks like an ass-backward skunk's roosting on my head, don't it?" She chuckled as she pulled the tricorn to her ears, but Jenna could see she was embarrassed. "That's what happens when a Hungarian tries to be a Swede, and can't get aholt of a bottle of Blondine."

"Oh, I think it's kind of exotic."

The older woman captured her in a one-armed hug. "Don't know what that eight-to-the-pound word means, but I'll take it for a compliment."

For the second time in as many hours, fever radiated through Jenna's shirt fabric—milder than Dan's, but an uncommon heat, nonetheless. While exposure to the elements had scorched the Cyprian's fair skin, her sunburn didn't extend beyond the vee of her shirt's placket.

Stretching to keep pace with Yolanda's lengthy stride, Jenna debated whether to mention it or not. She'd already discerned that it was medicine, not liquor, Yolanda nipped surreptitiously from a flask. But whatever that elixir was, it hadn't affected a cure.

Her voice barely louder than a whisper, Jenna said, "I've known from the start that you're hiding something from me. I think I've guessed what it is, but I wish you'd tell me yourself."

Yolanda halted as if she'd hit a wall. Tears welled in her eyes; she said, "I don't want you to know. Never thought you'd guess—"

"Please, don't cry. Don't you understand? I want to help you. There's nothing shameful in being ill, for heaven's sake."

Yolanda's eyes probed Jenna's brown ones. Parting her lips as if to speak, she hesitated and straightened to a soldierly stance. "I told you I had spells. Get a mite dizzy now and then, that's all. As long as I take my medicine, I'm strong as a bull and"—she winked jauntily— "twice as ornery." With that she started off again.

Jenna followed at her heels like a pup. "Dizzy from what?" she pressed, refusing to take Yolanda's flippant response for an answer. "Why did it upset you a moment ago when I first inquired?"

" 'Cause I didn't expect it, I reckon."

"You're feverish, Yolanda, and pale as my shimmy under that sunburn."

"Maybe so, but I haven't slacked a day yet, have I?"

"Of course not—"

Yolanda's tone was firm, but not unkind when she said, "Then until I do, I'd say my troubles is mine to keep and nothing for you to stick your nose into."

Sighing in resignation, Jenna crooked her thumbs into her jeans pockets. "If you say so, Miz Diamond. But please, promise if you're feeling poorly, you'll tell me—friend to friend."

Yolanda averted her gaze, answering sheepishly, "Yes, ma'am, I promise."

"Good."

Dan's bedroll was deserted when they reached camp.

"Appears the colic's hit again," Yolanda said sympathetically. "I sure hope Soupbone's right about A-rab's smeller."

Scuffling footsteps preceded Dan's appearance from behind a crag. Staggering, he was bent nearly double, clenching his midsection. He collapsed on the canvas fly and wrapped himself in the blanket.

"Never been this sick," he chattered. "Thirsty. Real thirsty."

Jenna stroked his flushed cheek. "Soupbone and Lanatk'll be back soon with all the water you can drink."

"Tell 'em to hurry. Please?" Eyelids fluttering, he rolled to one side.

Jenna tucked the blanket around him, then

peered up at Yolanda, her sense of helplessness almost overwhelming. "Isn't there anything more we can do?"

"Honey lamb, just knowing you're here is a comfort. There ain't no worse lonesome than being sick with not a soul around to care if you live or die."

In an instant Jenna was swept back to the frigid night when she'd miscarried the child she'd wanted so desperately. Guthrie hadn't been home for days; hadn't filled the woodbox before leaving to "mine some tinhorn gold at Cayuse Mike's gaming tables."

Perhaps sledging wood from the icy stack and lugging it into the cabin hadn't wrenched the baby from her womb. As Guthrie told her later, perhaps it was simply not meant to be—a mysterious act of God mere mortals can't understand, but must accept.

Whatever the cause, during those long, dark hours Jenna spent alone huddled beneath soiled, sticky quilts, all she'd wanted was a hand to hold.

She'd clasped her own. It had sufficed.

Yolanda cupped Jenna's elbow. "Let's us amble over yonder and let the boy rest. Long as he's sleeping, he ain't spitting cotton."

Leaning against the kitchen stores Soupbone had piled haphazardly before retethering his mules, Jenna picked up twigs and chunks of bark, absently chucking them into the dwindling campfire. Its flames flared and flattened like hungry, orange tongues.

"How long would you guess they've been gone?"

Yolanda shaded her eyes, gandering at the sun. "Not more'n two hours, I suspect. Seems like twice that, don't it?"

"I hope nothing's happened to them."

"Aw, Soupbone's a fractious old jasper, but plenty wily enough not to get them into a commotion he can't get 'em out of."

Jenna grinned, recalling the odd couple's departure: Soupbone cursing Jughead's snorting, balking skitterishness and Lanatk astride the august A-rab, looking for all the world like a down-on-her-luck, storybook princess.

"That's some strange lingo you used, explaining our situation to Lanatk," she said. "Are you sure she understood?"

"Jenna, I do believe if you didn't have nothing to fret about, you'd fret about that," Yolanda chastised good-naturedly. "Nigh all the hurdy-gurdy gals in the District is Injun of one stripe or another. Stirred up what they taught me, mixed in a dash of Frenchie Lanatk savvied from her people's dealings with trappers and traders and bingety-bang, we cooked up a parley."

Questions welled inside Jenna's mind, brimming like a drunkard's shot glass when the barkeep's back was turned. While she deplored idle gossip, wasn't it only natural to be curious about the stranger fate had dropped in their midst?

"What'll become of her after we arrive in Laketon her being so young and all?"

"Don't know she'll stay with us that long."

"You don't?" Jenna blurted, then grimaced, ashamed for brightening at the prospect.

Yolanda clucked her tongue, favoring Jenna with a sardonic smile. "Lanatk ain't fishing for a man. Leastwise, not yours. Even if she was and swayed him, that'd be as much your fault for not giving Dan the proper attention."

"Dan Brannum is not my man," Jenna whispered, her eyes pegged on the dozing trail boss.

"Could be, easy enough."

"Yo-lan-da!"

"Now, don'tcha be getting your socks in a knot. All's I was sayin' is that Lanatk has other fish to fry besides that beached 'un wadded up in the blanket. She's on a mission and nothing nor nobody's gonna fork that road."

"What kind of mission?"

The calico queen stretched out, crossing her feet at the ankles. "Everybody has one, borne of love, hate, greed—all manner of reasons. 'Cept a passel of folks die bitter because they never had the guts to do anything but stew in their own juice, waiting for it to come to them."

"So, what's Lanatk's mission?"

"To kill a varmint name of Uk-ley, or maybe she was clabbering 'ugly.' Whatever the handle,

he's the black-hearted son of a bitch that ravaged her."

"Killing him won't change what happened."

"I know, but she don't and won't listen. The
Bible says an eye for an eye, and that reads like
fair justice till you realize all that comes of it
is two half-blind hatemongers."

She chuckled derisively. "Odd book, the
Bible. Don't make it clear at all which circumstances call for pokin' eyes and which is the
turnin'-cheeks kind."

Shod hooves rang on stone. Gripping Yolanda's wrist, Jenna cried, "They're back."

She scrambled up so quickly she almost
tripped over her own boots. The mules, Cariboo, Blackie, and Mouse whickered nervously,
tugging at their leads like puppies worrying a
rag.

As he crested the hill, Soupbone raised a
brace of canteens. Behind him, A-rab let out a
rolling belch. The coosie ducked and jammed
his heels into Jughead's ribs.

On bended knee, Jenna gently shook Dan's
shoulder. He waved her away, muttering something unintelligible.

"Pouring water in your ear won't flush the
poison out of your belly," she said. "Roll this
way so's I can trickle it where it belongs.
That's it."

"Plenty more where that come from," Soupbone assured her, handing over a canteen.

"Sweetest little creek you ever saw not four miles north o' here."

Jenna splashed a measure into Dan's mouth, then tipped the canteen away. "Not too much, too fast."

He nodded, yet his mouth pursed for more.

"You're a lifesaver, Soupbone. Both of you."

"Hmmmph. I hate it, but if there's credit due, it goes to that humpbacked daughter of Beezlebub. Woulda never seen that rill what A-rab hadn't whiffed it and stomped over to stick her nose in it."

"Jaysus," Dan sputtered, lying back for a moment. "Never had a glass of oak-aged, gen-you-wine Kentucky sour mash that tasted near as good as that."

"Whoo-ee. You *is* sick, ain't you, boy?"

The trail boss gulped another swallow. "Bad as I ever wanna be till I hear them harps."

"I suspect a plate of boiled rice'd slide down your gullet easy. Mebbe some beef tea . . ."

Dan winced with the effort of propping himself on one elbow. "Druther you'd move the herd to that water. I'll be saddle-worthy by morning. Join up with you, then."

"No," Jenna answered sternly.

"Whaddaya mean, no?"

"I'm not leaving you by your lonesome."

With his brows meeting at the bridge of his nose, Dan looked more like himself than he had all day. "You will if I say so, by God."

Waggling her head stubbornly, she said, "Nope. I'm staying here with you."

"Alone?"

Yolanda nudged Soupbone. "Appears the boss is afeared for his virtue, too. Such high-mindedness is 'nuff to bring tears to a sportin' woman's eyes."

"Just lookin' at ya brings tears to mine."

Before additional verbal shots were fired, Jenna said, "Since you're moving the steers only a few miles, I'll help drive them, then come back."

Soupbone waved dismissively. "Not many straying places betwixt here and there. Soon as they spy that slough grass, they'll be content as hogs at a trough."

"I don't know about that," Dan muttered. "Who's gonna night-herd?"

Yolanda piped up, "Me and Lanatk."

At the mention of her name, the girl sidled closer to her mentor, but her gleaming white smile was directed exclusively at Dan.

Until Jenna caught Yolanda's glare, she didn't know her own mouth had puckered in a ripe persimmon moue. While Lanatk made a drinking motion and polished her belly, Jenna affected the polite countenance of a maiden aunt attending a niece's piano recital.

Lifting the canteen as if offering a toast, Dan said, "Thank you, Lanatk. You saved my—"

"*Merci beaucoup,*" Yolanda whispered.

"Huh? That's French, ain't it?"

"Of course, it's French, boss. Who do you think plundered the north country first? The I-talians?"

Dan's twangy version added extra syllables, but Lanatk understood, for she smiled even wider.

Jenna noticed, however, that the expression of happiness didn't extend to the girl's smoldering eyes. She pondered where she'd seen that kind of vacant dullness before. Immediately, images of the deer her pa'd shot every fall sprang to mind.

After he'd lash their hind legs to a mulberry branch to let the blood drain, the carcasses would twist in the wind, their eyes staring blindly across the prairie.

A shudder ricked Jenna's spine.

Chapter Seventeen

Dan chewed a mouthful of rice while thinking about how much he enjoyed having a gorgeous filly coddling and fussing over him like an ailing child. It was, as Soupbone'd say, "Jes' finer'n a frog's ass."

"Just a little more?" he wheedled, glancing over his shoulder at the kettle. "I'm plumb famished, woman."

The spoon clanked against the empty tin plate. "That's all you're getting for now," Jenna said. "As long as your belly's still in knots, there's no sense packing it too full."

"I haven't gone strolling for hours."

"Only because I'm taking such good care of you."

Scowling like a petulant boy, he crossed his arms at his chest. "Kicking a man when he's down is bad enough. You don't have to enjoy it so dad-blasted much."

"You would, if it was the other way around."

He chuckled. "Only from a distance. I'm like

a gored ox in a lamp factory around sick people. No help at all."

For an instant, Jenna's cheerfulness wavered like a cloud passing across the sun.

"Did I say something wrong?"

Smiling wanly, she shook her head. "No, I'm just weary, I guess. I reckon Yolanda's right. I fret too hard."

"Aw, I'm nigh right as rain again, partner."

"Who said I was fretting about you?"

Choosing to ignore the bait, Dan patted the blanket beside him. "I'm a heap on the grubby side, but my shoulder's soft."

Jenna hesitated, then scooted beside him. She sighed contentedly. Dan started to curl his arm around her, then thought better of it. He didn't want to risk spooking her.

"You do make a fine davenport, Mister Brannum."

"Happy to oblige, Miz French."

She giggled. "We sound like a couple of codgers on the porch swing . . ."

"After Sunday dinner . . ."

"Foundered on fried chicken, mashed potatoes, and rhubarb pie."

"Uh-uh, sodbuster. Fried beefsteak, fried potatoes, and pecan pie."

She fidgeted, sucking in her lower lip and gnawing it. "Won't be long before you'll be cutting into one of those fried longhorns."

"Yeah, I suppose that's right. This time next

month, probably. Don't mind telling you, I've been homesick as all get-out since I got here."

Jenna turned to him. In the dusky light, gazing upon her beautiful face was cruel temptation to a man trying desperately to control his emotions and desires.

"What about your claim?" she asked quietly.

"Signed it over to Chaney and slid it under the door the morning we left. Ain't worth the paper it's written on, but it'll give him something to light a stogey with, anyhow."

"Oh." She looked down at her hands, folded primly in her lap. "Then you are as good as southbound."

"What about you, Jenna? Where will you go? Back to your folks' place?"

"The prodigal daughter? That's not for me. To be honest, I haven't thought much about it."

"Think you might stay in Canada?"

She shook her head. "I love this country, harsh as it can be, but there's too many reminders—most of them, the kind I'd sooner forget."

Dan stared over her crown, absorbing the peacefulness that descends when day creatures retreat to their lairs and the night roamers are not yet wandering.

It seemed almost blasphemous to disturb the contented silence with a probing question, but he couldn't contain it any longer. "You're still in love with him, aren't you?"

Jenna tensed as if he'd struck her. Dan wished he could swat his words away like mosquitoes. The moment they'd slid out, he realized he didn't want to know; wasn't ready to deal with her answer.

"No, I'm not." She raised her chin, her eyes boring into his, reflecting pain, defiance, and confusion. "I never was. He used me, Dan, there's no denying that, but I used him, just as selfishly, to help me run away from a place I didn't have the guts to leave on my own."

"Lady, I think it takes a whole lotta guts just to admit that."

"What? That I'm as self-deluding and self-centered as the man I married?" She laughed bitterly.

Dan brushed away the tear wobbling from the corner of her eye. "It'd be so easy to blame everything on a fella folks knew to be a rascal, but you haven't. You've said very little about him and nothing unkind. You're a straight dealer, Jenna. Why, I'll bet you don't even cheat when you're playing patience."

She snorted indelicately. "That'd be pretty silly. I'd only be cheating myself."

"Yeah, but like my daddy told me, there's no face a man'll lie to, connive, and insult faster than the one he sees in the lookin' glass every morning of his life."

Jenna grinned wickedly. "Despite the getup, I'm not a man."

Dan brushed his lips across hers. "Oh, believe me, I've noticed . . ." He stopped when her fingers weaseled between them.

"Know what my pa always told me?" She eased ever so subtly from his embrace.

"I got a feeling I ain't gonna like it."

"He told me since I was a little girl, There's three things you never put your trust in: a strange dog, a dead rattlesnake . . . and a sick Texan."

Currying his mustaches thoughtfully, Dan drawled, "Well, now, I suspect that's dead-on, sage advice."

"Wh-a-at?"

He pecked her on the cheek, then cozied into his bedroll. "Just wait'll this cowhand gets well, Jenna darlin'. Just . . . you . . . wait."

Chapter Eighteen

Jenna awakened though her eyes remained closed. She languished, suspended between dream and reality—a lovely interlude when yesterday's trials seemed not only distant but resolved, and today's hadn't begun harrying her mind.

She pivoted her hips, gently wringing her spine and back muscles, shoulders tacking lazily along with the momentum. A peek between her lashes at Dan's bedroll brought a surprised blink.

Rather than the wool-covered, hill-and-dale outline she expected, his neatly tied, tarp-covered pallet looked like the dough cinnamon buns were sliced from.

"Mighty fine housekeeping for a fella dashing off for a stroll," she murmured, mildly resenting the abrupt end to her own slothfulness.

Legs folded Indian-style, Jenna stretched, tousling the witch's snarls from her hair. A shadowy form loomed at the northern horizon, footfalls echoing a beat behind their Stetson-crowned maker.

Dan's pace wasn't the tentative, shuffling gait of one recovering from a bout of abdominal misery. His heavy-heeled steps matched the solemn, rigid set of his features.

His gruff voice buckled Jenna's welcoming smile. " 'Bout time you showed signs of life, Miz French. Dawn'll break directly and the herd's waiting."

"And a cheerful good morning to you, too, trail boss." Clambering off her blankets on all fours, she smoothed them with the flat of her hand.

"Oh, well. Sorry." He snatched his bedroll from the ground. "Didn't sleep good. Don't mean to take it out on you."

As she folded the fly, Jenna scrutinized his taut, haggard face. Dysentery had certainly exacted a toll, but Dan appeared more vexed than peaked.

"Are you sure you're up to traveling? No sense in risking a relapse."

One knee cocked at a familiar, impatient angle. "I ain't enfeebled, you know," he muttered and reached to take her lashed bedroll.

Jenna jerked it away. "You're going to be if you don't tell me what's got you grumpy as a pig under a tub."

"Jay-sus Kee-rist, lady." As he itemized his troubles, one finger after another sprouted from its clenched brethren. "I got a passel of steers up yonder somewheres. With two green night riders nursemaidin' 'em, they could be scattered to hell and back, for all I know.

"My head's ringing like a farrier's anvil the day before the annual Fourth of July Futurity, and my gut's as shriveled as Abe Lincoln's pe—" He stammered, his cheekbones flushing crimson. "Well, as shriveled as he is."

Stifling a laugh, Jenna gained her feet and held out the bundle. "I'll be ready to go before you get the horses saddled, Mister President."

She wadded a clean shirt in her hand, smiled sweetly, and struck out in the direction from whence he'd come.

"Hey, where you off to?"

"For heaven's sake, Dan," she chastised over her shoulder, "tend to your own knitting."

"Jenna, don't." His edgy tone stopped her in her tracks. Before she could comment, he added, "It's too snakey thataway. Best you stay close by. I'll keep my back turned."

Snakey, my foot, she argued silently. Haven't seen one the whole time I've been in Canada. And after last night, I surely don't trust you to keep your eyes peeled east. A naughty shiver rambled through her. Or mine peeled west, for that matter.

"The sight of a snake won't put me adither. I'll holler if I need you."

Dawn's silvery sheen gave just enough light for safe navigation over the rocky terrain. Sculpted by glaciers and rutted by a millennia of seasonal freezes and thaws, the landscape's sparseness evinced a rugged dignity, not unlike the hard-earned crags and gullies etched in the faces of time-worn pioneers.

She recalled her mother often commenting on Bank of Hay Springs' president MacArthur B. Frederic's youthful handsomeness. The effusive money changer's two score and ten years had left few marks of their passage, which Jenna found about as intriguing as a freshly whitewashed wall.

The scars, wrinkles and worry lines her father bore aged him unduly, but like a storybook, each illustrated an event in Hank Wade's life, some shared with his daughter, some shrouded in mystery.

A natural alcove gouged in the rock caught Jenna's eye. She started unbuttoning her shirt as she hastened toward it. Wide as a buckboard, it was too shallow to shelter a thin man from the rain, but would serve well as a temporary hidey-hole.

The briny odor of dried sweat wafted into her nostrils. Her chemise was dingy and stained from daily wear, yet even had she'd owned another, there hadn't been time to crop and hem it for a makeshift undershirt.

With a resigned shrug Jenna slipped into her last reasonably clean garment, the flannel stiff from a lick-and-a-promise rinsing and being draped over a bush to dry.

Chin tucked to guide its horn buttons into their corresponding slits, she noticed the flattened butt of a hand-rolled reposed between her boots. Five, no six more tamped cigarettes littered the floor.

Jenna picked up the longest fag end and split the paper. Even without the crimped tobacco's faintly bittersweet aroma, she knew it'd been pinched between the smoker's thumb and forefinger a few hours earlier.

"Dan Brannum, you're a lying, conniving, cattle-thieving son of a bitch."

She hurled the remnants to the ground in disgust. "Had a nice long parley with your confederate last night, did you? Between pleading the backdoor trots and sending the herd east, there wasn't much chance of being discovered, either."

Jamming her shirttail into her jeans, she marched from the alcove. "You told me straight out that the Rocking B was as good as yours. I was naive enough to assume you meant your share of the drive would buy it back.

"But just how do you propose to separate the herd from the rest of us, dearest Dan? You're a rake of the first order, but I can't believe you'd murder all . . ."

A single, blood-chilling thought sent her reeling. Staring blindly at a wind-twisted spruce, a sinking, dizzy sensation assailed her.

God almighty, how could I have been so gullible for so long? Dan was never in cahoots with Cayuse Mike. A middleman shaves the profit. And Dan and his tobacco-loving crony don't have to *steal* the herd at all. If something happens to me, partner Dan becomes their legal owner.

Jenna swallowed hard, fighting for composure. Facts and conjecture ricocheted in her mind, spawning conclusions she'd have drawn much earlier had her emotions not gotten in the way.

Trail bosses don't ride drag, but Dan had insisted upon it so he could signal, or maybe even meet with his associate. That's why he'd been the sole nighthawk, too.

The cold camp she found. Shooting that crippled steer distracted her from telling Dan about it. Even if she had, he'd have invented a perfectly plausible explanation, showing her to be a nervous Nellie in the bargain.

Soupbone never understood why Dan chose her to lead General Sherman across that bridge, much less why he goaded the beast into charging.

With unbidden images of Dan's lips claiming hers, his arms holding her close, Jenna batted back tears. He's courted me, taking whatever liberties I'd allow before the inevitable occurred. It's all been a game, a vicious, cruel game of chess with me playing both pawn and vulnerable king dodging a checkmate I'm powerless to prevent.

Had General Sherman trampled me, it would've been dismissed as a tragic accident. And the night Cariboo got spooked? A horse pawing air has put many a rider in a pine box, no questions asked.

Dan kissed me then, too, and I've ached for him, deep inside—a yearning he must be aware of and eager to satisfy.

Bile scalded her throat. She wiped her lips on her sleeve.

Unless he's lying about that, too, we're less than three days out of Laketon. When will he get shed of me? Tonight? Tomorrow night? Dysentery must've skewed the bastard's timetable. There's not much time left to make ardent, passionate love before the next, and surely fatal, accident befalls me.

Every fiber screamed run, hide.

Jenna pivoted, then realized she was ensnared like a hare in a trap. There was nowhere to hide, nowhere to run, except to Soupbone and Yolanda. But Dan had them fooled, too. Without a shred of proof they'd never believe her accusations.

"What kind of crazy rain dance is that, woman?"

Heart hammering, Jenna whirled at the sound of Dan's voice. With his legs splayed and arms crossed at his chest, her grinning nemesis stood not fifty feet away.

"You've been gone so long, I thought you'd tumbled off the mountain."

And how convenient that would have been for you, eh? she snarled to herself. Wringing the dirty shirt into a lumpy, flannel rope, she strode toward him. "Forgive me for discommoding you, Mister Brannum."

She brushed past, and he grabbed her at the elbow. "Whoa, now, what put the burr under your saddle? I hollered soon as I saw you—"

"We've got a herd to move, remember?" Refusing to face him, she jerked from his grasp. "I suggest we get after it."

Muttering irritably, Dan followed her to camp. Cariboo craned his neck as she approached, ears cocked at the familiar footfalls. Jenna patted him affectionately, then wedged a finger between the cinch strap and his belly to check its tightness. The gelding whickered, his tail switching near her forehead.

From his high perch on Blackie's back, Dan drawled, "Holy Moses, ma'am, I hope that tack suits ya all right. Ain't saddled more'n maybe six or seven thousand horses in my day."

Retrieving the brush-tethered reins, Jenna grasped the pommel and swung up on Cariboo. Unwilling to dignify Dan or his remark, she heeled the chestnut's flanks.

Like it or not, I'm riding point, trail boss, she informed silently. Even a slow-witted greenhorn can track cowpatties straight to the animals that dropped them.

After a few tooth-grinding jolts, Jenna willed herself to relax, rather than sit as if her spine were tied to a fence post.

Later, she had no memory of the miles she traveled and admitted that a circus parade complete with a brass band could have goose-stepped beside her all the way to the bed ground without her hearing a note of "The Flying Trapeze."

From her vantage point it appeared the herd had browsed every sprig of grass bordering the rill, for not a green blade remained. Lowing plaintively, the animals milled alone and in clusters; none were the picture of contentment.

Yolanda leapt from behind the steer she was packing, hooting and waving her hat. Jenna returned the greeting with one hand, reining in Cariboo with the other. Dan eased Blackie up beside her.

"Why'd you—?"

"I wanted to talk to you within sight of the others, but out of their earshot." Dismayed by her trembling voice, she cleared her throat before continuing. "Since it's too late to fire you, I'm forced to let you continue top-handing the herd, but I'll watch every move you make from now on."

"What the hell happened back there, Jenna?" His head canted, a totally perplexed expression on his face. "I haven't done a damned thing—"

"Not yet, you haven't." She rapped the rifle's stock jutting from its scabbard. "And won't, if you value your own hide. I never trusted you, much as I wanted to . . ."

Her chest constricted, and she looked away. "From here on, Brannum, say the sky's blue and I'll glance up and check for clouds before agreeing. Got that?"

She dug Cariboo's ribs so sharply that he bolted. Tears streamed down her cheeks. The chestnut's three-beat gallop mimicked the litany pounding in Jenna's brain: I hate you, I hate you, I hate you . . .

Chapter Nineteen

"It's my fault, boy," Soupbone said mournfully after Jenna and Dan dismounted. "I misjudged how much water and grass it takes to satisfy a herd. Them bovines lapped that spring dry and clipped the fodder afore you could say John Barleycorn.' "

Dan clapped him on the shoulder. "Something in their bellies is more'n they'd have gotten where we were. If we're lucky, we'll find a place where they can eat their fill tonight."

Soupbone glanced toward the herd. "They've gone without forage for what, two ... three days now? Ain't gonna be any meat left on 'em worth frying."

"That they're more apt to balk and stay balked is what worries me," Dan countered. "Never been on a starvation drive, but I've heard plenty of stories about them—none of them pretty."

"Uh, boss," Yolanda said, "if you don't mind me asking, are you tracing a map to where we're going?"

Dan's eyes flicked to Jenna, his mouth flattening to a grim line. "No, but if Soupbone marked the North Star last night like I told him to, it's as good as."

"Shore did—"

"Any harm in suggesting a different route?" Yolanda scratched at her neck.

"Get to spitting it. We're burning daylight standing here dithering."

She hesitated, obviously taken aback by Dan's curtness, as was Soupbone.

"Well, boss, uh . . ." she stammered. "Lanatk knows this country. Her people's trekked all over, trading, fishing, and hunting since afore she was strapped to a cradle board on her mama's back—"

Dan grunted, making an impatient come-on motion with his hand.

"Grousy cuss, I'm agetting there. Lanatk told me a better, shorter way to get to Dease Lake. Said there's lots of little streams, fine for drinking and none too wide nor deep we can't wade."

As the trail boss's frown darkened, Yolanda's explanation all but burst out. "See that peak there to the northeast—the crooked one a fraction taller'n the rest? Head for it like a crow flies and we'll save ourselves five miles."

Dan pondered the white-capped, smoky blue range for a long moment. "What's an Injun know from miles, Yolanda? They measure by sunups and moons."

"That's what Lanatk said, 'a sun closer.' I ciphered the five miles part, boss."

Soupbone jerked a thumb at the saw-toothed mountains. "The shape them steers are in, that shortcut'd pay out in slaughter weight."

"Yeah, except according to Chaney, the lake's no more'n a mile wide itself. We angle too far east, and we'll miss it altogether."

Yolanda's chin set as stubbornly as Dan's. "Not with a native guide, we won't. She beats the bejesus out of a damn star. Where'll we be if the sky clouds over?"

"It got Columbus where he was goin', by God," Dan argued. "Lanatk's just a kid, and I don't mind saying, a shade addlepated from being wrassled the way she was."

Gooseflesh rippled Jenna's arms. It'd been as clear as window glass from the start that Dan intended to stay his own course—no doubt, one leading to a preplanned rendezvous with his henchman.

Yolanda huffed up into a six-foot-three, two-hundred-and-eighty pound colossus of seething maternal indignation. "Where Lanatk suffered is a damn sight south of her mind, Dan Brannum. If we were in Texas, it'd be different, but by gum, that girl knows the land she was raised up in."

In a quiet, even tone Jenna said, "Since we're not in Texas, I say we follow Lanatk."

"And I say we don't, Miz French." Dan trembled with ill-concealed fury.

Jenna stared him down, her courage borne of steely assurance that Lanatk had unwittingly diverted his scheme, at least temporarily.

"Boy, if you'll give us a better 'why not'," Soupbone prompted.

Dan remained planted like a statue and just as talkative. A melancholy pall flickered across his face. It vanished in a tick, too quickly for Jenna to swear she hadn't been mistaken.

Shaking her head slowly, Yolanda said, "Don't mean to gang up on you, boss, 'specially seeing as how you're still a mite green around the gills. Sure you're up to driving?"

His narrowed eyes bored into Jenna's. "That's a decision the beeves' owner'll have to make. Whaddaya think, Miz French? Do I go? Or stay?"

Soupbone glanced from Dan to Jenna. "Hey, what's with you two this morn—"

"Saddle up," she commanded. "Start the herd for that peak." She turned toward the remuda.

"Whatever happens is your responsibility, lady. It ain't mine anymore," Dan snarled.

She reversed herself, mouth curving into a smug smile. "How perceptive of you to realize that, Mister Brannum."

She paused again when he blurted, "That camel ain't going. If the squaw won't leave it, she ain't either."

"Agreed. Even I can see how skittish the steers are without the scent of a strange animal

hectoring them. Sorry, Yolanda, but you'll have
to tell her."

"Yes, ma'am."

"Is there anything else, Mister Brannum?"

His boot toe sent a rock sailing several yards.
"Nothing I can say in mixed company."

Approaching the graceful willow where the
horses were tethered, Jenna noted that Cariboo's russet coat was dappled by sweat-dark-
ened patches; beads dripped from his forelock
and ran down his nose.

"Shouldn't have lathered you so bad, fella,"
she said, scratching his soft muzzle. "But Brannum was priming to defend himself back there,
and I couldn't stomach any more of his lies."

The chestnut bobbed his head as if reassuring her.

"You're the only man I can count on"—she
chuckled softly—"and like as not, a feedbag full
of oats'd sway you in a finger snap."

Footsteps thudded behind her. Jenna
whirled, then sighed in relief.

"Honey lamb, you've been jumpier than a
striped jackrabbit ever since you rode in," Yolanda declared. "If Dan got too feisty last night,
say the word and this frail denizen'll check his
oysters for pearls."

Lord, lead me from temptation, Jenna
thought, and You'd best do it quick. Aloud, she
said, "No, he was too sick to be anything but
a gentleman."

"Uh-uh, no such thing as a Texas gentleman.

I'll swan, if the Alamo'd had a back door, the Lone Star state wouldn't have so many heroes, neither."

"Well, I suppose a bout of dysentery'd make an aristocrat out of a lecher."

Yolanda held up her hands as if in surrender. "Suit yourself. I ain't your mama nor his. 'Cept it's plain that something's put the blood in both your eyes."

Jenna fidgeted, picking burrs from her jeans, wanting desperately to share her suspicions. But what good would it do? Yolanda wasn't well, and fretting over Jenna or worse, confronting Dan, would only make a tense situation unbearable.

"A penny for your thoughts, lamb."

"Oh, I was just curious where Lanatk and A-rab disappeared to. Haven't spied—or smelled— a trace of either of them."

"Aw, she's curled up asleep in a draw 'bout a half mile south of here. Soupbone made her bed the camel away from the herd so's they'd quit ruckusing around. Me and her circled Mouse and Jughead till daybreak, but nary a steer ever hunkered down."

"You must be exhausted yourself."

"Naw, it's surprisin' how many winks you can catch in the saddle, long as your own snorin' don't get too loud."

"Think Lanatk'll come with us?"

"Probably. Soupbone's repacking the mules so's she can leg up on one of 'em." She grinned wickedly. "Old fool's plumb droolin' to gander at mountain peaks and not the ones on the horizon."

"Swing, flanker," Dan hollered. "Tea party's over. Mount up."

Jenna glared at him, yet slid her boot into the stirrup. As Yolanda passed in front of Cariboo, she asked, "Do you mind if I ride left of the herd today?"

"Nope. Them steers' butts look the same from either which-a-way."

Yolanda heaved herself on Mouse's back, the grulla grunting as she landed. Regarding Jenna quizzically, she said, "I reckon you've got your reasons for switching sides."

The lie sprang from Jenna's lips so easily it startled her. "Since Cariboo's a lot fresher than Mouse and water's so sorely needed, I figured I'd veer off now and then to do some scouting."

"Good thinkin', lamb," she agreed. "Just gimme a whistle or a wave so's I can shorten the string whilst you're wandering."

Jenna urged Cariboo to a canter. And if you hear a rifle shot, dear friend, she added silently, it won't be a river I've got pegged in my sights.

By midday, heat shimmers pirouetted across the rugged, seemingly endless expanse. The steers' tongues lolled, dry and lifeless. Like a bovine funeral dirge, their mournful lows rambled continually the length of the string.

Jenna's knees hugged the saddle when a

shaggy brute deliberately swerved into Cariboo. The chestnut stutter-stepped, then held his ground, forcing the steer back into line.

The frequency of such incidents concerned and confused Jenna. The steers had learned that horses meant ropes garroting their necks and usually shied from the larger, more agile animals. Other than a few ill-tempered ones, cattle preferred avoidance to confrontation.

"Yolanda, string 'em out," Dan bellowed from drag. "Don't let 'em bunch or they'll balk."

Only once had the herd lumbered along meekly enough for Jenna to vault up the slope for a look-see. The explanation she'd given Yolanda was rapidly becoming more truth than fib.

Her own mouth and tongue were gummy and tasted foul, but whenever the urge to sip the last teaspoonsful from her canteen grew too strong to deny, Cariboo's droopy neck stayed her hand.

She blinked in disbelief when General Sherman appeared, staggering through the middle of the line. "What the devil?"

The animals surrounding him stopped in their tracks. Those behind the leader started milling.

Jenna wrenched in the saddle at an outburst of frantic bawling. Steers plunged and reared around Yolanda, their bodies swirling like water down a drain. Cussing and hollering, she whipped a coiled rope to this side and that, beating their polls to no avail.

Dan spurred Blackie into the middle of the fracas, firing his pistol first at the sky, then close enough to the steers' noses to singe the hair.

Cariboo faltered a terrifying second with the force of the drag animals overtaking the lead. They closed rank like ants converging on a scrap. Jenna grabbed for the pommel, kicking out the stirrups with all her might.

Soupbone's hogleg boomed behind her. The herd surged forward. Shrill whinnies met screaming bawls. Hazy, acrid gun smoke lay like a blanket over their heads.

Jenna recoiled, vomit searing her throat. The steers' whipping tails flipped gobs of soupy green excrement in all directions.

"Swing 'em, Jenna," Dan bellowed.

The packs complicated throwing ropes in the animals' faces. Spotting General Sherman amid the turmoil, Jenna slammed her heels into Cariboo's flanks, spurring him closer. She lashed the lead steer time and time again, shrieking, "Git, goddamn you. Git."

The General ducked, then almost mounted the roan in front of him to avoid the stinging rope. Bellowing and snorting, he pile-drived through the crush.

"Take him, Soupbone," she yelled. "Keep him movin'."

More fell in behind the General. Seconds later, three balked and reversed themselves.

Gunshots volleyed at drag. Eyes streaming from the dust, Jenna turned around in the saddle, squinting to catch a glimpse of Dan. Her heart lurched. The drag steers were pounding their way toward her, Dan and Yolanda packing them tighter than cigars in a box.

Jenna geed Cariboo in a crescent, quirting his haunch with the rope until he breached the outside of the line. She prompted him to a canter, passed Soupbone and the saucer-eyed Lanatk astride a mule, then rode wide around the herd, circling back to its end.

Though sullen, lethargic, and prone to veer off alone and in groups, the steers plodded onward as if the break in ranks had never occurred.

With the other two drovers prodding the cattle from behind, Jenna proceeded to ride loops around the main body of the herd, cutting off wanderers before they strayed too far, balked, or turned again.

The chestnut's breathing became more ragged with each circuit. Snorting and waggling his head, Cariboo's normally graceful gait became choppy.

Coming up on the heard, Jenna shouted, "Dan, they're stringing all the way to Soupbone. Lanatk's with him, no worse for wear."

At his wave she added, "I'm gonna scout ahead for water."

He twisted sharply in the saddle. "The hell you are."

Silently apologizing to her flagging horse, she snapped the reins. Trooper that he was, Cariboo broke into a smooth canter, Dan's spluttering epithets lost in the measured rat-ta-tat of hooves hammering solid rock.

Once well in front of the herd, Jenna slowed him to a walk. Her hopes rose like soap bubbles in the breeze as the sparse terrain surrendered to myriad, ever-thickening species of vegetation.

Cariboo whuffed at the air and greenery, then whickered his disappointment.

"Don't get discouraged yet, fella," Jenna said as they were drawn into a broad, downward-sloping canyon. She gauged the walls at a hundred feet in height, their stair-stepped surface striated with every color of the rainbow. Nature had not only provided a lofty crow's nest but also a ladder with which to reach it.

Pulling up near the canyon's shady side, Jenna dismounted, leaving Cariboo's bridle reins dragging.

Fascinated by the variegated hues and polished feel of the stone, she climbed one ledge, sidled to another, scaled it and several more, all the while pressing her palms and face to the wondrously cool wall.

The chestnut neighed and stamped a forehoof, the echoes reverberating sharply. Jenna looked over her shoulder, amazed at how high she'd already ascended. "Rest easy and blow, boy," she called. "Be down in a—"

Boulders pelted down from above and to her right. Cariboo backed, then volted wildly. Swiveling her head at the sound, Jenna's breath caught in her throat.

Not fifty diagonal paces from her, an enormous, mangy grizzly crouched on a ledge. Shiny, black button eyes stared at her without blinking.

She clung to the wall, paralyzed. Cruel droplets of sweat trickled down her ribs and between her breasts. She pinched the edge of her tongue between her teeth to keep from screaming.

The bear shuffled forward. A murderous, five-clawed paw stretched to the next level. With ease belying its girth, it rumbled onto the slab. A vile, suffocating stench swept past her.

Shaggy head craning toward her, the grizzly's snout quivered as it inhaled her scent.

She heard hooves—dozens of them. The bear rose up on its hind legs to its full seven-foot height.

"Jen—"

It's Soupbone, she thought. Please, please, do something before this stinking nightmare tears me to shreds.

Mouth open and drool oozing from the corners, a growl thundered in the grizzly's chest. Its porcine eyes seemed to suck the very marrow from her bones.

Boots clattered on the rocks beneath her. A cartridge clacked into its chamber.

Silence.

Jenna shivered, her fingernails scraping stone. Shoot, damn you. Why don't you shoot?

With the terrifying realization that whoever held the rifle wasn't going to fire, darkness descended like a curtain, tunneling her vision.

The bear swayed, forepaws dangling at its abdomen. A vague moaning commenced. It peered at her as if unsure whether to attack or retreat.

Inhaling as deeply as she dared, she murmured, "I won't hurt you. Never meant to trespass on your lair."

Slimy drool gushed down the grizzly's chops. It remained rooted to the ledge.

"Kill me if you want," she continued, her voice as soothing as a lullaby, "just have mercy and be quick about it. If I move, I know you'll be on me in a flash. But that beats hell outta cowering against this cliff, waiting for you to rip my heart out."

She had the strangest feeling that the animal was considering what she'd said, or at least, the way she said it. The animal certainly wasn't starving or it would have attacked immediately.

"I can't take much . . ." Jenna stifled a gasp when the bear dropped to all fours. Pausing to smell the breeze, it rocked around until its ridiculously stubby tail was to her.

An eternity crawled by before the grizzly

scaled the canyon wall and vanished from sight. Panting and too weak to move, Jenna slumped, letting her arms slide to her sides.

She was startled when a hand cupped her elbow. "Lean on me," Dan said softly.

Jenna shook her head. "I-I'm all right. I don't need—"

"Anyone," he finished gruffly. "Especially me." Border-shifting his rifle, he retraced his steps.

It was Dan who'd had the animal in his sights. Waves of nausea hurtled through Jenna. *Would he have let the bear maul me? I heard the rifle cock. Why in God's name hadn't he fired?*

Stooped as a dowager, Jenna eased down the ledges. Near the floor she heard Soupbone say, "Gloryoski, boy, Jenna come a flit from being that griz's supper. Why in tarnation didn't ya plug the brute?"

"Didn't have a clear shot," Dan answered curtly.

"Whaddaya mean you—aw hell, never mind. Just don't never ask me to take you deer hunting. I'd get plumb riled if a twig cheated me out of a pot of venison stew."

Yolanda scooped Jenna into a crushing hug. "Honey lamb, that's the bravest thing I ever did see. Lanatk's eyes like to popped."

Jenna managed a wan smile. "I suppose she's seen what a bear can do to a person."

"That ain't it a'tall. Said if you was a feller,

you'd be a big-medicine shaman. That you surely conjured up Yek; that's one of their highest falutin, hoodoo spirits, to protect you from that hootz which her people believe can savvy humans."

Thinking back to the grizzly's inscrutable expression prickled the hair on the back of Jenna's neck. "Oh, horse apples. I might as well have chattered in squirrel. Mister Griz just didn't find my aroma particularly appetizing."

"Listen here, missy, Lanatk believes what she believes with her whole heart. It ain't our place to scoff."

"I'm not making fun of her, honest I'm not." Jenna felt as brittle as eggshells left from last season's hatchlings.

Yolanda harrumphed, grasped her by the shoulders, and sat her down on the bottommost slab. Hollering over the lowing herd, she asked, "Boss, any objections to me and her taking a rest? One of us is about played out."

Dan shrugged, which both women assumed to mean no.

Squatting beside her, she patted Jenna's knee and said, "Don'tcha talk, just listen whilst I tell you a story Lanatk told me. Might be a hunnert-proof bushwah, but it's a good 'un, anyhow."

Jenna nodded, leaning back against the cool stone.

In a hushed, dramatic tone Yolanda said, "It seems that once upon a time, there was this chieftain's daughter who said some real disrespectful things about the hootz—them's bears, you know.

"After that, every time she'd go berry pickin' with her girlfriends and left her basket sitting somewhere's with nobody watching it, lo and behold, it'd be tipped over and the berries strewed every which-a-way.

"Then, one evening, she was dawdling along behind the other gals when this bodacious, sweet-talker of a fella stepped out from behind a tree. Love at first sight it was. She run off with him back to his den and he took her for his wife.

"Would've been pure-de-romantical if that shiny new husband hadn't—lickety-switch— changed back into a bear and held her captive like a slave.

"Eventually, the bride's tribesmen slayed that hootz-man and freed the gal, but ever since then, the womenfolk's been mighty careful not to say anything disparagin' about bears. 'Specially when they're out berry picking."

Jenna stared across the canyon. As she did, images of the bear's feral features melted into Dan's handsome contours then shape-shifted back again.

Chapter Twenty

Propped by a forearm resting on the pommel, Jenna absently scratched Cariboo's mane. Day's end should find them in Laketon. She contemplated a crazy quilt of notions, perceptions, and observations.

Soupbone stirruped his fingers to boost Lanatk aboard the mule. With A-rab set free, it was easy to forget the brooding young woman's existence.

Jenna chuckled. In Yolanda, Lanatk had surely acquired the largest, loudest, orneriest guardian angel one could divine. But the wise, often brutally candid calico queen would be a splendid mentor in spite of, or perhaps because of, her occupation.

As it happened, Bear Canyon, as Jenna would forever call it, was the gatekeeper to a lush, verdant valley. Both animals and humans had slaked their thirst, eaten their fill, and rested there.

Gazing upon the spruce-bleachered hillsides, where three streams merged into a nameless, crystalline river, looming mountain peaks where winter's white blanket never abated, and the meadow's brilliant jade carpet strewn with every wildflower in Mother Nature's delicate palette, it was difficult to believe that arid, desolate barrens neighbored this glorious site.

Wondrously pastoral though it may be, Jenna mused, like Eden, a wily serpent or two lurks in our midst. But when will they strike? That question had haunted her sleep and festered now, like an ulcer.

Yesterday afternoon, while the cattle dog-trotted into the river, wading almost belly deep for nigh an hour before lapping the sweet, icy water, she and Dan reached a truce of sorts.

He'd approached her, hat in hand, as she rubbed down Cariboo. "Never let it be said I don't give credit where it's due, Miz French. You didn't panic when the herd balked, and riding circles around 'em afterward is what kept another mill from kicking up."

He sounded sincere, and that galled Jenna enormously for some inexplicable reason. Granny Detheridge's oft-repeated advice to confuse the enemy by maintaining an aura of flawless courtesy compelled a curt "Thank you."

Grass rustled as he angled closer to Cariboo's hindquarters. Immediately, Jenna feigned intense interest in a crusty spot near the animal's jugular groove.

"I don't rightly know what brought it on, but

it appears that the further we keep our distance—"

With an irritable snort she intoned, "Isn't now as good a time as any to start?"

Backpedaling a couple of steps, Dan continued, "Like I was saying, spreading out and staying that way'd be better for both of us."

"I'll not argue that."

His lips bowed in the hypocritical fleer undertakers adopt when told of a townsman's imminent demise. "Hmmph. Reckon there truly is a first time for everything."

Turning to swipe the rumpled wool across the chestnut's withers, Jenna stifled the urge to hurl accusations and generally besmirch Dan's minimal, despicable character.

"So, I'll be taking supper at the bed ground."

"Please do."

"Breakfast, too."

Jenna's shoulders ached from exertion. If Brannum rambled on much longer, Cariboo'd end up as bald as a cannonball.

"I'm sure that's for the best."

By the shadow he threw, his Stetson had found its home.

His right hand anchored on the corresponding hip. Jenna didn't need to see the scowl on his face to know it was there.

"You gonna help rope them beeves in the morning? Just 'cause they're blind don't mean I can do it by my lonesome."

She spun on a heel. "What do you mean they're blind?"

Clearly pleased to have gained her full attention, Dan drawled, "Steers get dry enough, their tear ducts parch. When that happens, milky stuff coats their eyes to protect 'em, but then they can't see the broad side of a barn at three paces."

More to herself than Dan, she said, "That's why they were so clumsy, bumping into each other and Cariboo."

"Shouldn't last long. I suspect they'll see the butcher's sledge before it coshes them."

Jenna winced, her stomach taking a lurch. "You're a bastard, Dan Brannum."

"Nope, I ain't. My mama was holy wedlocked long before I came squallin' into the world."

She flounced the saddle blanket, showering them with horsehair and dust. "How easily we'd have been spared that if only your mother had invested a dollar in a female preventative."

A low growl rumbled up Dan's throat. "Lady, fat cows from poor bulls ain't the only critters you can't tell apart. Damn shame you aren't half as smart as you think you are."

He stalked away, then stopped short. "Be at the bed ground, first light. The faster we get where we're going, the happier I'll be."

"As will I, and I certainly intend to get there in one piece."

Now, astride Cariboo on a rise adjacent to the night's camp, she waited for Dan's wave signaling Soupbone to move out. She and the top hand hadn't made eye contact, much less exchanged words since yesterday's verbal parry.

Yolanda and the cook tried six ways of Sunday to find out what caused the rift and to cajole them into repairing it. Failing that, they'd made no bones about their disappointment in the couple's "damfoolishness."

Jenna groaned, noticing the Amazonian cowhand break from the herd and trot toward her. She sat back more properly in the saddle, expecting a last-ditch, kiss-and-make-up plea.

"Ain't been shuttled from one boss to another like this since I was a chubby tyke in ringlets," Yolanda bellowed. "All of a sudden, this drive's got all Indians and no chief."

Shaking her head, Jenna replied, "Obviously, you're upset about something. What, is about as clear as mud."

"You and Dan swapping evil eyes leaves the rest of us not knowing which way to jump nor how high."

"Yo-lan-da."

"I'm agettin' there, dad-gum-it." She jerked her head toward the north. "Lanatk says there's a buncha draws branching off ahead, all except one ending up in a box canyon. Since she knows the right way to go, I asked that old buzzard if'n probably me and her oughta ride point instead of him."

Sucking in huge gulps of air started a coughing spell that hurt Jenna to hear. Knowing better than to inquire about the older woman's health, she vowed silently to force her to see a doctor when they reached Laketon.

"Sorry for the croupin', honey lamb. Anyhow, Soupbone sent me to ask Texas tall, dark, and handsome. I did, and he scratched and twiddled and chewed his cud awhile, then mumbled something about asking you.

"I've rid about five miles in the same spot already this morning, and I figure there ain't nobody left to ask 'cept General Sherman, and he's probably tired of having Soupbone's skinny butt in his face for however many days we've been pioneering this godforsaken country. So what's it gonna be: a yes or a no?"

"Heaven above, after all that, I pretty near forgot the question. Just teasing, don't get grousy." She grinned. "Of course, you can ride point. In fact, it'll be grand watching the looks on those townsfolks' faces when three women ride in at lead and at flanker."

Yolanda's brow furrowed. "I hadn't thought of that."

"No matter. Head 'em up, point gal; we're burning daylight."

They hadn't traveled far before Jenna's eyelids began drooping like counterweighted window sashes. Cariboo's rocking-chair gait was gentle torture for one who'd hardly slept in thirty-six hours.

Worse, the rimrocked gorge they'd entered

acted as a natural cattle chute, which made driving the herd as easy as shooing ducks to a pond.

With every mile the bedraggled, trail-weary steers jogged evermore quickly, a spry spring to their step as if they knew their journey was nearing its end.

Owl-eyed between yawns, Jenna scanned their staved flanks replete with weeping sores. She couldn't help wondering whether their eagerness came from ignorance of their fate or eagerness to depart this burdensome, exhausting world.

A gunshot echoed from the front of the line. Jenna's head snapped front and center. Another winged off the rocks. Cariboo whinnied, hindquarters swerving.

The cattle bellowed and balked in confusion.

Bam. Bam. Ba-bam.

The reports were measured, deliberate, not a random fusillade.

Soupbone and Dan raced past her, rifles clenched in one hand, reins in the other. "Stay back," Dan commanded.

Jenna's eyes darted the length of the canyon's jagged lips. She trembled like a dry leaf in a gale.

Yanking up the Sharps, she swung its barrel right, then left. Answering volleys boomed from the point position.

It's all a diversion, Jenna thought. Must be. She whipped side to side. Any second now . . .

sun'll glint off gunmetal up there. Gotta kill him or he'll kill me.

The terrified steers bucked and pitched. Cariboo lurched, spun, screaming in frustration and fear. Dust boiled up into a choking fog.

A string of shots cracked ahead—repeaters.

Silence.

A single report.

Bullets rained in response, thunking, pinging off the bluffs.

Nothing, then one shot.

Jenna's gut flip-flopped. She hawed the chestnut cruelly. *God damn, you fool woman. It's a real ambush. Dan and Soupbone don't have repeaters. They're pinned down by those that do.*

Cariboo churned, twisting and lunging through the rolling sea of cowhide. Jenna's heart squeezed. Lanatk's mule was being carried along with the tide of animals surging away from the gun battle.

The canyon bulged. Jenna spotted Dan and Soupbone hunkered behind a dead General Sherman, their rifles propped on his pack.

Yolanda? Lanatk? A bullet whined past Cariboo's nose.

Jenna ducked behind his neck. Hind legs tucked, forefeet stiff, he juddered to a halt. She spiraled off the saddle, her shoulder and hip bearing the brunt of the fall. Rifle cradled across bent arms, she scrambled, belly-crawling on knees and elbows, beside Soupbone.

"I told you to stay back," Dan snarled.

A slug thudded into the steer's carcass. Jenna scooted nearer the cook. Bullets peppered on all sides. Pungent white smoke pierced her nostrils and burned her eyes.

"Go to hell, trail boss."

Crouching low, he drawled, "Appears I might directly, if them jakes up yonder have their way."

Jenna peeked through a crease in the pack canvas. Two rifle barrels spaced fifty feet apart angled from the adjacent rimrock.

One shooter lay prone, his derby's brim jutting out from a spruce's trunk like curved stubs. The other, a southpaw, squatted behind a flat-topped boulder, swiveling out on the balls of his feet to bring his weapon into firing position.

She hunched, his rifle's report and the bullet's ricochet resounding almost simultaneously.

"Where's Yolanda and Lanatk?"

Soupbone's good eye searched her face, then averted downward. "The sumbitches shot Yolanda. Dunno if she's dead. Big ol' she-ox's crumpled out yonder in the draw. Can't get to her."

"Lanatk?" Jenna whispered around the lump forming in her throat.

"Dunno. She grabbed my hogleg off'n the other mule and took off arunning. Ain't seen her since."

Teeth grinding and steel edging her voice, she asked, "How are we fixed for ammunition?"

"We ain't," Dan grunted. "Our extra cartridges were on the kitchen mule. Soon as lead started flying, it bolted for tall timber."

Finger curved round the trigger, he slithered up the barricade, squinting at the ambushers' position.

Soupbone rolled toward him. "Reckon if we waved the hankie they'd leave us be?"

"Not hardly."

The instant Dan got a clear shot, a volley thundered from the ledge.

"Yaw—jaysus. Shit—"

He whirled backward, a hand clapped to his chest. Gasping for air, he tipped his palm. Blood smeared the skin; a crimson ooze rimmed the neat hole in his shirt.

Jenna's pulse hammered in her ears. A white-hot rage screamed for revenge. She eased the Sharps barrel into the wedge of fabric. Sight leveled precisely, she said, "Soupbone, take a potshot at that jasper behind the tree."

"I ain't got but two bullets."

"Do it!"

She flinched at the roar of his carbine. The second gunman whipped from behind the boulder to return fire. Jenna smiled malevolently, index finger pulling the brass trigger.

The rifle butt mule-kicked her shoulder. She hardly felt its impact. The sniper's skull exploded in a star burst of brain, blood, and bone.

He toppled off the precipice, dead before his body hit the ground.

"Well, I'll be," Soupbone wheezed. "Damn fine shootin', gal."

"Lucky's more like it." She swallowed hard. "I was aiming for his chest."

"Think we can skunk the other one, the same way?"

Raising up cautiously, she said, "Not at this angle, but maybe I can . . . oh, no . . ."

"What?" Soupbone craned for a look-see. "Lord God Almighty."

With the stealth of a panther, Lanatk emerged from the trees behind the other assassin, clutching Soupbone's long-barreled revolver in both hands.

"Hey, I ain't dead yet," Dan groaned. "What's going on?"

"Lanatk's getting the drop on the other feller," Soupbone cried. "Hell, we can't cover her. 'Fraid we'll hit her instead of him."

"Fire wide then, you fool!"

Arms extended and elbows locked, Lanatk raised the hogleg chin high. Her target reeled onto his back and sat up, rifle arcing with the motion.

Four guns fired at the same instant. When the haze cleared, the shooter was toppled on his side. There was no sign of Lanatk.

"Oh God, did he shoot her?"

"Dunno. Don't rightly think so."

"Cover me in case he's playin' possum."

Jenna sprinted into the draw, falling to her knees beside Yolanda.

From beneath her breasts to her groin, her blood-soaked clothing clung like a second skin. Her lips quivered with shallow, raspy breaths.

Jenna reached to rip her shirt open and examine the wound.

"Don't, honey lamb. Too late."

Clasping her friend's cool, clammy hand, tears streamed down Jenna's cheeks. "No, please, we'll get you to a doctor—"

"Listen, just listen. Gotta put my soul . . . to rest a-fore—" Yolanda bit her tongue and almost crushed Jenna's fingers in a viselike grip. Eyes fluttering open, she exhaled deeply. "This was all my doin' from the start . . . all mine.

"Mike Duncan come to me, promisin' five thousand dollars to bring the herd to this canyon. Said Dan turned him down . . . better me, anyhow. You'd never suspicion it . . ."

Jenna's mind whirled as dizzily as a child's string top. "I don't understand—can't believe—"

"Hush. Lemme speak my peace. I got the cancer, lamb. Had a month, two at most. Needed money bad, and Duncan knowed it. Got me a little girl, Marianna Elizabeth. My folks is taking care of her in St. Louis."

Yolanda smiled, her round face taking on an ethereal beauty. "She's almost four. Prettier'n an angel. Her daddy was a sailor. Run off when

I got in the family way. Gave me the pox, too. Doc said that's why my baby was born blind."

Bending closer as Yolanda's voice slurred and softened, Jenna felt as if her heart were breaking.

"Had to have lots of money . . . for Marianna's special school and all. Nobody was s'posed to get hurt."

Her head lolled. "Shoulda knowed. Be sure to ride point, Duncan tol' me. Saved hisself five thousand—"

She rallied, her free hand flailing as if catching fireflies. "Lanatk didn't have no part in this. Used her." Grief tightened her features. "Used you."

Finger-combing Yolanda's damp yellow-brown tendrils, Jenna crooned, "It's all right. Everything's going to be all right. Duncan'll pay every penny he promised, and I'll see that Marianna Elizabeth gets it. I'll take it to her myself."

Yolanda's china blue eyes stared blindly into eternity. After brushing a palm over the lids to close them, Jenna bowed her head, sobbing.

A strong hand gripped her forearm, pulling her to her feet. Seeing a tear wobble from under Soupbone's eyepatch was almost more than Jenna could bear. He hugged her close, rocking her from side to side. When she quieted, he escorted her away from Yolanda's lifeless form.

"You heard?" she asked.

"Yeah."

"All of it?"

"Enough."

Something in his tone made Jenna step back. While she wiped her nose and eyes on her sleeve, he fidgeted with a black derby.

"Dan knew for sure yesterday that Yolanda was in cahoots with Duncan. Told me so, last night. We didn't know about the baby, though, nor the cancer. Shines a different light on the whole caboodle."

More questions than answers tumbled in Jenna's brain. She rubbed her throbbing temples, her attention riveted on the hat. "That's what the shootist—oh, Lord, I forgot all about Lanatk."

"She's gone. No, no, the vamoosed kind, gal. Found my hogleg atop the ridge right where she cut loose with it. Found this, too."

He flipped the derby crown-side down, pointing to a line of lettering burned in its band.

"Frank Utley," she read aloud. "The North West Mounted Police might be real interested if we can prove he was on Duncan's payroll."

Soupbone grunted. "You ain't tracking the right rabbit. Don't that name mean anything to you?"

"No, and I'm too addled for riddles."

"When Lanatk joined up with us, Yolanda said the bastard what roughed her up was named—"

"Uk-ley," Jenna blurted. "Frank Utley. No

wonder Lanatk ran away. Killing him completed her mission."

"Huh?"

"Never mind. I guess she exacted justice for what he'd done to her."

"Mebbe. Mebbe not. Three of us drew down. Sumbitch's got two slugs in him." Soupbone chuckled, but with scant humor. "Figure either yours or hers went wild."

The teasing remark fell on ears too numb to appreciate it. "Utley terrorized a near-child and likely murdered a good woman. Leave him and his partner for the buzzards. We've got a grave to dig and a wounded man to see to."

Soupbone glanced over his shoulder at General Sherman's carcass. "Whilst I start on the first, you rig a travois for Dan. He's in no shape to ride."

"He will be all right, won't he?"

"Gal, the faster we get the herd rounded up and back on the trail, the better his chances. The bleeding's stopped, but that bullet's lodged deep."

Chapter Twenty-one

After three days of fever-hazed writhing that Dan scarcely remembered, it appeared he'd walk out of his dismal Laketon hotel room rather than be carried out in a pine box.

Judging by the agony he'd inflicted, the boomtown's doctor, a Milwaukee hatter in his former life, might well have used a pick axe to extract the bullet from Dan's chest.

He knew he should be grateful to be alive—to Soupbone for his vigilance as much as to the ham-fisted haberdasher. Instead, only seventy-two hours separated from the Grim Reaper's clutches, Dan was as restive as the "borehole" allowed.

Timid knuckles rapped on the door. Dan slapped his knees with the quarter-folded newspaper—a weeks' old edition of *The New York Times*.

"Whadday want?" He winced, his wound punishing him for his gruffness.

"It's Jenna. May I please come in?"

Covering his bandaged, bare chest with the

muslin sheet, he drawled, "Ain't up to stopping you."

His fingernails rasped on his stubbled cheeks. As the door creaked open, he wished he'd let Soupbone give him the shave and haircut he'd offered the day before.

Jenna's bright smile lit the dingy cubicle like a thousand lanterns. Dan had barred her from visiting, thinking it would also lock her out of his mind. He'd tried to forget how beautiful she was, her loveliness heightened by her skin's toasty vigor, contrasting with her new dress's frothy, mint green color.

"Soupbone tells me you're better. That you'll be fit as a fiddle in a week or two."

"Fever broke yesterday. Don't remember much before that. Been kinda out of my head, they say."

She settled in a barrel-backed chair, careful to avoid the jagged stumps of two missing spindles. What sunlight leaked through the filthy windowpanes burnished her hair's auburn hues. A faint, citrus scent dispelled the room's mustiness.

Strictly business, Brannum, he warned himself. Too much water's flowed under the bridge. Let it go. Someday you might even convince yourself it's good riddance.

"You do know about Yolanda?"

Dan nodded. "I don't bear her any grudge, either. Duncan had her backed in a corner with only one way out. Truth is, I was right fond of her even after I knew she was the inside man— so to speak."

Jenna pondered the envelope lying in her lap beneath her clasped hands. "I thought it was you."

"I know." He laughed bitterly, then groaned. Adjusting his sling offered some relief to the knifelike pains shooting down his back.

"What did you call me in your mind, Jenna? I can't think of anything foul enough for a man who tries to make love to a woman he's fixing to have murdered."

She stared at him, her face so stricken he almost felt sorry for her. Almost. He'd never loved a woman—anyone—the way he loved her. She had the steel to defy him, the soft femininity that made him ache to hold her, take her for his own, protect her.

In loving her, he'd entrusted her with the power to hurt him more brutally than a hundred slugs ever could. And she had. There'd be no second chance given.

"Dan, can't you understand? I knew Cayuse Mike wasn't going to let a fortune slip through his greedy fingers."

"But why me? Why not Soupbone? Why'd *any* of us have to be in on it? Duncan was smart hiring an insider, but he damn well could've stolen the herd without one."

Her lips compressed in a thin line. "Soupbone just didn't seem the type."

"Oh, and I've got 'cattle thief' branded on my forehead, right?"

Under the sheet his hand balled into a fist. Jaysus, take it easy. Send her packing before you bust that scab, tussling with her.

"If you'd ever, once, shared your suspicions with me, none of this would have happened," she argued. "I saw the cold camp the morning you had to shoot that steer. It was you who stampeded General Sherman right at me on that bridge. Somebody, we now know either Utley or the other gunman, spooked Cariboo the night at the river.

"Then, the morning after we lagged behind because you were sick, I found cigarette butts, fresh ones, not a hundred yards from where you'd strolled into camp a few minutes earlier, *and* it was you that got so angry when I set out in that direction in the first place."

She sat back smugly, flicking her hair from her neck. Short strands clung to her temples, glossy with perspiration.

"Miz French, I ain't heard such oratory since Tom Harold McCutcheon was running for Bexar County justice of the peace. Nor such a load of bull dung, neither."

"It is not! I—"

"Went looking for trouble and pushed, shoved, pinched, and kneaded me to fit the neat conspiracy you'd divined in that distrustful, man-hating mind of yours."

"I did no—"

"The hell you didn't. I was trail boss. Like I told you from the start, it was my job to get the herd here to Laketon. Not only didn't you tell me about those camps, the jake in the woods, none of it, you didn't tell Soupbone, either.

"Damn you, Jenna, you coulda gotten that old man killed—yourself killed—all because you can't keep from slapping Guthrie's lying, conniving face on every man you meet."

Dan sighed, a twinge of guilt nagging him for the fat tears staggering down her cheeks. More softly, he added, "You made a mistake marrying him. All right. Your pride got bent out of whack for it. All right. But it ain't fair to make every fella that cares for you pay for your husband's transgressions."

"Does that mean *you* care for me?"

His eyes pegged the tin ceiling, its whorls and angles presenting no revelations and no easy lies. There was a time, a few days ago, when he'd wanted to lash out—hurt her the same way she'd hurt him. Now, he only wanted her to leave him alone.

"I uh, I'm feeling a mite puny again all of a sudden. Maybe you'd best go."

The rustle of petticoats indicated she'd gained her feet. Dan was startled when her hand brushed his bare shoulder. Leaning over the edge of the bed, Jenna kissed his bristled cheek tenderly.

"I guess this is good-bye, then. I'm riding out for Glenora in the morning."

She tucked the envelope under his hand. "There's a bank draft inside for your forty percent of the profits. Between the steers' slaughter and hide price, selling the remuda, the fire at the mercantile giving Soupbone the brilliant idea of auctioneering the freight, we made $41,291.63."

Dan glanced at her, then looked away. He let out a low whistle.

"Minus expenses and the five hundred apiece I decided to pay Yolanda and Soupbone, that is, if you don't object—"

"Nope. They earned every nickel of it."

Her voice caught, but she persevered. "You're just shy of sixteen thousand dollars richer, Mister Brannum. I truly hope it's enough to buy back the Rocking B."

Throat constricting, Dan felt as if he were strangling on his Adam's apple. His heart commanded him to stop her. It seemed to shrivel when his head refused to cooperate.

As Jenna glided toward the door, he croaked, "What about you? After Glenora, I mean."

She half turned, chin tucked and quivering. "St. Louis, to call on Yolanda's folks. I'm told it's a grand city. I may settle there."

He nodded. "Take care of yourself, Miz French, and be happy. I wish you well."

The door almost closed behind her when it swung open again. Her posture as straight as a militiaman's, Jenna's eyes captured his for a long moment.

"I love you, Dan Brannum," she whispered. "I just couldn't leave without telling you that."

In a whirl of green cotton, copper hair, and lemon verbena, she was gone. The room darkened as if the shades had been drawn.

Chapter Twenty-two

Jenna's eyes wandered to the hotel's upper right window as she trotted past astride Cariboo. The glass reflected nothing but hazy blue sky and cotton boll clouds.

It's just as well, she thought, ignoring the murmur in the back of her mind that said otherwise.

Laketon's main street was a churning melee of plinkety saloon tunes, mud, pack animals, barking dogs, dung, and every stripe of humanity.

How gaming houses and saloons acquired faro tables, expansive backbar mirrors, pianos, and barrels of whiskey, while flour, coffee, and beans remained scarce and dear was a mystery shared by most wilderness boomtowns.

Hammers rang and a tingly scent of cedar drifted from where the new mercantile's hewn frame rose from ashen rubble. Josiah Fountainbleau'll be open for business before noon the next day, she guessed, as would the neighboring Miner's Supply and Sam Hayle's Cigars & Tobacco, also charred in last week's fire.

Slapdash boardwalks teemed with silk-hatted gamblers, native doxies flaunting their turquoise petticoats, buckskinned trappers, merchants, veteran prospectors, and gawking, spit-polished greenhorns.

Jenna bowed her head, trying to be inconspicuous, which was impossible in a District where white women were as rare as heatstroke.

"Keep it lively," she quietly encouraged the chestnut.

It seemed every pair of staring eyes knew an oilcloth packet full of bank drafts and cash was tucked inside her slubbed woolen sock. Slanting her heel properly downward caused a corner of the parcel to jab her instep. She didn't dare adjust the cache until well out of sight.

Laketon's environs tapered to a tent village with dozens more canvas castles being erected by the hour. Sounds of commerce clashed with the raspy scrape of whipsaws cutting lumber for sluices and wingdams, steamboats whistling in from the lake, the groans of countless, cradlelike long toms, and sifting elusive, dull yellow flakes from tons of worthless sediment.

Jenna was well along the trail before most signs of the gold-fevered invasion diminished. Tree stumps from finger-girth to footstool-sized littered the track as densely as hairbrush bristles.

"Why, we built the herd a better road than

this," she muttered as Cariboo picked his way around the jagged obstructions. "Fifty cents toll per horse and two bits charged for me on principle. That's broad daylight, cold-blooded robbery, as sure as I'm born."

Overhanging limbs arbored the mucky path, their leafy ends teasing Jenna's face and hair. She stayed to the center as best she could, yet now and then, hastily lopped branches swiped at her like a cat's paw jousting from under a fringed davenport.

She gave wide berth to a scruffy quartet trekking toward Laketon. Chin tucked, but alert for false moves, Jenna tipped her hat at them in silent greeting.

"Mornin', uh . . . ?" The snaggletoothed stranger peered at her, his lips sliding into a grotesque smile. "Why, lookee here, fellers. It's a woman a-straddle of that fine steed."

Cariboo shied when the speaker latched onto the bridle strap. Jenna's hand crept toward the Sharps's stock.

The youngest of the group, a scarecrow of a lad not a day over eight, dawdled a toe in the mud as if embarrassed. His two older companions, doltish louts, judging by their slack expressions, leered at her as if she were a dance hall floozie.

"Whoo-ee, she's a purty thang, ain't she, Delbert?" one nigh drooled in response. "Why, she couldn't pass fer a man in a bat cave on a moonless night."

Jenna's finger curled around the trigger guard. "I'll thank you to turn loose of my horse, mister." She eased the rifle from the scabbard.

"Aw, we ain't aimin' to do you no harm, honey," Delbert wheedled. "Jes' been a huge, long while since we met up with a sweetheart that weren't of the sportin' persuasion. Cain't fault a feller fer appreciatin' beauty when he sees it, can ye?"

Cariboo's ears flattened with the snap of the cartridge being chambered. Jenna swung the rifle into firing position, its bore aimed square at the bridge of Delbert's bulbous nose.

"I said, let go of my horse."

His grip loosened a fraction before his features tensed in a cunning smirk. "Mighty big gun for such a little lady. Sure you know how to use it?"

Jenna stared him down, hoping more fury than fear showed in her eyes. "The best way to find out is to stand right where you are for about five more seconds."

"Leave her be, Del," one of his flunkies said, pulling at his arm. "We ain't walked alla way from Kain-tuck to get our heads blowed off six mile from the diggin's."

Hoofbeats approached along Jenna's back-trail. Much as she wanted to, she dared not risk a glance. Delbert was as burly as he was vulgar. He'd wrench the Sharps from her hands in a second.

"C'mon, Pa," the boy said, his tone too flat

and world-weary for a mere child. "The ol' jasper ridin' up looks like law to me."

Cariboo neighed what was undoubtedly an equine obscenity as Delbert shoved his muzzle away. Whirling, he cuffed his son. "Ain't no laws up here, Runt, 'cept them Nancy-boy Mounties. Ain't did nothin' wrong even if'n there was."

He stalked off, the other two thugs at his heels.

Lips quivering, the boy paused a moment, rubbing his red-rimmed ear. Raising aged brown eyes to Jenna's, he said, "Sorry to trouble you, ma'am," and scampered away to rejoin his father.

Jenna twisted in the saddle for a glimpse at the ol' jasper' edging his mount close behind. She gasped.

"Gonna swaller a flock of skeeters with your mouth flapped wide, gal."

"Soupbone! What in the devil are you doing here? And, heavenly days, that isn't Jughead, it's Mouse. Why'd you buy him back from the liveryman?"

Scrubbed pink as a parson, sporting a freshly barbered beard, hair, and a sleek, moosehide eyepatch, the cook relaxed against the cantle.

"I figured you might want company on the ride south. Somebody besides them riffraffs you was parleying with, anyhow. And yeah, this here's Mouse, and I bought him 'cause I damn well wanted to."

In the minute it took to slip the rifle into its scabbard and haw Cariboo beside him, a suspicion hatched in her mind.

"Did Dan send you to nursemaid me?"

"Well, I had to sit and cogitate real hard for a day or three—" His lips puckered like a kiss before he spit a hefty stream of tobacco juice into the brush—"but by God, I got that idea all by my own self. Miracle, ain't it."

Jenna fidgeted with the reins to hide her disappointment. "I thought you joined the cattle drive to earn a grubstake to prospect up here."

"So'd I, when I done it. 'Cept I've never had this much hard coin in my pocket, my whole life. Sudden-like, it appeared plumb stupid to pour it down a hole in the ground, trying to prize out more."

"Good thinking, I'd say."

He curried his sculptured chin whiskers, chuckling. "Truth be told, nobody's ever accused a prospector of having a lick of sense, but this argonaut's had his toes froze all he can stand. I'm going where the sun'll warm my bones. Where I'll break a sweat if I get too rambunctious."

"Any place specific in mind?" she asked drolly. "Such as Missouri? I hear St. Louis is a lovely city."

"Ain't decided yet, but even a rambling man knows home when he sees it. Maybe knows it better'n them that stays put."

"Soupbone, much as I'd enjoy your companionship, I don't need a chaperone."

"Never said I was one. It's reckless for anyone, man or woman, to ride this trail by their lonesome."

"Once I reach Glenora," she cautioned, "I don't plan to tarry more than a day."

Brown spittle splatted the tree. "I'll do my best to keep pace, gal."

"And I won't be bossed."

He looked pointedly at her. "Me neither, by gum."

"Nor will I abide partaking of strong spirits before we're safely back in the States."

Planting his heels in Mouse's gray hide, he drawled, "All right. See that you don't, then."

Laughing, Jenna wheeled Cariboo, falling in a couple of lengths behind Mouse. Once a point rider, always a point rider, she thought, shaking her head.

Rest and ten dollars worth of oats and sweet hay had certainly revived both horses' flagging energy and spirits. The riders stayed ever mindful of deadfalls that could lame an animal with one misstep, but kept a steady, ground-eating pace.

Frequent encounters with north-bound travelers were curtly accomplished, for they appeared no more eager to stop and chat than Soupbone and Jenna were.

Occasionally, the couple had to vault their mounts completely off the trail to give leave for a single-wheeled "go-devil." Two prospectors could transport five- to six-hundred-pound loads in the crude, buckskin-bound wheelbarrows, their splayed sidewalls demanding every inch of the trail's skimpy width.

Jenna felt guilty as Chauncey and Tristan, unemployed English actors who hoped to make their fortunes reciting Shakespeare to the assembled multitudes, struggled their go-devil across a particularly rough stretch.

"Egad, this oxcart will be the death of both of us," Tristan whined. The veins in his slender neck stood out like bell cords.

"I will let the world wag and home will go I," Chauncey recited in stentorian tone. "And drive my plow as I was wont to do."

Tristan smacked him with his pancake cap. "Not bloody likely, old chap. Bring up your end, or you won't live to see Mother England again."

Frowning, Jenna nudged Soupbone. "Why can't we help them?"

"Because none but an addlepate takes on a chore he knows he ain't equal to, then bellyaches until he's blue-faced when he can't do it. Nobody forced them lubbers up here, and I'll wager if that contraption was fulla dust, they'd sprint like prairie hens."

Jenna saddled up, grateful for the small favor of her money stash shifting atop her shin. As Cariboo surged through the bordering tangle and onto the trail, Chauncey bellowed, "Good

night, good night. Parting is such sweet sorrow,
that I shall say good night till it be morrow."

She snorted, not bothering to wave at the
blathering thespians. "If Pa had those two
staked near the windmill, our well'd never have
gone dry."

The trail veered west across the Tuya River,
then south to follow the northern rim of the
Grand Canyon of the Stikine.

A thousand feet below, the river's white-
capped rapids glistened, their churning, lusty
rush to the sea hushed by the awesome, ter-
raced canyon walls.

"You'd think the earth had a split clear to its
core," Jenna whispered. "I've never seen anything so beautiful and so wildly frightening."

Birds plummeted, swerved, and soared with
the chasm's capricious wind currents. Stands of
spruce crowned both sides of the gorge, with
regiments of braver kindreds miraculously finding root on the tiered precipices.

"Will you look at that?" she gasped, pointing
at a herd of shaggy, white mountain goats grazing amid the conifers. "Those ledges don't appear wide enough for a snake, much less a
goat."

Soupbone's leathery tan blanched to a butter-
nut shade. "Best pray they's broad as boulevards
on this side. Beyond that rise, the trail follows
a shelf jutting out over the river."

Naturally, Jenna was compelled to peer down
again at the Stikine, shrunken to creek size by

such lofty heights. She tottered backward on rickety knees.

"You're joking, right?"

"Uh-uh."

"And I suppose if there was a way over the top, the trail would have been cut that way in the first place."

"Yep."

Shrugging off the woozy sensation that crept through her like a chill, she climbed aboard solid, surefooted Cariboo.

"If a couple of moon-calves like Chauncey and Tristan negotiated it, I reckon we can—as long as we get moving before my backbone turns to yellow mush."

Soupbone nodded, his cheek bulging in earnest as he worried the plug chucked inside it. "We'll have to walk these nags most of the way, I suspect. And whilst you're parleying with the Lord, you might ask Him real nice to put the kibosh to any pilgrims starting out at t'other end."

She groaned at the thought of reaching an impasse with another party headed in the opposite direction. Her mother's stern voice echoed in her ear: Don't borrow trouble when there's more under your own bonnet than you can mend.

Sometimes, that's a whole lot easier said than done, Mama, Jenna retorted silently.

The heart-pounding, gut-knotting, unadulterated terror of those first steps along the silt-strewn promontory would be etched permanently in her memory.

Other than the stranglehold she kept on Cariboo's flimsy reins and continually stifling the urge to latch onto Mouse's tail to anchor her free hand, the rest of the trek was a sensory blur: dust hectoring her eyes; the grulla's musty odor; the hypnotic sway of his hindquarters; fear's metallic whang coating her mouth and tongue; the rhythmic cadence of hooves and heels thudding on solid rock.

When the ledge met blessed, firm ground, Jenna didn't know whether to collapse with relief or sing thankful hosannas.

"Aw, that weren't so bad, now was it?" Soupbone teased, though he looked as spent as the middle man in a chain gang.

"The last time I was asked that, I'd just swigged a gravy ladle full of castor oil."

Wiping his sweaty brow on his sleeve, he said, "If there's one thing can be said about the Cassiar, it damn sure ain't boring. Can't never tell what lies beyond the next bend."

"Well, nothing could be worse than that little jaunt." Seeing him trying to smother a wicked grin brought a blurted, "Could it?"

He waved a hand dismissively. "Nah."

"Soupbone?"

"We got a little cutbank to mosey the horses down in the morning, but then it's easy going the rest of the way."

"A little cliff, huh? Just how little is little?"

" 'Tain't more'n a thousand feet, I expect. Hell, it's no hazard atall for a pair o' billy goats like us."

Soupbone wrenched in the saddle. "Lord above, Jenna, it sounds like a swarm of bees buzzing back there."

She gave him a look no elder could possibly consider respectful.

Raising a palm, he said, "I swear on my sainted mother's grave that the trail gentles now, all the way to Telegraph Creek."

"If I recall, you also said we could mosey the horses down that cliff."

"We moseyed 'em—"

"No, they moseyed themselves," she corrected. "We skidded the whole dad-blasted way on our butts."

"How long you gonna chew my gizzard for ripping the haunches outta your britches?"

"Oh, probably until the choir starts to sing 'Weeping Sad and Lonely'."

Favoring her with a singular evil eye, he resumed the more proper equestrian position.

By their next rest stop, bygones appeared to have become bygones. While Soupbone pried open airtights full of beans and peaches, Jenna was drawn to a mound of discarded supplies.

She took scant satisfaction that the enormous piles of tools, ruptured sacks of flour and rice, vintage muskets, silver tableware, books, clothing—enough loot to stock three mercantiles—they'd encountered farther up the trail had winnowed considerably.

Here, two shaving mugs, several pair of city shoes, a case of White Ribbon Secret Liquor Cure, and a rusty hearing horn had likely been lugged a thousand miles only to be yanked from their backsore owners' rucksacks and abandoned.

"Come 'n get—gal, what is it that makes you so all-fired curious about what them pilgrims have jettisoned trailside?"

"Not curious, so much as angry," she shot back. "There's so much wastefulness being done; it's positively sinful."

With a kick at the rotting heap, she stormed to where he was contentedly munching on a smoked, salted strip of mackerel.

"Tear into one of them bloaters. They's passable for a cold camp, and it's a fair stretch till supper."

"I thought you weren't going to be bossy."

"Hmmph. Didn't know you was gonna get epizootic."

Glaring as she chewed, she argued around a mouthful of fish. "I'm not a horse and I don't have distemper."

"You're acting pure-de-distempered from where I sit."

"Well, it galls me that we labored like ... darkies, driving that freight to Laketon, and we've seen bales and barrels and mountains of stuff lying from hither to yon—not to mention the dead and dying pack animals."

She shuddered, recollecting the scores of flyblown corpses and emaciated beasts of burden left tied to trees. When she opened her eyes, Soupbone was studying her intently. "Doesn't any of that bother you?" she asked.

"Wish I had the coin it took to buy that plunder, but it ain't my bailiwick to lose sleep over other fool's damfoolishness. God created the world, but I don't reckon He put you nor me here to fix things for Him."

She stroked the cushiony grass. Granny Detheridge and Yolanda had possessed wisdom, as did Soupbone. Like crow's-feet, swollen joints, and liver spots, it was supposed to come with age.

Rubbing her thumb across the back of her unmarked hand, Jenna wondered why youth was denied that sagacity. It seemed that by the time a person had it, she'd be too old to need it much.

Dan's beloved, chiseled features shimmered behind her eyes. He'd shown wisdom in avoiding this narrow trail, its indescribable obstacles, and the scores of nomads traversing it.

He was brave, too, to have even attempted trail-bossing the oddest caravan of pack animals and hands across country few, if any, white men had ever trod.

Jenna missed him like an amputee mourning a severed limb. You're a helluva man, Dan

Brannum. If only I'd been woman enough, trusting enough—

"You may raise six kinds of Cain," Soupbone said softly, interrupting her reverie. "But I don't think your nervous flusters have got anything to do with that junk."

Jenna smiled halfheartedly. "Oh? Say it's female weakness and I'll demonstrate otherwise."

He paused to wash down the last of the salty bloater with a gulp of river water. "We'll make Telegraph Creek tomorrow. Glenora, before nightfall, if you want to push on. I reckon you're skittish about Cayuse Mike and the squabble you're due for is coming faster'n a locomotive."

"Can't say I'm looking forward to it. Can't say I'm not eager to have it out with him and over with, either."

"You're kinda stumped that there ain't been a ruckus along the way, too."

She nodded. "Dividing the money between us after we started out calmed me considerably, but I'd have bet every penny that Duncan would send a bushwhacker to relieve us of it."

Soupbone repacked the burlap supply bag and rolled it to secure against the pommel. "Pity the poor shootist that jerks my boot off to get at it. He'll think he's the guest of honor at a skunk convention."

"I understood Cayuse Mike's grapevine to be faster than Western Union," Jenna said as she stood to brush grass and dirt from her backside.

"But maybe he hasn't gotten word yet that we made it to Laketon."

"Yeah. Could be, he ain't."

The knife edge to his voice betrayed him. Jenna knew better, regardless; yet for once, she'd have welcomed a convincing bit of deceit.

Chapter Twenty-three

Captain Moore's tollway skirted a sprawling Indian fish camp at the confluence of the Tahltan and Stikine rivers.

Along the gravel bars men hauled in willow traps chocked with salmon struggling to escape and race for the spawning grounds upstream.

Tons of gutted coho and scarlet steelheads hung from poles to dry before their turn inside the crude smokehouses. Like giant macabre beads, the heads were strung on separate poles, with delicate roe packed in willow baskets for smoking.

A plentiful river harvest meant full bellies rather than hunger come winter, so all but the tribes' youngest members were involved. Yet, hard as they worked, smiles beamed from every coppery face.

How marvelously uncomplicated their life seems, Jenna mused, then chuckled softly. Probably because I'm not living it.

She had spent the last ten miles doing her level best to think about anything besides journey's end or Dan Brannum. The former, especially, put the flocks of butterflies nesting in her innards on fluttery wing.

Soupbone didn't help much, for he glanced over his shoulder at her so persistently, Jenna feared his head might shear off at the neck like a worn-out bolt.

The plan she'd divined during the sleepless night seemed flawless; the odds of the old buzzard cooperating with it at best, seventy-thirty. Providence would simply have to intervene.

As they neared the river port, the gold-fevered pilgrimage, both four-legged and two, increased. Most of the pioneers were as friendly as half-grown pups, and flushed with the solid surety that untold wealth would be theirs before autumn flamed the foliage.

Cresting the hill that formed Telegraph Creek's eastern boundary, a veritable throng milled along its main thoroughfare. At the riverbank a double-decked steamer discharged its load of human and animal cargo. Verily, news and ongoing reports of Thibert's, Tifair's, and Loozon's strike must have headlined every newspaper in America.

"Soupbone . . . hold up a minute."

"Anything wrong?"

"I need to talk to you where we won't be overheard." Scanning the bowled terrain, she added, "There, that shady grove of alders looks nice and private."

They left the horses to graze, settling them-

selves in a pool of shade. Because his most fe-
rocious scowl had long ago lost its daunting
affect, she forged cheerfully ahead. "From what
I've been told, Guthrie wasn't much of a poker
player—"

"Hmmph. That's same as saying Abe Lincoln
weren't much of a mule-skinner."

"Please, Soupbone. Hear me out."

He sucked in a corner of his mouth, nodding
with obvious reluctance.

"I need an ace for a hole card when I meet
with Cayuse Mike who, I've decided, truly
doesn't know or has just been informed, of our
success. After all, a henchman stationed in
Laketon couldn't have gotten more than a couple days' head start on us."

"An Indian runner'd double that."

Jenna rolled her eyes heavenward, mustering
her patience. "Except it makes absolutely no
sense that he'd hire gunmen to kill us and steal
the herd, then let us waltz away with the
profits."

"Good point."

"Thank you. All right, we agree there's a
chance we've got the temporary drop on him."

"Only till we ride into Glenora."

"Exactly. That's where the hole card comes
in. I want you and most of the money aboard
the next steamer departing for Wrangel. That'll
put you and the loot on the American side of
the border before I call on Duncan to tell him,
among other things, that if I don't join you by

tomorrow afternoon, Fort Wrangle's commander and the Northwest Mounted Police will be notified of his ill-fated venture into the cattle business and my disappearance."

Soupbone adjusted his eyepatch as he was wont to do when pondering something of importance. He took on a puzzled expression, then drawled, "By damn, it just might work."

"All I'll need is enough cash for my own steamer passage, to reimburse Mister Twyford for the merchandise we freighted and our supplies, and the nine hundred Guthrie owed Duncan."

"Best take fifteen. Cayuse Mike's hell-bent for tacking on interest." His brow furrowed. "The only part I ain't keen on is you riding the twelve miles betwixt here and Glenora by your lonesome."

Jenna rocked on her haunches. "I'm not terribly keen on it myself, but I do think it's safer for both of us if we split up. And, all this foot traffic on the trail should lessen the risk of an ambush."

"By Duncan, yeah. Problem is, there's plenty more cat-eyed bummers stalking these hills like them four that pestered you outside of Laketon."

"I sent them skedaddling, didn't I?"

"Sure enough, 'cept what if they'd gotten real nasty? Could you truly have plugged that fella at close range?"

In her mind's eye she saw Delbert's young

son, hand clapped against his head, apologizing for his elders' behavior. The child had a poor excuse for a father, but thanks to the War, thousands didn't have one at all.

"Yes," she lied, bold as brass.

"Uh-huh. Well, would Lady Black Bart kindly mull a couple of suggestions?"

A grin served as Jenna's answer.

"Since any bloodhounds what might be sniffing around is gonna be asking after a freckle-faced, passable pretty female, how about if I saunter on into town, check the steamboat schedule, secure me a ticket, and get us some decent grub to gnaw on whilst we're waiting?"

Thumb cocked under her chin and index finger tapping her cheek, she feigned intense deliberation. "By damn," she drawled, "I think *that'll* work for sure."

Chapter Twenty-four

Dusk's gray veil was falling by the time Jenna completed her uneventful ride to Glenora, the gloom as beneficial for her as for anyone watching from the shadows.

Just as she'd expected, the boom had put the bustle to the Stikine's only other river port gateway to the gold fields.

That, too, offered both relief and vexation. Melting into a crowd lent some security as long as its members were too drunk or distracted by dreams to notice her gender and Scotch-Irish coloring.

Cariboo whuffed the air, his ears taking a double-barreled bead on Goodacre's Livery. Clearly, the animal remembered the barn's warm stall and well-filled troughs.

The beginnings of Jenna's wan smile faded. So much for well-laid plans, she thought, slowing the chestnut to a walk.

Soupbone had sold Mouse, profitably, before boarding the steamer, yet Jenna hadn't considered what she'd do with Cariboo when she arrived at her destination.

She patted his sweaty neck, murmuring, "Maybe because I hate like the devil to leave you behind, old fella."

Goodacre would give her a fair price and Cariboo the care he deserved, but the liveryman or his stable hand might also alert Duncan of her whereabouts—intentionally or not.

To Cariboo's whickering disapproval, Jenna urged him past the stables, heading directly for Twyford Chaney's mercantile. When she dismounted and wrapped the reins around a post, the gelding favored her with a disdainful look.

Inside, the storekeep was behind the counter, totaling the bill incurred by three gents hovering over his scrap of butcher paper like buzzards on carrion.

Jenna sidled into a dark corner, studying the labels on an assortment of shelved airtights as if they were museum pieces.

It seemed as if a week passed before the tinhorns gathered their plunder and took their leave.

"Sorry for the wait, sir," Twyford called. "Those boys— Why, a thousand pardons, Miz French. I didn't recognize you in that hat and trail duds."

She smiled as she strode toward him. "No insult taken, Mister Chaney. In fact, I'm relieved you didn't."

"So you and Dan got the herd through, did you? Never doubted for a second that you would." Before she could respond, he asked,

"Where is that long, tall Texan? Bending an elbow over at the Kingchautch?"

"He's uh—Mister Chaney, I've got a world of things to discuss with you. When will you close up for the night?"

She jumped when the merchant slapped the counter with the flat of his hand. "Right now seems as good a time as any." He proceeded to the door and shot the bolt.

"I keep a private kettle boiling in the back. Got a couple of comfortable sippin' chairs, too."

Between the warmth of the bachelor's tiny quarters, the cushioned rocker, and heady aroma of fresh-brewed Arbuckle's, Jenna almost pitched into a swoon.

Chaney sighed as he slumped in the other spindle-back. "Whenever you're ready, I'm all ears for the whole story. Don'tcha dare leave out a thing."

She chuckled at his boyish enthusiasm, then launched into the adventure as instructed. The granite pot was as close to drained as Jenna was when she finished.

"Sorry to hear about ol' Yolanda. She wasn't a bad sort, for a whore, anyway. But are you sure Dan's on the mend? I'm pretty fond of that fellow. He's honest as the day is long. Not many like him in this neck of the woods."

His words brought a wave of sadness. Several seconds passed before she could trust her voice not to tremble.

"I'll wager he'll be striking out for home before July's over."

Chaney's blunt chin bobbed. "Well, the day he gets here, I'll stand him to all the Forty-rod he can guzzle."

"That's one of the things I want to discuss," Jenna said, drawing herself up straighter. "I don't think it's wise for Dan to come back to Glenora."

"Why not?"

She related her and Soupbone's plan to outfox Duncan, all the while hoping the affable storekeep wouldn't betray her trust.

"I'll pay whatever it takes to get a message to Dan that it'd be dangerous to show his face, or back, here again. He'll be the only one left that Duncan could use for a whipping post."

"A Tlingit boy I know'll hot-foot the warning to him. It's your safety I'm concerned about. Duncan isn't going to hand over that kind of cash with a smile, Miz French. Rumor has it, he's done away with many a man for a lot less than that."

"With Soupbone waiting in Wrangel, Duncan would be foolish to do me any harm."

Chaney drummed stout fingers at his temple. "Except you could be six feet under before that old argonaut realizes something's gone wrong. Accidents do have a habit of happening to those who've ruffled Mike's feathers."

Jenna sucked in her lower lip. That potentially fatal flaw hadn't occurred to her. Worse, it was too late to divine an alternative.

"I'll do what I can to protect you, as long as you understand that I can't be too bold about it. Duncan has this town in his watch pocket, and that includes me."

Boring hard into his eyes, she asked, "Does that mean he'll be privy to all I've told you, soon as I'm out the door?"

"No, ma'am, it does not."

"Thank you, Mister Chaney."

"Don't thank me, yet," he said with a chuckle, though there wasn't much humor in it. "For what it's worth, I don't think taking on Duncan tonight is a very shiny idea. Better to hide out here and call on him right before your steamer boards."

Jenna glanced warily at the neatly made cot that claimed an entire wall.

"Hey, now, I'm not suggesting anything improper. I'll find me a poker game at the Kingchautch, which I'm known to do with regrettable regularity."

"Then I'd be delighted and forever grateful to take you up on your hospitality. She paused, adding, "But there's a speck of horse trading to be done before I do."

Chaney took on a puzzled expression when she leaned to tug her trouser leg from inside her boot. His face flushed rosy, and he averted his gaze as she crumpled the leather upper and pulled down her sock, exposing a length of calf only a husband had a right to ogle.

Though amused by his discomfort, she hastily rearranged her attire in a more decorous manner. Unwrapping the oilcloth packet, she extended a sheaf of bank notes. "That's what's owed against the goods we freighted to Laketon."

A slimmer pile changed hands. "This should settle up the supply bill, with a smidge extra, for interest."

"Miz French, I kind of wish you'd waited until morning to give me this. Best way I know to go broke playing poker is to feel prosperous."

She jerked a thumb toward the street. "At least if you bust, you'll have transportation out of town. Fourteen hands worth of smooth-mouthed, Sunday horseflesh is tied outside needing an owner that won't mistreat him. His name's Cariboo, and you can keep him, sell him, whatever you wish, but please, do me the honor of accepting him as a gift."

"Are you sure? Much as I've hankered for a good mount to ride back and forth to Telegraph, like everything else, horses are dear-priced around here."

Grinning mischievously, she said, "Cariboo might not seem such a bargain after you've fed him a while."

Several greenbacks tucked under the bank notes were counted and held out to the stunned storekeep. "That should be enough for passage on tomorrow's steamer, if you wouldn't mind securing it for me—and only if no one'll wonder about it later."

Tucking the cash into his shirt pocket, he assured her, "I spend half my life hauling freight back and forth from the riverbank. "The *Hope*'s due in before noon, and Captain Parsons and me's foamed our mustaches many a time. He'll keep it under his hat."

The *Hope*, Jenna repeated silently. To set sail for the States on a so-named ship seemed wondrously auspicious. All she had to do was live long enough to board it.

That dire thought reminded her of the night's final transaction. "Now, I still owe you for the rifle and other personals, but if you're agreeable, I want to trade it for a revolver and ammunition."

"I don't have a single derringer in—"

"The forty-four caliber, six-shot Army Colt you had when I bought the Sharps would suit me fine, Mister Chaney."

A groan, as if his lungs had suddenly sprung a leak, rumbled from his lips. "I've never known such a gun-savvy woman. Makes a man kind of nervous."

"My father always wanted a son and had one until Mama forced me into petticoats and hair ribbons," she replied. "I reckon I'm not a particularly feminine woman, but my abilities are quite diversified."

"Oh, no doubt about it, ma'am. The Colt's

yours, dead-swap for the Sharps. Anything else?"

Grimacing as she tried to squelch the yawn prying her jaws, she shook her head. "Goodness. Excuse me for my rudeness."

"Miz French, after all you've been through and what you're facing tomorrow, I don't know how you keep slapping one foot in front of the other."

When he rose, the rocker chirruped a farewell. "I'll fetch your possibles off, uh . . . Cariboo, wasn't it? Then you can lock up after me."

One step took him halfway through the doorway. He turned, gazing at her for a long, thoughtful moment. "It's none of my affair, but you're a fine-looking, sandy-crawed woman, Jenna French. For the life of me, I can't feature why you and that Texan didn't hitch up to the same wagon."

She sat motionless, battling for the composure Chaney seemed determined to wrench from her. "What's done is done, Mister Chaney."

"No, ma'am, I flat don't believe that, and surely hope you don't either. Other than dying, what's done can damn well *always* be done over. All you gotta have is the want to."

Chapter Twenty-five

Jenna's brushed kid boot crossed the River Queen Saloon's threshold at the stroke of twelve-thirty. Up since dawn and as nervous as a Jezebel at a tent revival, it'd been the longest morning in memory.

She clutched a moose hide pouch at her waist, one forearm supporting its bottom. It was awkward, but in all other positions she'd tested, the soft leather hugged the Colt's long-barreled outline like a mitten.

"Show me to Mister Duncan's office, please," she said to the swarthy, pock-marked man tending bar.

His gimlet eyes rambled from her widow's peak to her mint green hemline. "Women ain't allowed in the front door. Go round back to the service entrance." He chuckled wickedly. "It's special-made for them that services the boss."

Jenna marched behind the line of hooch hounds standing shoulder to shoulder, swigging their dinners. Politeness had founded her inquiry. She knew quite well from her previous visit where Duncan brass- and mahogany-appointed lair was located.

"Hey, lady," the mixologist bellowed. "You deef or something?"

"Aw, leave her be, Serge," one of his customers slurred. "Whaddaya think she's gonna do, shoot him?"

Only if I have to, Jenna answered silently.

The barn-sized, smoky room was alive with gamblers' patter, the ping of silver coins, clacking chips, and the sharp kiss of billiard balls.

With a genteel nod toward the players, she negotiated a hallway and knocked on a six-paneled door.

"What is it now, Serge?"

Plastering on a sweet, Southern-belle smile, Jenna swirled inside, gushing, "I hope you don't mind me barging in like this, Mister Duncan."

A dumbfounded expression caused his jowls to sag comically, but he recovered in the blink of an eye. "Of course not, Missus French. This is a delightful surprise."

He sprang from a high-backed swivel chair and darted around the desk to proffer his guest a seat. She settled a fraction clumsily, for the chairs Duncan provided visitors had considerably shorter legs than standard.

The bag lay heavy in her lap. An uncommon warmth seemed to emanate from it. Jenna tucked her elbows to her ribs, hoping to hide the moons of perspiration she knew were darkening her dress.

"I only learned a few hours ago that the cattle drive was successful. Bravo, dear lady. You're to be commended for your efforts."

"More to the point, Mister Duncan, you're to be compensated for your investment." She eased the pouch's drawstrings open, careful not to expose the revolver or her travel voucher.

"This draft, in the amount of seven hundred dollars, reimburses you for the cost of the cattle," she said curtly, sliding the instrument across the desk's gleaming oxblood surface.

Duncan peered down his nose at the note without acknowledging its presenter.

"The second covers the gambling debt my deceased husband incurred, plus two months' overdue rent on our cabin."

"Most businesslike, Missus French. Again, I am compelled to commend you. There is, however, a slight discrepancy between the amounts you've tendered and the balance my bookkeeper recorded in the ledger."

Jenna pressed her knuckles against the revolver's grooved cylinder. "Oh? How much of a discrepancy?"

Pulling a handled quizzing glass from his breast pocket with one hand and flipping ruled pages with the other, Duncan was a study in diligent fact finding.

Jenna watched as his manicured index finger crept down a column and felt a peculiar admiration for the articulate fraud. Had Guthrie not told her, she'd have never guessed Cayuse Mike Duncan was illiterate. He managed his various enterprises, both legal and illegal, with a head for figures and an incredible memory.

"Ah, here we are," he said, pegging an entry at the bottom of the ledger. "I'm afraid you're still five hundred dollars in the red."

"That's simply not possible! Why, you told me yourself how much Guthrie borrowed to buy the herd and about his unfortunate run of cards."

Steepling his fingers, Duncan peered over their spire. His well-practiced somberness was surely designed to put the squirm in his victims' backbone.

"Just like a bank, I must charge a reasonable percentage of interest on outstanding debts."

Jenna paused for a quick mental calculation. "Fifty-five percent is hardly reasonable, Mister Duncan."

He splayed his hands and shrugged.

"Would you be willing to negotiate?"

"I'll listen to your proposition."

She took a deep breath, letting it out slowly. "If you disregard the interest I supposedly owe, I'll do the same for the interest on the five thousand dollars you owe Miss Yolanda Diamond."

Duncan chuckled, then threw back his head and laughed long and hard. "Where did you ever get the idea that I owed that harlot a copper-cent?"

"From her," Jenna replied evenly, "shortly before she died from two bullet wounds. The gunmen you hired gut-shot your point rider like a rabid dog, Mister Duncan."

"That accusation is not only preposterous, but impossible to prove." His lips parted in a malevolent, feline smile. "After all, neither that grotesque old whore nor the shootists are in any condition to testify."

Jenna gained her feet, swinging the Colt into position with one fluid motion. She took steady aim with both hands around its plow-handle grip. "I shot the man who murdered Yolanda. Don't think for an instant I have any qualms about killing the man who hired him. I'll take her wages now, if you please."

Duncan raised his arms, palms out, his owled eyes locked on the revolver's bore. "For God's sake, I don't keep that kind of cash in my desk drawer."

"No, but you carry twice that in the money belt under your shirt."

"How could you know . . ."

"My husband told me last Christmas Eve. After a customer spilled whiskey punch all over you, Guthrie brought you a clean shirt. You were too drunk to notice that he didn't completely shut the office door when he left."

"The conniving bastard, I—"

"Get up, Duncan . . . slowly. Right hand—

two fingers. Remove the derringer from your left pocket."

The pearl-handled hide-out clunked on the desk.

"Left hand, right pocket, the same."

Its twin thudded beside it. She snatched them up and laid them on her chair's seat.

"Off with the jacket, tie, and waistcoat. Let them drop behind you."

As he complied, Jenna was taken aback by the pure hatred emanating from his every pore. Her revolver wavered not an inch as she reached behind and turned the lock.

Cuff links bounced to the floor, then an arm fell to his side as he began unbuttoning his shirt.

"Yank the tail out of your trousers, Mister Duncan. Keep both hands where I can see them."

The canvas money belt bound his waist like a truss. At a half-inch thick by four inches wide, it must have been as uncomfortable as a millstone.

"Sidle around the desk—whoa, that's far enough. Unbuckle that belly bank. *Both hands.* I'll not remind you again."

Jenna wriggled her tingling fingers, trying to rekindle the circulation. The Colt felt as heavy as an anvil.

"Count out five thousand and make it snappy."

He dealt the bank notes into a stack like a poker hand. His lips mimed the running total.

At least my unlearned foe can count, Jenna thought. Sweat trickled between her breasts. Chaney'd told her the steamer would cast off shortly after one. No clock adorned the walls. How much time had passed since she'd arrived? Ten minutes? Fifteen?

"Faster, Duncan."

A venomous glare shot from the corner of his eye. Another sheaf left its cotton confines. He licked his thumb.

Jenna's arms trembled visibly. She ground her teeth as if that would bolster her endurance. It was reassuring to notice that Duncan cut a far less imposing figure stripped to the waist with his braces dangling near his knees.

She was startled by the crash of glass shattering outside the door. Muffled guffaws, probably from the billiard players, drifted into the office.

The fifth stack was still shorter than its neighbor. Jenna's pulse galloped through her veins. "That's close enough, Mister Duncan. Consider the difference your dad-blasted interest."

She edged backward. "See that pouch? Fill it, quick."

Yolanda's legacy disappeared into the hide bag. Jenna chanced a single-handled hold on the revolver to wrest a flour sack from her dress's pocket. She tossed it at Duncan.

"Stuff your clothing in that. No dawdling, and I'll not brook a false move."

She moved to the opposite side of the desk for a clearer view. As she'd suspected, like most who relied on thugs for enforcers, the Scotsman was no hero. Powerful only by proxy and lulled into complacency by his reign of intimidation, he was a gutless wonder without his henchmen at his back.

"Now, take off your trousers."

"What?" Duncan blustered. "Missus French, this is an outrage."

"Do it." Jenna angled the barrel at crotch level. "Put 'em in the bag."

Tugging the fabric over his polished highlows, his ruddy face gleamed with sweat.

"Drawers, too."

He glanced at her, then nodded in resignation. Stark naked but for his shoes and gartered socks, he tossed the plump sack beside her without being told, then cupped his privates protectively.

A fist pounded the door. "Everything all right in there, Mister Duncan?"

By reflex, Jenna almost whirled at the intrusion. "Tell him you're hale and hearty."

"What if I don't?" he sneered.

"Then I'll blow your fool head off."

"Which would bring Serge blasting through the door. He'd kill you before you drew another breath."

The brass knob rattled. "Boss? You got that woman in there with you?"

A wicked chuckle rumbled up Jenna's throat. "Oh, but I'd still have a tiny chance of escape, whereas you'd be cold, stone dead."

Duncan's chin jerked up. "Get back to the bar, Serge."

"You sure, Mister—"

"Leave me be."

The expectant silence was a hundredfold more frightening than Serge's intrusion. Jenna fumbled in her other pocket for the precut lengths of rope it held. She flipped two of them into his lap. "Lash your ankles to the chair legs ... no, spread 'em, Duncan. Modesty be damned."

It pleased her to see he shackled himself tightly. His arms curled behind the chair, awaiting the inevitable.

She hesitated. Her heart hammered in her chest. She must lay the Colt down to manacle him. And Duncan knew it.

Kneeling behind him, Jenna steadied the revolver with one hand. The other snaked the rope across his wrists. God love the lousy coward, he didn't so much as wiggle.

Jenna grinned in triumph and proceeded to hog-tie him in record time.

Wadding his handkerchief into his mouth, she said, "Even if you free yourself, I reckon you'll be loath to sprint through the gaming room, *Cayuse* Mike."

She stowed the Colt in the plump pouch. Just as she'd practiced that morning, her voluminous skirts and petticoats hid the flour sack straddled between her thighs.

Poised to release the lock, Jenna turned. "For the record, you've been repaid every dollar Guthrie owed, plus interest. And I have not taken a nickel more than Yolanda's due."

She breezed into the saloon, closing the door firmly behind her.

One billiard player peered at her curiously for a scant second. Jenna bobbed a farewell and glided toward the entrance. Stepping as lively as a duckwalk gait allowed, her passage caused several leering jakes to nudge their fellows and point.

Jenna's steel nerve faltered. A swoony sensation blurred her vision. Any second, voices would holler "Stop, thief," and grimy hands would grab her arms.

Eyes flicking across the sea of faces, she read their expressions like a signboard. Good Lord, the randy hooch hounds thought Duncan's hearty pleasuring had put the hitch in her stride.

Jenna bit her tongue to stanch the giggles quivering her belly. Oh, if you only knew, she thought. Calling Mike Duncan "Cayuse" is the same as calling Abe Lincoln "Shorty."

Bright sunlight almost blinded her as she stepped out on the boardwalk. Every instinct screamed run. It was damnably difficult to ignore them.

Rounding the corner of the building, she made straight for a row of ramshackle privies. Her prayers were answered; the third from the left wasn't occupied.

After hooking the string latch over a bent nail, a whirlwind commenced inside its rank, filthy confines. Jenna spraddled her legs; the flour sack thumped the dirt floor beside the money bag. She ripped off the dress and petticoats, pearl buttons flying in every direction. Shoes, stockings, garters followed.

With the mound of fabric covering the glory hole, she yanked down the burlap bag she'd tacked to the ceiling before sunrise. Socks, Levi's, flannel shirt, and boots were donned in a flash; the other ensemble shoved down the ragged hole. Jenna twisted her hair off her neck, secured it with pins, and clopped a knitted hat over the wad.

Leather pouch tucked inside the burlap bag, she departed the privy, leaving Duncan's belongings where they'd fallen.

Cutting a wide berth around the saloon, she reentered the street a hundred yards above it. No alarm appeared to have been sounded.

At the riverbank the *Hope*'s stack belched clouds of black smoke. One gangplank had already been raised. Crewmen were wrestling with the other.

Jenna rose on the ball of her foot to sprint

for the boat. An iron hand clapped her arm and spun her around.

"Think you're a trickster, eh?" Serge's stinking breath blistered her cheeks. "One of the reg'lars saw ya sashay outta the shithouse."

The *Hope*'s steam whistle trumpeted its departure.

She hied back and kicked her captor's shin with a brute force borne of six weeks in the saddle. Serge roared like a bull. His grip loosened. Jenna tore free and ran pell-mell for the *Hope*.

"Grab that bitch," Serge bellowed. "She robbed the River Queen."

A crewman pitched the last mooring rope onto the deck. Heavy footfalls thundered behind Jenna. She slammed through the people milling at river's edge.

The crewmen leaped aboard the steamer's flat prow.

"Wait . . ." she screamed, waving frantically.

He wheeled, spotted her, and shook his head.

Water flumed from under Jenna's boots. She vaulted for the prow. Teetering on its edge by one foot, her slick sole caught, then skidded backward.

A bear-sized hand snagged her wrist. The crewman jerked her onto the planks, almost pulling her arm from its socket. Jenna's knees buckled, and she collapsed on all fours, panting like a winded dog.

"You all right?" her rescuer asked, patting her on the shoulder.

She nodded.

He chuckled merrily. "I s'pose it's kinda late to ask if you've got a paid passage, eh?"

Chapter Twenty-six

"Well, you sure took your goldurned dear sweet time a-getting here, gal," Soupbone hollered through cupped hands.

Jumping from the *Hope*'s rickety gangway onto Wrangel's wharf, Jenna grinned at him, knowing his scowl was as bona fide as a politician's epitaph. He shied when she hugged his shoulders and pecked his cheek.

"Cut the floweredy stuff, woman. Ain't been two days since I saw you last."

Laughing, she turned and waved at her rescuer, Terrance McGuyver. High atop the upper deck, he clapped his cap over his heart and bowed.

"Got mighty friendly with Christopher Columbus there in a twelve-hour boat ride, didn't you?"

Weaving her arm through Soupbone's, Jenna tugged him into a stroll. The dock was a jumble of baled hay, crates, cartons, and barrels of every size and description. Like drunken swabbies on shore leave, they zigzagged through the maze of freight.

When the passage widened, Jenna explained, "For your information, Terrance, that sailor, saved my hide back in Glenora. If not for him, I wouldn't be here"—she waggled the water-stained burlap bag under his nose—"or have this to show for my escapades."

"Hmmph. Looks like you're toting a helluva big tater in there."

Lowering her voice to a whisper, she corrected, "Five thousand of them, to be exact."

"Good God, you wangled Yolanda's bounty outta that scalawag?"

"Will you hush, for heaven's sake? I didn't acquire it only to lose it to a cutpurse."

His expression was equally dumbfounded and suspicious. "How'd you do it? And I mean chapter and verse, gal."

"Let's just say, the Army Colt I'm using for a paperweight helped convince Duncan to pay off his debt."

Soupbone halted as if he'd slammed into a mountain. "That was part of the scheme from the get-go, wasn't it? A little detail you kinda forgot to mention to me."

"You heard me promise Yolanda—"

"Uh-uh. I heard you lend comfort to a dying woman. Making good on what Guthrie owed Cayuse Mike was crazy enough, considering the way he double-deals."

"Maybe he doesn't have a conscience, but I do," she countered, then glanced over her shoulder. "Can't we walk and talk, too? I feel silly standing here arguing in the middle of the wharf."

Soupbone started off, hands clasped behind his back.

Jenna buckled her chin defiantly and matched his pace. I didn't want to latch on to your scrawny old arm again anyway, she sneered to herself.

"You are the most fractious, stubborn, knot-headed female I've ever met in all my born days."

"Why, thank you, Soupbone. Sometimes you say the sweetest—"

"That'll do. I'm not joshing a bit. If I'd known what aces you really had stashed up your sleeve, I'd have carried you screaming bloody Nell aboard that steamer from Telegraph Creek."

"Which is why I didn't tell you."

The pier curved as it intersected with Wrangel's boardwalk. Across the inlet amber torchlight silhouetted Fort Wrangel's stalwart log palisade. Outside the gate carved Tlingit totems loomed like giant, mute sentries.

I might as well be promenading with one of those poles, Jenna mused, stealing a peek at the stoic old coot beside her.

She nudged him gently with her elbow. "Come on, everything squared up fine in Glenora, and Marianna Elizabeth'll have the money for that special school."

Soupbone chucked the edge of a warped

plank with his heel. "Aw, no use floggin' a dead horse, I reckon."

"Nope. What's done . . . oh, never mind."

"Truth of it is, since you managed not to get yourself killed adoing it, I'm right proud of you for keeping your word to Yolanda. I figure she'll rest easy now."

"I truly hope so."

"And them boat passages to San Francisco? They're taken care of as far as Seattle, anyhow. Hafta make arrangements when we dock there for the last leg to Califor-nee."

"When do we leave?"

"In the morning. Half-past nine."

Jenna chuckled. "Pretty sure I'd make it to Wrangel today, weren't you?"

"If you was a horse, I'd put a fair bet on your muzzle to win."

An odd rasp to Soupbone's voice gave her pause. His hand reached up and fidgeted with his eyepatch.

"If it don't kibosh your plans, gal, I'd like to take the train with you to St. Louis. See that the little girl's being taken care of proper, and all."

Wriggling her fingers in the crook of his arm, she answered, "I'd like nothing better. Why, horseback, steamer ships, then a train? We'll be the best-traveled pair of boon companions the country's seen since Lewis and Clark."

"Hmmph. Don't know about you, but I ain't

gonna make it much farther afoot without some supper warming my innards."

"I'm about two shakes this side of starvation myself."

He pressed her hand against his gristled ribs. "Seeing as how you're such a wealthy widder lady, if you'll stand me to supper and tell me how the hell you connived Cayuse Mike Duncan outta five thousand spondulicks, I'll chew real quiet and listen real hard."

"Soupbone, my friend, you've got yourself a deal."

Chapter Twenty-seven

Dan breathed in the musky-sweet tang of horsehide, green hay, leather, and manure peculiar to stables as he strode through the open double doors of Bailey's Livery.

After spending the last month cooped up in steamboat compartments, crowded railcars, and a mail coach, that familiar aroma raised his spirits like a letter from home.

He dropped the satchels he held in each hand beside a bank of saddle trees and scanned the building's interior. A wiry gent wearing a knitted hat, bibbed overalls, and a tattered, Sunday-go-to-meeting shirt with cut-off sleeves was pitching fresh straw into one of the stalls. He paused midswing when Dan approached.

"Are you Mister Bailey?"

"Been known to answer to that handle," the liveryman replied, dabbing his sun-creased face with a kerchief. "Been known not to, on occasion. What can I do you for?"

"A horse and tack, for starters."

"To buy or let?"

"Let."

"How long?"

Dan grinned, amused by his rapid-fire twang. "A day, two at most."

"Five dollars." Turning, Bailey forked another mound of straw over the cross-hatched gate. "In advance."

"Kinda steep, ain't it? Your stock rigged with silver shoes or something?"

The man cackled heartily. "It's been a hundred and two in the shade for over a week. I've got ten more stalls to muck, water to lug from the pump, and a dozen nags to feed and curry. You want a bargain? Come back when August's burned itself out."

Dan's mouth puckered ruefully at one corner as he dredged five silver dollars from his pocket. The coins clinking in his hand gained Baileys' full attention.

"What kind of mount'll this king's ransom get me, anyway? Best not be a blindered plow-puller."

Bailey's mouth hinged wide enough to afford a bird's eye view of his celluloid-colored molars. "Golly Moses, son. You're about as larksome as watching grass grow. Aren't you going to haggle the price at all?"

"I wasn't, but seeing as how it means that much to you, parting with three of these'd suit me a lot better."

"Doesn't suit me worth spit."

"Four?"

The liveryman scratched his crepey, dirt-ringed neck. "I reckon five'd do the trick."

"But . . . you"—shaking his head in bewilderment, Dan dropped the Liberties into Bailey's extended palm.

"Much obliged. I've got a fine blood bay mare in number eight with your name . . . well, she'd be branded with it, if I knew what it was."

Dan introduced himself, then followed the odd little man down the aisle. With speed borne of long practice, he bridled the animal and led it from the stall.

"Ol' Cornsilk here'll go five miles better than your behind can stand. She's gentle-hearted, pretty as they come, and sound as the day is long."

"Yeah, well, I ain't aimin' to marry her," Dan drawled. "Though much as she's costing me, maybe I oughta."

Smoothing the wool saddle blanket over the mare's back, Bailey wheedled, "I suspect you're bound for the gold fields up north. Most are that come through Hay Springs."

"Nope. I'm not traipsing any farther than the French's place."

"French? I don't recollect anyone by that name around here."

"Hell's bells, of course, you don't," Dan muttered, his innards sinking to his boot tops. "And I have no idea what Jenna's maiden name was."

"The only Jenna I've ever heard of's Jenna Wade. Her folks' farm is about ten miles east of town, but she married and left home three, maybe four years ago."

"That's my—that's her," Dan said, whistling with relief. "How do I get there?"

Bailey's hazel eyes narrowed. "Seems strange you have to ask, being a friend of hers and all."

"We met up in Canada and were a mite too busy driving cattle to exchange particulars."

"The devil you say. That's a story I'd buy the Three Roses to hear told." He bent to double-check the cinch. "Head due east, third farm to the north'll be the Wades. Drucilla's a bit tetchy about strangers. I'd advise you to stow that hip warmer at the gate post."

Dan hooked his smaller satchel's handle over the pommel. It was probably foolish to tote his fortune in plain sight, but he trusted himself far beyond a banker's safekeeping. "Mind if I leave my other bag here until I get back?"

"No trouble atall." With a sly wink Bailey added, "No extra charge, neither."

A brood of Rhode Island reds squawked and scattered as Dan turned into the Wade's yard. He chuckled and said, "Sorry to disturb your tea party, ladies."

Dwarfed by two, towering mulberry trees, the tin-roofed, clapboard house had a sit-a-spell-size front porch banked by well-tended flower beds. A barn and smaller outbuildings flanked the house, and Dan caught a whiff of a hog lot, but most of the Wade's arable acreage was devoted to corn.

While he threaded the mare's reins through the hitching post's ring, the outline of a woman appeared just inside the screen door.

"Hallo the house," he called. "I'm looking for the Wade place."

"You found it. State your business, young man." Drucilla Wade's reedy voice had less "howdy" in it than a rattlesnake's buzz.

Dan stopped in his tracks, told her his name, and asked after Jenna.

"I haven't seen my daughter in years. Don't expect to, anytime soon." She turned away from the door.

"Uh, ma'am? Missus Wade?" He glanced toward the crunch of boots on parched grass. A lanky man sauntered into view just as Dan asked, "Can you tell me if you've gotten a letter from Jenna since she left Canada?"

"Whether I did or didn't, I doubt if your name would've shared space on the envelope, Mister Bran—"

"For goodness' sake, Drucilla," the man blustered. "I'd like to think if Jenna called on this feller's folks, they'd at least give her something to wash away the road dust for her trouble."

Sticking out a hand, he said, "Hank Wade. Pleased to make your acquaintance."

"The pleasure's mine, sir," Dan said sincerely.

"It's hotter inside than out, but to stay on my

wife's good side, I reckon we'd best find a couple of the horsehair monstrosities in the parlor."

Dan fell in beside Wade, groaning inwardly. He'd hoped for a private talk with Jenna's father. Judging by Drucilla's demeanor, he should have known better.

The stuffy front room harbored all the trappings of a place designed to impress company: the aforementioned horsehair settee and sidechairs draped with starched antimacassars, piecrust tables, fern stands, bric-a-brac galore, and most of the wallpaper hidden behind giltframed ancestral portraits.

Clearly, Hank was intimidated by such splendor as much as Dan was. No sooner than they'd eased themselves onto the fancy chairs, Drucilla whisked in to serve them glasses of cool, springwater tea and settle primly on the settee.

While the sweet refreshment slid down Dan's parched throat, he peered over the hobnail tumbler's rim at his hostess. Beyond Missus Wade's slender build, he detected no trace of mother-daughter resemblance. The sparkle in Jenna's eyes and her easy smile favored her father's, but she was hardly his "spittin' image" either.

Averting his eyes from Drucilla's haughty gaze, he did a double take at one of the wall's oval paintings. Dan's belly flip-flopped.

Though she was wearing an old-fashioned gown and revealing enough décolletté to give a man sinful ideas, Jenna Wade French had been captured in oil in all her flirtatious glory.

"How long ago was that painting done?"

"Along about eighteen twenty-three," Drucilla answered. "That isn't Jenna, Mister Brannum. It's a portrait of my mother, Kathryn Kennedy Detheridge."

"Lawsy, she was a beauty, Dan," Hank murmured. "And a corker from the word go. Kate came to live with us after she buried her sixth husband. She died several years ago, and not a day goes by that I don't miss her."

"Hmmph. One would think she was *your* mother, not mine."

He continued as if he hadn't heard the remark. "Every Saturday night, Kate and Letitia Bailey—those two were peas from the same pod—would come in here, sneak a splash of whiskey into their lemonade and play five card draw until they got too tipsy to tell jacks from queens.

" 'Shenanigan Night' they called it. Used to drive Drucilla to distraction."

"Of course, it did. Not only were both of them absolutely dotty, their antics were a terrible influence on Jenna."

"I met a Mister Bailey at the livery in town," Dan piped up, knowing scabs from old wounds were in danger of breaking open. "Is he any relation to—"

Her humorless laugh stilled his question. "The older she gets, the more easily she fools people. There is no Mister Bailey and never was. That was the infamous Letitia, masquerading as a man, as she's done for a quarter century."

"Well, I'll be . . ." Dan stifled the expletive before it rolled off his tongue. He couldn't check the grin spreading across his face. "But why?"

"Like my mother, God rest her deranged soul, Letitia delights in scandalizing and embarrassing the entire town."

"Horse apples, Drucilla. Letitia Bailey knows horseflesh better than most know their own boot size. Trouble is, strangers are mighty skittish about a woman doing a man's work, so, she capers about in overalls and laughs all the way to the bank."

"Well, I maintain that if she knew her business, the ruse wouldn't be necessary."

"And how many barns have you mucked out wearing petticoats, my dear?"

As the Wades's debate flourished, Dan sat quietly, staring at Kate Detheridge's painting. I do believe, he mused, that Jenna's acorn fell but one generation from the tree.

But physical beauty wasn't all she'd inherited from her grandmother. It takes brains and grit to take life by the *cojones* and shake it for all it's worth, all the while shouting "Devil take the hindmost" to society's shackle-bearers.

Yeah, and only the purest kind of fool

would've let a woman like that walk out the door.

"Yoo-hoo," Drucilla trilled. "Are you still with us, Mister Brannum?"

"Oh, uh, sorry. You were saying?"

"Actually, I was apologizing for rambling on so. I'm sure you have better things to do than listen to our family skeletons rattle their bones."

Her hint was as subtle as a twelve-point newspaper headline. Swallowing a smirk, Dan replied, "No, ma'am, it's me owing the apology, along with my thanks for you folks' hospitality."

Hat in one hand and glass in the other, he rose, searching in vain for somewhere he could safely dispense with the latter. Finding none, he thrust it toward Drucilla, who graced him with a patronizing moue.

"I, uh, if you don't mind my asking again before I go, has Jenna written you in the last month or so?"

"Mister Brannum, charming as your company has been, you never explained why our daughter's whereabouts should be any of your concern."

Dan fidgeted with his Stetson, worrying its brim as he spun it slowly through his fingers.

Jenna's father sidled around his haughty bride. "We got a long ol' letter from her last week, dated July twenty-ninth—"

"Hank!"

"—saying she and her companion were in St. Louis."

"Her companion?"

Glaring at her husband and then Dan with hell-furied scorn, Drucilla stomped from the parlor.

Hank cupped Dan's elbow and steered him toward the door. "I hope you understand, the quicker you're on your way, the faster I can get to making amends." He chuckled, adding, "I really don't want to sleep in the barn until Christmas."

"Did Jenna mention how long she'd be staying in St. Louis? Or even whether she might settle there?"

"Not that I recall, but I'd be real surprised if she she did. Unless I miss my guess, my little girl's too accustomed to fresh air and wide open spaces to cotton to city life."

Dan swung up in the saddle and reached for the reins Hank held up to him. "Thank you, sir, for everything. And I sure hope my coming here hasn't caused a ruckus between you and Missus Wade."

Hank waved a dismissive hand. "Aw, don't you worry about that a bit. Me and her's been snapping at each other for twenty years, come October. I'm sure there's better ways of enduring, but it's the only one we know."

Dan tipped his hat, kneeing the bay into a swing toward the road. Funny, he thought. Jenna's folks are a tad shy of their twentieth anniversary at the same time their daughter's on the brink of her twenty-first birthday.

"Hey, Brannum?"

Dan looked back over his shoulder. "Yeah?"

"If you do meet up with Jenna, tell her I love her."

"I surely will, Mister Wade," he assured Hank, adding to himself, right after I tell her that *I* do.

Chapter Twenty-eight

It is the soul that sees.

Silently, Jenna mouthed the words of the maxim that spanned the width of the narrow schoolroom's back wall. She couldn't decide whether the sentiment's location was appropriate or ironic. Painted in blocked, white lettering above the wainscoting, it bridged two rows of double desks that faced the opposite direction, a moot observation, perhaps, since the children who occupied the seats were blind.

Maybe it was placed there intentionally, Jenna mused, to remind sighted teachers and visitors that the students are children who happen to be blind, rather than blind children, which puts the emphasis on the affliction.

When Jenna shared her theory with Miss Parsons, one of the school's instructors, she confirmed, "That's precisely why, Missus French, though not many grasp the distinction." With a wide smile, she added, "Watching our charges caper about during recess might, shall we say, open others' eyes more fully."

The journal's string-stitching creaked as Miss Parsons closed it. She caressed its tooled leather cover with slender fingers. "I'm terribly sorry, Missus French, but I find no record of an inquiry being made in the name of 'Diamond,' and there would be, had one been made.

"Some parents have proven reluctant to enroll their children, believing that our institution's policy smacks of charity. In those circumstances, we visit their homes, several times if necessary, to disavow that notion."

Disappointment hovered over Jenna like a thundercloud. For three weeks she and Soupbone had battled August's cloying heat while rambling from one end of St. Louis to the other.

They'd called on every Diamond listed in the city directory, every shoestring relation within a ten-mile radius. Soupbone made inquiries at police station houses, and Jenna checked every hospital, just in case Yolanda had given birth at one of them.

The School for the Blind was their last hope. At four years of age, Marianna Elizabeth was too young for enrollment, but if Yolanda or a family member had contacted the school, a home address might have been mentioned and remembered.

"I simply don't know what to do . . ." Jenna whispered. "We've hit a box canyon everywhere we've turned."

Miss Parsons cleared her throat. "If I may be so bold, I have two suggestions that might relieve your quandary."

The teacher removed a sheet of stationery and a pencil from her desk drawer. "On the off chance that your friend was Catholic, as many city residents are, Father Francis Xavier at the Cathedral of St. Louis of France will surely recognize the name."

As Jenna tucked the letter of introduction into her reticule, Miss Parsons pushed away from the desk to speak to her more directly. "The Missouri legislature does underwrite most of our funding, so I presume the cost of Miss Diamond's personal expenses are your primary concern. Over a period of years, transportation costs, additional reading books and learning aids, and enough clothing to properly outfit a growing child does add up to a goodly sum. More will be needed if Miss Diamond chooses to continue her education or pursues one of the trades we provide training for, such as proofreading texts written in Braille, weaving, and cooking."

Miss Parsons took a deep breath, then laughed heartily. "My, my, I am taking the long way around the barn to make my point."

"No, I'm fascinated, truly. That Marianna Elizabeth could support herself after she's grown was something I never divined."

"I'm proud to say, many have since the school opened over twenty years ago."

A corner of Jenna's mouth pursed. "In all honesty, that also makes my inability to find Yolanda's daughter all the more disheartening."

"Which returns me to the suggestion I intended to make before straying from the subject. If Father Xavier is unable to help, consider setting up a trust in Marianna Elizabeth's name for a period of, say, ten years.

"If her guardians have not communicated with us by then, and they surely will long before its expiration, the funds could revert to the school and be used to offset expenses for many less fortunate children."

Jenna mulled the idea for a moment. "What a wonderful compromise. Putting the inheritance directly into Marianna Elizabeth's hands is still my fondest hope, but knowing there's an alternative if that proves impossible is very comforting. And I think Yolanda would approve."

Miss Parsons walked Jenna to the front entrance, hesitating before she pushed open its heavy oak door. "This may sound odd, but I hope we don't meet again, Missus French."

"So do I, Miss Parsons. With all my heart, so do I."

She found Soupbone where she'd left him, sprawled on a bench, taking what slim advantage the shady side of the street afforded.

A flock of potbellied pigeons paid her little heed as she plopped down beside him. The birds strutted like drunkards trying desperately to act sober. "Coodle-coo, coodle-coo," they warbled, their eyes seeming to revolve with each blink."

"Nasty, ain't they?" Soupbone opined, drawing lustily on a fine two-bit cigar.

"You know, they truly are. I can't feature why so many folks feed the rascals. It's even odds a body'll get splattered with droppings just walking under a tree branch or awnings as it is."

"Hmmph. I reckon city folks are a mite tetched anyhow, living where you can't stretch your legs proper without stepping on somebody's foot."

"You're not particularly fond of this 'Gateway to the West,' are you?"

"After telling you that about fifty thousand times, you mean you finally gave a listen? I ain't built to rub shoulders with my feller man, and the sooner I get away from the sumbitches, the better I'll like it."

Jenna related both of Miss Parsons's suggestions. "If our call on the church goes the way of all the others, I don't know how we can honor Yolanda's wishes except by putting her money in trust."

A perfect smoke ring puffed from Soupbone's lips. It sailed upward, spinning like a lazy, gray halo, then shattered and vanished. "Don't have no qualms about putting the money aside. Ain't nearly so keen on hoofing it clear to the river landing to pester that padre. I don't figure a gal like Yolanda did much pew warmin'."

"She wasn't born a prostitute."

"Well, we don't rightly know she was Catholic, either, but sure as cows make milk, you're gonna make me go with you to find out."

His knees cracked as he gained his feet. "I s'pose if that ol' she-ox ever did beller them cater-clysms, Father What's-his-name woulda noticed."

Backdropped by the cluster of steamboats docked along the Mississippi's bank, the cut stone cathedral's belfreyed spire rose ever vigilant above the smoke-smudged pilothouses.

A reverent silence fell over Soupbone and Jenna as they mounted the granite steps and passed between the Corinthian columns supporting its massive stone architrave. Pausing inside the cool, candlelit narthex, Jenna peered into the chancel. Stained glass windows softly illuminated a silver and blue expanse so beautiful her mind seemed incapable of absorbing it all.

She was startled when a door creaked open behind her. An elderly man, dressed head to toe in his calling's somber black robes, stepped into the foyer and introduced himself.

Jenna proffered Miss Parsons's letter.

The priest nodded as he read it, murmuring, "To be sure, if there is anyone in this city devoted to the Lord's work, it is Laura Parsons."

He clasped his hands at his waist and asked, "How may I be of service, Missus French?"

"We've been searching for weeks for the family of a friend of ours, Yolanda Diamond. It's terribly important that we find them, and Miss Parsons thought you could help."

Father Xavier worried his chin, staring at the marbled floor. "Diamond, you say. I'm sorry, I don't recall anyone by that name among my parishioners."

"Yolanda was a monstrous big gal," Soupbone blurted. "Stood better'n six-foot-tall in her socks. Don't mean to speak ill of the departed, but she was a mite shy of comely, too."

"For goodness sakes, Soupbone—"

"Well, consarn it," he whispered, "I thought it'd help the padre here if I described her."

A sheepish smile spread across Father Xavier's face. "And it did. I daresay, even in a city the size of St. Louis, there could not be two women of that stature."

Jenna fought off a nigh overwhelming impulse to hug the dignified, white-haired man. "You're acquainted with the family, then?"

"Yes, but the woman you described is known to me as Adelaide Diamont. Her mother, also named Adelaide, and father, Percival, have a flat above their grocery at the corner of Olive and Broadway."

"Hal-le-lujah," Soupbone bellowed, instantly clapping a hand over his mouth.

The priest chuckled merrily. "Don't chastise

yourself, my good man. What better place is there to shout hosannas than in God's house?"

His benevolence didn't prevent Jenna from gracing her companion with a blistering glare. Without disclosing the nature of Yolanda's livelihood, she told Father Xavier the reason behind their search.

"It saddens me to learn of Adelaide's, er, Yolanda's death. If you'd be so kind, please tell the Diamonts that I will call on them this evening."

"We will, Father," Jenna promised, "and thank you for your help."

They accomplished the six blocks between the cathedral and their destination at a spry pace. Soupbone took Jenna's arm to cater-corner the intersection from southeast to northwest.

Eyes locked on the three-story, redbrick building that housed the A and P Grocery, she balked the moment her heel touched down on Olive Street.

"C'mon, gal. I won't stroll you in front of no dray."

"Please, let me rest a spell and catch my breath."

The cigar stub he'd retrieved from his pocket and relit wobbled between his lips. "The best way to get past telling that little girl that her mama ain't coming home is to get it done and over with."

"Coosie, I think you're part gypsy."

"Naw." He exhaled a long drag from his stogie. "Long as we was caught up in finding Yolanda's folks, it was real easy to forget why we was looking. That 'why' flew home to roost no sooner'n we bid adios to the padre."

"You are coming with me, aren't you?"

"I don't suppose propping up the building with my backside'd make me much of a boon companion, now would it?"

Jenna snuggled against his arm affectionately. "Nope."

"All right, then, let's anti-goggle yonder and get it done."

For a midmorning Thursday, the store seemed unusually well patronized. Housewives and turbaned Negress cooks wielding split-oak market baskets pinched and prodded myriad displays of vegetables and fruits.

Black-waistcoated clerks dickered prices, scampered up and down ladders to reach boxes and tins stacked to the ceiling, and fed coffee beans into a roaring grinder's mouth.

Jenna tapped a young employee on the shoulder. "Where might I find Missus Diamont?"

His downy upper lip puckered with indecision. "Mister Diamont's the butcher. Maybe you ought to ask him."

"I'd rather not disturb him. Please, would you mind fetching Missus Diamont for us? It's very important that we speak with her privately."

"Yoo-hoo, boy," a matron warbled from another aisle. "Have you gathered my order yet? I don't have all day to wait."

The flustered clerk pointed to a narrow stairway. "The Diamonts' apartment is up there, end of the hall. Bell cord's beside the door."

Jenna was taken aback when a petite, stunningly beautiful woman answered the bell's summons. Her silver-streaked, strawberry blond hair was braided into a coronet, appropriate to her regal bearing.

"Missus Diamont, we're friends of Yolanda's, uh, Adelaide's—your daughter's. May we come in?"

"Yes, but of course," their hostess replied in heavily accented English. "It was Yolanda's papa who named her for me, and only he who called her Adelaide." With a sweeping gesture she added, "Please, the chairs by the windows are most comfortable. Pardon me for a moment, and I will bring the refreshments."

"No, Missus Diamont, don't trouble yourself on our account."

"It is a hot day, and the throat becomes dry from talk. A little tea and some cookies, eh?"

When she was out of earshot, Soupbone muttered, "I ain't never seen folks so damned partial to tea and cookies. Everywhere we've gone, that's all we've got. Lordy, what I wouldn't give for a beer and some sodie crackers."

Jenna giggled, more from nervousness than from amusement. "Mind your manners, and I'll buy you all the lager you can hold after we leave."

He was still smacking his lips in anticipation when Missus Diamont returned bearing a pine trencher. Only a thread of the cups' gilt banding remained on their cracked surface, their rosebud pattern as faded as their owner's gingham dress.

Once they were served, she perched on the edge of a bench, looking expectantly from one guest to the other.

Jenna sucked in a deep breath and let it out slowly. "Ma'am, I guess it's more proper for us to exchange pleasantries—"

"My daughter has gone to the Lord, has she not?" At Jenna's nod, Missus Diamont flinched. "I have known this in my heart for many weeks. A mother does, I believe, feel when the one she carried within her ceases to draw breath."

"Yolanda was a dear friend, Missus Diamont. She was a brave woman and had a gift for making us laugh when times were the hardest. I'm sorry we're the bearers of such sad news."

"Oh, but it is well you are. It is far gentler to hear of death from friends than from strangers. Tell me, please, how you knew my daughter."

With the same diplomacy she employed with Father Xavier, Jenna described their adventure, admitting only that Yolanda had been diagnosed with cancer. As she'd hoped, Missus Diamont concluded that the disease had taken her daughter's life.

A wry expression washed across her porcelain features. "A cow . . . how do you say . . . drover, eh? If only Doctor Schwann were alive to know of that. Yolanda was born many weeks too early. Ah, she was so tiny, with pale yellow fuzz on her head like a baby chick. The doctor said she would die, but I told my Percival that she would not." She shrugged her shoulders impishly. "The doctors, they do not know everything, eh?"

"I'd reckon not," Soupbone drawled. "It appears Yolanda growed a passel afore she was done, too."

"And so quickly, Mister Soupbone. Like a weed, she grew. Her chums, they made me so angry. I wanted to yank their hair, the way they teased her. But Yolanda, she never said anything unkind about them, though her pillow slip was damp many mornings when I awakened her."

Soupbone and Jenna sat quietly, allowing Missus Diamont to voice her recollections and by doing so, reveal a side of Yolanda they'd have never known.

"It grieved me when Yolanda sat home with us night after night while the other girls attended the dances and parties. Percival, he did not mind, for it relieved him of worries the father of a daughter has when remembering his own youthful mischiefs.

"Then, that sailor, Jimmy Mathers, came calling. I did not care for him, but when Yolanda said, 'Mama, Jimmy says I am pretty. Oh, if you heard him talk, you would think I was slender and graceful as the swans at Forest Park. Anyone can say the words, Mama, but he makes me believe them, inside.'"

Missus Diamont's teacup quivered as she took a sip. Misty blue eyes met Jenna's. "You know, I am sure, the result of their involvement."

"Yes, ma'am. A lovely little girl named Marianna Elizabeth . . . who sees with her soul."

Missus Diamont glanced toward a hallway. "She is napping still, but a wee peek into her bedchamber will not disturb her."

The trio tiptoed like burglars into the small, sparse room. Starched cotton curtains embroidered with jaunty red and yellow tulips riffled in the light breeze drifting from the Mississippi. Marianna Elizabeth lay asleep on a quilt-spread cot, her cornsilk sausage curls fanning across the pillow. Tears sprang to Jenna's eyes. Yolanda had not exaggerated. Her daughter was as beautiful as the angels depicted in the paintings in the Cathedral of St. Louis's foyer.

As they crept out, Soupbone seesawed a kerchief under his nose. "Fumes off'n that river'd choke a horse," he muttered. For good measure he feigned a cough as they returned to their seats.

"Marianna Elizabeth is my joy. She shares a world through her ears and touch unknown to us who have eyes."

Their hostess squared her shoulders and raised her chin. "She does not remember her mother. My husband and I allow her to believe we are her mama and papa."

Soupbone said, "If you're a-feared that we or anybody else'd fault you for that, you got another think coming, ma'am."

"Bless you, Mister Soupbone. Percival, he works very hard, but the groceries, they are fickle. The spoilage, it eats the profit, eh? But in love for Marianna Elizabeth, we are rich."

He extracted the envelope he'd carried in his jacket for weeks. "Yolanda's last wish was for her little girl to have this to pay for the special schooling and such she'll need."

Missus Diamont regarded him quizzically, sliding her finger inside to open the flap. Squinting at the bank draft, her head shook slowly from side to side.

"Jenna's talked to the gal at the blind school and swears the place is finer'n a frog's—uh, that it'll larn Marianna Elizabeth all her brains can hold."

With tears streaming down her cheeks, Missus Diamont covered her mouth with both hands. "Five thousand and five hundred dollars? Mother of God, it is a miracle you give to her."

"No, Missus Diamont," Jenna corrected softly, "it's Yolanda who did the giving. We're only her messengers."

Chapter Twenty-nine

Dan breakfasted alone in the dining room of Birdie McCarthy's St. Louis boardinghouse, save for the caged finches twittering from every corner. The clerks, brewery workers, a dock hand, and a bank teller who called Birdie's home had long since left for work.

"Aye, it's a regular toff, ye are," she teased Dan for his leisurely lack of employment.

Yesterday he'd tossed the letter Twyford Chaney had messengered to him in Laketon into the ashcan behind the boardinghouse. The storekeep's hilarious description of Jenna's "armed robbery" had gotten Dan laughing aloud. Chaney's solid admiration for her and his aside that if Dan didn't pursue her he was the biggest damfool on the North American continent put him on the trail for Telegraph Creek within the hour.

But second chances don't nary ever work out, he reasoned as he pushed his food around the plate. He knew before he left and was certain-sure after that jaunt to Hay Springs. Chaney was well-intentioned, but wrong. What's done is done.

Birdie bustled in carrying a dented copper coffeepot. Dan chuckled under his breath. His landlady never simply entered a room, she stormed it, chattering the continuation of a conversation she'd had in the meantime with herself.

"So, it's leavin' you are and breakin' my poor heart," she wailed in her singsong brogue. "Haven't stayed here a week and already givin' up on your lady friend."

She clucked her tongue as she topped Dan's coffee cup. "Clean your plate o' that hash 'n eggs, or I'll bar the door till you do. Mark me words, won't be fare near fine as Birdie's on that steamer to New Orleans."

Dan forced a mouthful of beef and riced potatoes down his gullet. "If Jenna ever was here, she's left the city by now. I can't feature why that Hoseah Abercrombie fellow at the Blind School'd never heard of her, but he hadn't, so that's that."

"If I was twenty years younger and fifty pounds lighter," Birdie said, fluffing a mass of rusty gray curls, "I'd make you forget that woman, sure as you're born."

He grinned at the barrel-size boardinghouse owner's flirty antics. If not for her unflagging good humor, his stay in St. Louis would have been doubly depressing. In his mind's eye, he'd fantasized encountering Jenna promenading along a broad, tree-lined avenue on a balmy September afternoon.

Nothing like letting your imagination run like a derailed locomotive, Dan thought. You've rambled from one end of the city to the levee, searched a thousand faces, and damn near got arrested when you grabbed that one gal by the arm and swung her around. Might as well be looking for a sprig of loco weed in a hay barn.

"Dan, me boyo, it weights my heart to see you so daunsy," Birdie said, plopping down on an adjacent chair. Elbows anchored on the table, she bridged her chapped hands and nestled her chins on the span. "Haven't known you long, but sometimes folks just takes to one another, easy like."

Chewing the dregs of his meal, he winked a confirmation.

"I read eyes the same as some reads books, lad. There's shadows in yours that don't come from not finding that woman. I'd say, you'd given her up for gone before you ever crossed my threshold."

He stared at her, discomfited by her perception. Dan thought himself adept at hiding his emotions. Jenna was the first who'd seen through the facade, and now Birdie.

"Well, Jenna's 'purtier than a spotted pup under a red wagon,' as my daddy'd say. Her kind of spunk doesn't go begging. Writing her folks about that 'companion,' told me she'd found somebody else."

"Saints preserve us! And they say it's women that jumps to conclusions. Who's to say your sweetheart didn't meet up with a woman friend?"

"I thought of that," Dan countered. "And I'd bet my last dollar if it was a female Jenna'd partnered with, she'd have called the gal by name."

"Not for . . . well, maybe—yeah, dash it all, it's right you are. And that her friend's a school-marm from Paducah, has three sisters, four brothers, and a mole on her left cheek, like as not."

"There you go."

"I'm awful sorry, Dan," Birdie murmured. "Maybe while you're chugging downriver, the girl of your dreams, a swoony Southern magnolia will shimmer across the deck in the moonlight."

"Nope."

"A cajun darlin' then, in New Orleans—"

"Uh-uh."

Birdie's button eyes almost disappeared in fleshy folds. "I hear there's senoritas, by God, swarming around Corpus Christi like bees in a hive." Her strident tone challenged him to defy her a third time.

Dan shook his head, chuckling. "Damned if you ain't a romantic fool, Birdie McCarthy, and plumb full of blarney to boot."

He shoved his tin plate away from the table's edge and reached for his coffee. "I reckon this old cowhand's gonna stick to chasing four-legged heifers from here on out. The two-legged variety's just too hard to brand, especially when a fella's a mite slow with the iron."

The boardinghouse owner's expression clabbered. "Can't say this plump colleen didn't try to keep you from leaving. Grand it's been to make your acquaintance, Dan Brannum."

"I'll miss you, too, Birdie. But there's a man I gotta see about a ranch down San Antonio way. That's what I shoulda done when I left British Columbia behind me, instead of trying to rope thin air."

Chapter Thirty

Like a gritty cyclone, dust swirled around the stagecoach well after it rolled to a stop at Fort Gibson. Soupbone, seated closest to the door, pulled himself into a hunchback's stance before stepping out.

Jenna fidgeted while her fellow travelers exited with due haste. She was surprised to find that the Indian agent who'd whined about his finicky bowels for well over a hundred miles had tarried long enough to assist her from the coach.

"Thank you, Mister Izzenthorpe. And I do hope your health improves."

He sniffed at his handkerchief before patting his shiny pate. "I expect Oklahoma Territory will try my delicate constitution to its limit, Missus French, but your concern is appreciated."

He scurried off toward the nearest privy, and Jenna entered the shanty that served as the stage station. Not finding Soupbone among its inhabitants, she ventured outside again.

The long-abandoned military outpost that shared its name with the town had fallen into a rubble of stone ruins. Gandering about in pioneer fashion, other than a few walnut groves and the Neosho River, there were no amenities worth risking heatstroke to investigate.

"This *is* Indian Territory, isn't it?" she muttered, giving the single street's false-fronted buildings a hasty once-over. "So where in the devil are all the Indians?"

On many a night her father had regaled her with deliciously gruesome tales of whooping, swooping raids on earlier Nebraska settlers, complete with scalpings, sundry tortures, and the kidnapping of women for unspecified, but certainly lascivious, purposes.

Despite a prairie childhood, Jenna'd never seen a Plains Indian, though she'd spent innumerable hours crouched in the farm's root cellar with her mother and grandmother. That not a single bare-chested, breechclouted, raven-maned warrior stalked Fort Gibson's bleak environs was a crushing disillusionment.

Up the road a ways, however, a one-eyed, trail-grimy old jasper was shaking the kinks from his knees. As she approached, Soupbone planted his hands on his narrow hips.

"Well, now, if this place isn't just scenic as hell, I'll eat my dad-blamed satchel."

"When we left St. Louis, you said you wanted to see the country," she replied drolly.

"Not where she bends over, I don't."

Dipping a shoulder, he spit a stream into a wheel rut. "How come you didn't want to go to Kansas City? I heard it's a right rollicksome cowtown."

"I got more river port than I wanted in St. Louis, thank you very much."

"As I recall, Colorado didn't light your wick, neither."

Jenna shrugged, intently watching two bluejays bicker on a sycamore branch. Soupbone's scrutiny felt more scorching than the sun's white-silver glare.

"You gave me your word at Wrangel, Jenna."

"About what?"

"Sleeving aces. You're doing it again, and I don't like it one iota."

Her lips parted to give him what-for, then closed for lack of ammunition. The old coot's not entirely correct, she thought, silently defensive. What I won't admit to even to myself doesn't count as a secret.

"It's not me that left Canada bound for somewhere to warm my bones."

Soupbone crooked a finger and pointed to the towering ghost-barked sycamore. "Plant your haunches in the shade, gal. We got us some palavering to do."

"Can't it wait until later? I'm parched from—"

"Aw, quit sniveling like Izzenthorpe and do as you're told."

His uncommonly brusque tone brought Jenna's swift compliance. She knew he was more disappointed in her than angry. Regrettably, his attitude was justifiable.

For a few tense moments his thumb and forefinger sheared wispy blades of grass like a scythe. "There's a fair lot of things I gotta say, most of which I should've told you clear back in Laketon, but didn't. All I want outta you whilst I'm doing it is a sharp ear and a latched mouth. Understood?"

Jenna giggled. "So much for palavering."

Continuing as if he hadn't been interrupted, Soupbone said, "I had me a wife, once—Julianna. She was prettier'n a china doll. Tiny, and blithe as a child.

"I met her on a Sunday, and we got married the next. By then I'd knowed her my whole life. We had a year, Julianna and me, to love each other as strong as a man and woman can before a fever took her and the baby she carried in her womb.

"Life don't get no harder than burying everything you'd ever love in a goddamn pine box. I grieved, then I got rampageous angry, wishing to God I'd never met her 'cause if I hadn't, half of me wouldn't have got tore out when she died.

"Took a while, but I finally realized that having just one year to hang cobwebs on the moon with Julianna was more love, and joy, and happiness, than most men get in a lifetime.

"Been meandering this planet for nigh a

quarter century now, and I ain't never seen but two others that might, if they found the guts to lay bare their souls to one another, have the kind of love me and Julianna had. I reckon you know who I mean."

Jenna shook her head, her chest so tight she could scarcely breathe. "If there ever was anything between Dan and me, it's too late to mend it. He told me as much before I left Laketon."

A rough, callused hand wriggled into hers and squeezed. "If you believe that, gal, why're we here? If you wanted to go to Wichita, there's easier ways of getting there. The only other direction the Shawnee Trail goes is due south."

"Soupbone, I swear I wasn't keeping secrets—"

"Aw, I know you weren't. I just figgered it was high-time you faced yourself in the mirror. Waking up one morning kinda by accident in south Texas wasn't good enough."

"But what if we get there, and Dan tells me to turn tail, pronto?"

"Would you sooner not ever know?"

She smiled wanly. "Ask me again in an hour. Whatever I answer, it'll change about that fast."

"Do you love him like you've never loved anyone your whole life through?"

"Yes."

"Think that'll change in an hour? Or a month? Or maybe twenty-five years from now?"

"Uh-uh."

Grinning like a dog with a ham hock between his paws, he drawled, "You know, suddenlike, I'm getting a powerful notion that it truly ain't Wichita we're going to."

Chapter Thirty-one

Dan smiled ruefully at the forged iron Bar Double-R eyebolted to the ranch's peeled log gate.

Josh Reed's fifty-two-hundred-acre spread had been his second home. A hearty welcome was assured from his father's best friend whereas breaching the neighboring Rocking B's boundary—his old home—would surely get a shotgun leveled at Dan's chest. That disparity might have been easier to accept if the two ranches weren't nigh identical in size and layout.

Dan closed his eyes, breathing deeply. Had a mythical phoenix dropped him blindfolded into the San Antonio Valley's verdant folds, he'd have known instantly that he was home, just by the land's heady, distinctive aromas.

As he kneed his mustang to a trot, two Mexican boys who were gamboling in the tassled bluestem froze like startled deer. They whirled and sprinted for the house like barefooted roadrunners.

Flanked by Suki Reed's beloved yellow rose-bushes, the two-story, hewn log *hacienda*'s wraparound porch lent a shady reprieve on sweltering summer days. Rectangular *troneras* cut in the dormer, and the ground-level window shutters were grim reminders that in the event of an Indian raid, a rancher's home was also his fortress.

By the time Dan reached the yard, Josh Reed was leaning against the open door's facing. Nudging five foot ten in his high-heeled boots, the cattleman's burly frame belied the wavy, snow-white mane flowing from his battered, felt John B.

Anchoring his hawkish features, Josh's oft-broken nose testified to a misspent youth, but as Micah Brannum quickly learned, Josh'd "stick with a friend right up to hell's hottest backlog."

"Howdy, stranger," he drawled to Dan, his expression deadpan. "By that Running W brand and saddle, I'd reckon your mount hails from down Corpus Christi way."

Dan wound the reins around the hitching rail. "Yep. Richard King himself signed the bill of sale. Heard the horseflesh wasn't worth shootin' here in these parts."

"Cocky little shaver, ain't ya?"

"Always have been, Josh."

Both men grinned ear to ear as the bear hugs and backslaps commenced. Grasping Dan at the elbows, Josh eyeballed his visitor. "You've filled out some since I seen you last. Been too long, son."

"Longer than I allowed when I left, that's for sure." Dan squinted toward the door. "Where's Suki? She getting shy in her old age?"

"Every year, her and some other gals flock together at the shank of September over to McAllister's place. She'll be back next Friday or Saturday with a spring wagon load of pickles, jerked venison, jalapeno jelly, and the hen cluckings."

"The boys?"

"Joel, Paul William, Jeffrey, and James ought to be loping in any day from driving three thousand head north to Montana. Parker was fit to be tied getting culled from that enterprise, but a buckskin mare he was breaking pitched him nigh across Bexar County, then trounced him a lick. Came a gnat's whisker from breaking his back."

"No wonder it's such a quiet Sabbath morn around here."

"God's truth is, this grissel-heel's kind of enjoying it," Josh admitted. "Fallen into all manner of bad habits. It's real comforting to know that being civilized ain't entirely permanent."

They were still laughing when Benito de Vaca, Reed's *segundo*, rode up astride a black-speckled mare. It's supposedly lucky, medicine hat marking was an appropriate choice for a foreman renowned for his superstitious nature.

De Vaca was leading Josh's starred sorrel—

its empty stirrups flapping against his saddle's tooled fenders.

"*Que milagro, hola amigo*," de Vaca called, waving at Dan. "For many weeks, the *mayor*, he has expected you."

To his employer he added, "The new *presa* is progressing well, Senor Reed. Your inspection, I think, can wait until tomorrow."

While Josh and his foreman discussed the dam project further, Dan ambled away to reacquaint himself with the Bar Double-R ranch.

Unlike Richard King, whose *vaqueros* were replacing his expensive cypress post and pine-plank fences with newfangled barbed wire, mesquite *corrales de lena* still served Reed's purposes as they had the Spanish and Mexican *hacendados* for three centuries.

To the south, one-room adobe *jacals* housed the *peons'* and *vaqueros'* families under their thatched roofs. Cooking was done inside grass ramadas behind the huts, and most plots also contained a hog pen, a chicken coop, and a garden.

Because the majority of Reed's ranch hands were Mexican, an adobe, saddlebag house adjacent to the *hacienda* quartered his unmarried, anglo employees. Connected by a roofed dog-trot, one cabin was a combination bunkhouse and living quarters, with the cookhouse and dining hall occupying the other.

Dan wondered if Alabam, the Negro cook,

was still rustling up the fluffiest biscuits and fork-tender fried beefsteak he'd ever tasted.

He let out a low whistle. Gooseflesh riffled the hairs at the nape of his neck. Jaysus, Alabam was *our* belly-cheater, not the Bar Double-R's. It's damned spooky, confusing the two ranches even if Pa did pattern ours after this one.

"*Que le vaya bien,*" de Vaca called, ending Dan's reverie.

"Yeah, uh, *gracias*, Benito. *Nos vemos.*"

Jerking a thumb at the door, Josh said, "Pot's boiling inside."

"Am I going to need a spoon to shovel it down my craw, as always?"

"Hmmph. If it ain't strong enough to kick up in the middle and carry double, it ain't coffee."

A stairway divided the living room from a smaller parlor and the dining room. The former's clay-chinked walls displayed woven Mexican rugs, stretched antelope skins, and mounted deer heads interspersed with framed daguerrotypes. A massive stone fireplace claimed an entire side of the room.

Dan groaned as he settled into a cobbler seat rocker, laying his head against its carved panel back. Other than the few days spent recuperating in Laketon, he'd been on the move for five solid months. Suddenly, he felt every mile, and at least double his twenty-four years.

Proffering a cup of stout, syrupy Arbuckle's, Josh said, "I got your wire from Nebraska the same day as I got your letter from British Columbia." He chuckled low in his throat. "The way you spelled 'profit' gave me pause, son. Couldn't help wondering if you spell 'shit' with one 't' or two."

A flush rose up Dan's neck. "After coming down with the dysentery, four of 'em sounds about right. Since when did you take up schoolteaching?"

"I've got a better question. Since when is Omaha a crow's fly between Telegraph Creek and south Texas? From your letter, I expected you back months ago."

"It's a long story, Josh."

The older man snorted. "I guaran-damn-tee, it won't hold a candle to the chin session I'm in for when Suki gets back."

Dan laughed, recalling Josh's feisty, salty-tongued wife's exuberant storytelling. There wasn't a cowhand alive who could out-windy, out-cuss, or out-drink Suki Jane Reed, and to a man, they adored her for it.

Balancing his cup on the rocker's bent arm, Dan described his first encounter with Jenna French and their partnership, ending with his unsuccessful attempts to find her and make amends.

"If Suki were here, she'd have you back astraddle of that mustang and aimed for Nebraska in two shakes," Josh replied. "But I'll warrant that if you and that gal were meant to be together, the cards would have fallen different."

Dan nodded. "It took roving a few thousand miles, but I finally got it through my bony skull, that's the way the hand plays."

Josh's shrewd hazel eyes challenged that statement, then softened with affection and a measure of sympathy. Dan knew what the older man was thinking: Texas was hell on women and hell for men without them.

Currying his droopy mustaches with the stub of his left index finger, Josh said, "So, you're fancy-free and lugging a fifteen thousand, two-t profit from that cattle drive. Not bad, son. As I recollect, you left the country with a fire in your belly and ten bucks in your jeans."

Feet flat on the floor, Dan leaned forward, bracing his forearms on his knees. "That fire's smoldered for over three years, Josh. Like I wrote you, I want my home back."

"I understand that, but there's surely been complications since you left. More of 'em than you can shake a stick at."

"Such as?"

"First off, there's a damned army of *banditos* headquartered between the Goliad and Nueces rivers. They divvy up in bands of about forty and are raiding ranches right and left, either rustling beeves over the border or crippling them with hocking knives and skinning 'em."

"Good God, I thought hocking knives were outlawed three hundred years ago."

"Guess somebody forgot to tell the *banditos* about it," Josh replied drolly. "Fact is, it doesn't take but a second for a mounted man to slice an animal's hamstrings with one of those curve-bladed devils. Worse, the bastards just kill 'em to sell the hides and fat, leaving the meat behind to rot."

"Is that why you sent such a big outfit north this year?"

"Partly, but mostly for the same reason the *banditos* are on the prowl. The market's good and promises to get better."

Josh rose and reached for Dan's cup to fetch refills. Over his shoulder he added, "Me, McAllister, Vic Rubio, and a few others have enough *vaqueros* patrolling around to cut our losses."

"I take that to mean Darrin's been hit pretty hard."

"Depends on how you look at it."

"C'mon, Josh. It isn't like you to make me fish. I'd appreciate your giving me the lay of the land instead of having to pull it out of you like bad teeth."

"I've got nothing to say that you want to hear."

"Probably not, but spill it anyway."

Rather than reseat himself, Josh hunched over his chair's oval panel, cradling the iron-stone cup in his work-scarred hands. His jaw ruminated the subject at length before he addressed it aloud.

"Even before the *banditos* started harrying us, the Rocking B didn't have enough cattle left to fill a fair-to-middlin' *corrales de luna*"—he hesitated, then all but snarled, "Your brother, the sorry jackass, has got me so riled I can't pussyfoot worth spit. If you don't want it straight and proddy as hell, tell me now, son, because it's not gonna come out any other way."

Dan couldn't help smiling. Josh's bristles didn't stand and salute without enormous provocation. At the moment, the rancher looked angry enough to gnaw the sights off a six-shooter and swallow the cartridges for dessert.

"Darrin's my brother and I reckon I love him—the memories of us growing up together, anyway—but I'm long past ignoring or defending his sidewinder antics."

Josh snorted. "How Micah could sire a whelp too dumb to drive nails in a snowbank, I don't know, but in Darrin's case, he surely did.

"When you left, you probably weren't past the Nations before Darrin took a leaf from Richard King's book and tried setting himself up as a *patron*. Same as King done, he hied off to Mexico and convinced a passel of villagers to throw their plunder in their *corretas* and follow them oxen north to the Rocking B.

"*El Patron* Brannum did luck into a few decent *vaqueros* amongst the lot—not to mention several blossoming ninas to frolic with."

Dan thought of Lanatk and the degradations

Utley committed against her. Acknowledging that his brother needed the same stimulation set his stomach churning. "I'll wager my sister-in-law didn't take kindly to that."

Josh's leathery face had disgust stamped all over it. "Alyssa Sue packed up and shipped out to Waco sure enough, but according to Suki, it had more to do with the lack of bulls in *her* pasture than the herd of heifers in Darrin's.

"Beyond the fornicating—a side road I'd sooner avoid—it came to light pretty fast that Darrin's notion of nabobery had a big chock under its wheel: The *peons* he imported weren't slave labor. Since a *patron's* supposed to provide for them and he lacked both the money and inclination to do so, they said, *Vete a la cingada, cabron,* took their oxcarts, and went home, *pronto*.

"With no *vaqueros* on the spread, Darrin started selling livestock for eight bits a head."

"Naw, even he can't be that stupid," Dan roared. "Hell, Richard King's *segundo* told me steers're bringing fifteen, eighteen dollars per at Abilene and Dodge City."

Josh waggled a palm to silence him. "Well, that whiskey's been baptized a mite, son. Almost exactly a year ago, Black Thursday slapped the whey out of Wall Street. Cattlemen weren't scalped as badly as we feared, but it put the knock-knees in a heap of Texas bowlegs for a while.

"No, where your brother truly dug his own

grave was by cozying up to Charley Tremain's son, Neville."

"The same Charley Tremain who owns the bank in San Antonio?" Dan asked, anticipating both Josh's confirmation and the next boot poised to hit the floor.

"Umm-hmm. Behind Charley's back, Sonny Boy helped his best drinkin'-and-whorin' friend Darrin mortgage the Rocking B to the moon. Darrin went through the money like a jack rabbit with a prairie fire at his tail, plowing not a half-dime on the ranch itself."

Dan's lips set in a thin line. "I couldn't tell much from the road when I passed, but enough to see that the place appears deserted."

"Oh, Darrin's living there, all-hat-and-no-cattle-style. That's about all can be said." Josh sidled around his chair and sat down, his nose scant inches from Dan's.

"What's owed against it's twice what it's worth, son. Much as I wanted to buy it and hold it until you came back like you asked me to, I just couldn't afford to borrow against the Bar Double-R to do it."

"I'm glad you didn't," Dan said softly. "The day after I mailed that letter, I sorely regretted asking."

"That's not—"

"Hold on, it's my turn at speechifying. This whole deal's going to work out in the wash better than I expected.

"Sure, paying off that mortgage is bound to

cost me more than I bargained for, but if Charley Tremain's bank's got the place tied up, Darrin can't put the kibosh to me buying him out."

Hoofbeats tattooed a cantering gait on the hard-packed lane. Josh craned his neck to glance out the window. "It's damn well about time he showed up."

"Who?"

"Parker. A lot of good it did telling Benito to point him home. Six bits gets a dollar, that boy was sniffing around Anna Maria Gaspar's petticoats instead of helping dam that arroyo."

Dan grinned. "Your moss-horns are showing, old man. I'd damn sure cut a rusty with a pretty senorita before I'd spend the afternoon hauling dirt out of a hole in a *mecapal*."

If anything, Josh's expression turned more dour. Before Dan could ask why, the cattleman said, "I'm sending Parker to nose around San Antone. Late as it is, he'll have to stay in town tonight and ride back in the morning."

"What do you mean, 'nose around'? Is there a ruckus kicking up that you're not telling me about?"

Josh gripped the cup's handle so tightly his knuckles blanched. "I happened upon Charley Tremaine yesterday when I was picking up some supplies. You know how Charley is—always looks like he just found out his mother-in-law's moving in with him.

"Never saw him so chipper and was compelled to ask why. Said he was on his way to an appointment with an eastern syndicate owner interested in the Rocking B. That if the negotiations progress as he expected, he'd have that millstone off his neck by Monday noon."

Dan slumped in his chair feeling as though his chest were being crushed by a vise. The phrase "a day too late" throbbed in his mind.

Within hours the Rocking B wouldn't be Brannum land anymore. It wouldn't matter a damn to a Yankee syndicate who had cultivated it and defended it with their sweat and blood; nor that they were buried on a knoll overlooking the river valley they'd loved almost as fiercely as their two sons.

Dan's pulse pounded in his ears like a sledgehammer on stone. *I could have been here a month ago, easy, if I hadn't dallied to hell and back chasing after that . . . that woman.*

Chapter Thirty-two

"Consuela outdid herself on these huevos ran-
cheros," Josh said, digging a fork into his spicy,
sauce-smothered fried egg and tortilla. "Made
'em special for you, I'd reckon. She'll be heart-
broken if your dinner plate's not cleaned any
better'n breakfast's was."

Dan stopped pacing midstride to take a sip
of his coffee. Since sunup, he'd stalked back
and forth across the Double Bar-R's front room.

The Regulator pegged twenty past eleven—
three whole minutes later than the last time
he'd glowered at it.

"Damn it, son, wearing a slough in my floor
won't get Parker here any faster."

"I can't help it, Josh. I'm jumpier than a preg-
nant fox in a forest fire."

Dan'd pulled a crick in his neck, jerking his
head toward the window at every real and imag-
ined sound. But . . . hallelujah and praise the
Lord, those hoofbeats weren't phantom cozens.
He spied the dust boiling up behind Parker's
galloping dun mare.

Arms crossed at his chest, Dan was waiting in the yard when the copper-haired, eighteen-year-old hard-reined his horse to a halt.

Ornery showed in every freckle on the boy's face. Dismounting like an express rider, he crowed, "Ain't she a pegger? Buttermilk can stop on a quarter and give fifteen cents change."

"Uh-huh. Ruin her mouth with those shenanigans, and she won't be worth a plug nickel."

"Don't waste your wind, Dan," Josh chimed in from the porch. "Young'un thinks he's got all the answers. Shoot, his ears aren't dry enough to hear the questions yet."

Parker's downy lip buckled at a corner. He'd obviously heard that song before and wasn't fond of the tune. Dan chuckled to himself, allowing that he wasn't so many years removed from that growing uppity stage himself.

"How about it, Parker? I suspect that trip to town stuck a few answers under your hat brim."

"Yep, it did." The boy sighed, averting his cornflower eyes. "She's sold, Dan. A man name of Harry Glasscock paid cash on the barrelhead for the Rocking B. Darrin's supposed to be skedaddled by nightfall. Glasscock's paying him a bonus to take possession so quick."

His chin came up to meet Dan's stony gaze. "It don't please me atall being the one that has to tell you that."

Chucking Parker lightly on the shoulder, Dan

said, "Aw, hell, I never did understand that 'killing the messenger' stuff. I'm beholden to you for doing the scouting for me."

Dan took a sniff, then a second. "Whoo-ee, boy. It appears you hoisted a couple of beers in my honor while you were at it." Smacking his lips, he drawled, "Standing downwind, I can pert-near taste 'em."

His father drawled, "Yeah, well, there's nothing like toting dirt to clear them cobwebs, now is there, Parker?"

"No, Pa," he droned sluggishly.

"And no time like the present to get started, eh?"

"I reckon not, Pa."

"And an extra good day's work just might make me forget to tell your mama *all* that's gone on since she left."

Parker hastened into the saddle as quickly as he'd cranked out of it. He'd paled considerably, his freckles seeming to hover an inch from his face. "Oh, I surely do hope so, Pa."

The younger Reed trotted across the yard, spurring his dun to a canter when he reached open ground.

"Looks like Suki's put the fear of God in ol' Parker," Dan said, laughing.

Josh deadpanned, "Suki could put the fear of God in God when she's riled."

Beyond the scythed circle meeting the rutted lane, a vast, undulating sea of bluestem and wildflowers rippled gently in the breeze. Dan squinted to the east, battling the melancholy that threatened to engulf him. "I will lift up mine eyes unto the hills," he whispered, "from whence cometh my help."

The psalm his mother had so often quoted lent him no comfort. Josh had mentioned the fire in Dan's belly. As if stirred by a poker, those embers glowed orange, flared, and caught flame.

Spinning on one heel, he said, "I'm heading for the Rocking B. There's things that need settling between me and Darrin."

"Let it go, Dan."

"Nope. Can't."

"All right, then, I'm going with you."

"There's no need—"

"Damned if there ain't. Don't know if I'll keep you from killing your brother or help you do it, but I'll stand by you, just like I did your daddy for more'n half my life."

The sight of the Rocking B's overgrown, untended front acreage put steel in Dan's jaw. Tumbledown *corrales de lena* were testament to the maltreated *vaqueros's* lackadaisical construction and absence of maintenance.

But it was the *hacienda's* shutters hanging drunkenly from their hinges, the spavined porch roof, the hundreds of empty liquor bottles and ruptured airtights sprawling across the yard like autumn leaves that clawed at Dan's gut.

He heard Josh mutter, "The son of a bitch."

Slowly, Dan shook his head. He knew a fair-sized complement of cuss words, but they all lacked the teeth to sufficiently villify his older brother.

A two-seater buckboard harnessed to a pair of matched bays waited alongside the porch. With its yellow-enameled spoke wheels and a box pinstriped in red, Dan thought the rig was gaudier than a Bourbon Street whorehouse.

Tethered to a corner post, Cutter, his father's elderly grulla, regarded Dan balefully. Two bulging, leather satchels were lashed behind the saddle's cantle. A blanket-rolled bundle was wedged in front of the pommel.

"It appears that Glasscock jasper beat us here," Josh said. "Must be in a powerful hurry to boot Darrin off the place."

A feral growl rumbled up from Dan's chest. Much as he despised his brother, at least he was a Brannum. Sale or no sale, that buckboard's driver was a low-down, carpetbagging trespasser.

As Dan started for the porch, Josh snared him at the crook of the arm. "Let me go in first, son."

"No," Dan snapped, feeling instantly contrite for his misdirected hatefulness. "Gimme one good reason."

"Because I asked you to."

He hesitated, then stepped back to let the older man by. The plank door trilled open on rusty hinges. Inside, a musty odor, like a dowager's attic, filled Dan's nostrils.

Their boot heels echoed in the cavernous room. Only spectral outlines remained of the furniture, pictures, knickknacks, and books that had once decorated his home.

Voices wafted from the office at the back of the house. Josh hied up on the balls of his feet, gesturing for Dan to follow suit.

"I believe this occasion calls for a toast, don't you?" Darrin slurred. "Here's to Micah and Evangeline Brannum, who had the wisdom to recognize prime Texas cattle land when they saw it, and to Harry Glasscock, who has the financial resources and acumen to make it . . ."

The pompous salutation trailed off when Josh's bulky frame breached the office's threshold. Casually, he anchored a palm against the opposite facing.

Leaning into the sleeved, human railing, Dan was taken aback by Darrin's florid dissipation. A grimy sweat stain jagged his paper collar with fleshy folds wattling above the button. The snifter of amber liquor he held aloft quaked in his grasp.

Dan's eyes flicked downward, riveting on an ungodly straw chapeau adorned by a riot of flowers and peacock feathers. He'd partially glimpsed the gent seated beside her before Darrin purred, "What a surprising, albeit fitting addition to the festivities."

All too vividly, Dan remembered his brother

using that same condescending tone when telling him to move his gear to the bunkhouse or get off *his* ranch. Blind fury washed the entire room in a crimson haze.

"Allow me, if you please, to introduce you to my baby brother . . . Danny boy."

"Goddamnit, lemme at him," Dan roared, struggling to break through Josh's blockade.

The woman swiveled in the chair, her hat's wide brim lofting upward. Full, cherry lips widened into a gloating smile. "Hullo, Dan. How nice to see you again."

Jenna's companion rose and offered his hand. If not for the eyepatch, Dan would never have recognized the grinning, clean-shaven, expensively attired man as Soupbone.

Dan's eyes bored into hers, his icy, venomous hatred so intense it should have seared her very soul. She'd committed the ultimate betrayal: robbing him of his birthright.

Turning stiffly, he strode through the front parlor and out the door.

Chapter Thirty-three

Jenna tugged at Dan's Levi's, her other hand grabbing for the cantle. "You're gonna listen to me," she shouted.

Without looking down, he peeled her fingers off the crumpled denim. Pressing his knees to the fenders, he urged the buckskin into a lope.

Stumbling backward, Jenna wrenched off her hat and bunched her skirt and petticoat in her fists. She sprinted across the drive's grassy center. Thorns shredded her stockings, slicing her skin like razors. Whaleboned corset stays tortured her heaving ribs.

As Dan's horse rounded the bend, it slowed a fraction. Jenna jumped in front of the animal, hollering and waving like a madwoman.

The buckskin whinnied and reared, forelegs churning the air as it did so, the tip of its left hoof uppercut Jenna's chin. She was knocked over from the impact and collapsed into a frothy heap of beige tarlatan, eyelet lace, and white cotton unmentionables.

The next thing she knew, Dan was cradling

her to his chest. He whisked the handkerchief from her cuff and dabbed the corner of her mouth and tender chin. "Crazy, goddamned female," he snarled. "Like to got us both killed."

Tasting the salty blood that oozed from her mangled tongue, she drawled, "Told you, I wanna-ed to talk to you."

His features set as rigid as a statue. Bending her into a sitting position, Dan grasped her upper arm and helped her to her feet.

With a curt tip of his hat, he murmured, "Well, now we've talked. Good day, ma'am."

Jenna punched him hard on the shoulder. "I've had all I'm going to take of your stupid, arrogant, Texas bullheadedness."

"Then after walking out on me in Laketon, you should've stayed gone."

"*Me*? Walk out on *you*?" She knew she was shrieking like a harridan and she didn't care a whit. "You *told* me to leave."

"And you didn't balk an instant, did you?"

"What the . . . I . . . you—"

"Lady, I went from one end of God's green earth to the other looking for you. Wrangel, Victoria, San Francisco, Hay Springs, St. Louis—and where do I find you? Sipping brandy, billin' and cooin' with my son of a bitchin' brother in what used to be my goddamned house."

Circling each other as warily as tomcats, Jenna glimpsed Soupbone, Darrin, and the man that had accompanied Dan lined up posse-style on the porch, watching and eavesdropping on every bitter word.

"I don't bill and coo with anyone—"

"Tell me something I don't know, Missus French."

"Is that why you're so angry? Because I didn't drop my shimmy at the first wink? Hurt your pride, did it?"

Clenching his hands into fists, Dan warned, "You're plowing rocky ground, lady."

"Did you assume if you found me, I'd fairly swoon into your arms *and* your bed?" Her fingers combed the hair from her forehead, wadding the strands into a ball.

"God help me," she murmured, "I probably would have, simply because I love you. Worse, I was stupid enough to think you cared for me."

He snorted, staring out over the rolling hills. "Uh-huh. A passel of muddy water's clearing right fast. This whole shebang's another one of your schemes, ain't it?"

"I don't know what you mean."

"You couldn't keep to the tracks in a handcar, could you? What Jenna wants, Jenna goes after, the snakiest way possible. When I couldn't abide your double-crossing up north, you just set your cap t'other side and hied south."

"Dan, you're not making any sense."

"Oh, yes, I am." He jerked a thumb in the direction of the ranch house. "That lonesome old man'd do anything for you, including swallowing whatever horseshit excuse you connived to buy this place."

"No, that's not it at all," she cried. "We were told that someone else was interested in buying the Rocking B."

"That's pure folly, gal. I know for a fact that Darrin mortgaged it for twice what it's worth."

"I swear to you, Mister Tremain at the bank told us another rancher—a Joshua Reed—had made inquiries. Nobody'd seen you in town, we were afraid your brother'd sell out before you got back—"

"C'mon, Jenna. Even if that's partly true, and I'll credit it is, I can't wait to hear why you had to spruce up like a five-dollar Jezebel, flimflam Soupbone into a catalogue suit, and pass him off as a highfalutin Yankee named—for Christ's sake—*Harry Glasscock*."

The despair and desperation that sent her reeling scant seconds earlier switched in a pulse beat to teeth-gritting hostility. "Because we thought insinuating that we had deep pockets would dissuade the other buyer from trying to compete with us. To do that, we had to dress the part. I assume you've sported more whores on your arm than ladies, but I assure you, my attire is completely appropriate for a woman of my station. And it seems that Soupbone's mother had an odd, if not cruel sense of humor, for Missus Glasscock named her firstborn 'Harry.'"

Dan's snicker blossomed into laughter. "Jaysus, no wonder he goes by Soupbone. His right handle musta got him whomped half to death in the schoolyard."

Jenna's lips curled into a feline smile. "How reassuring to see that you believe something I've said."

"Doesn't matter if I take the whole sermon for gospel," he shot back evenly. "It's the why behind it all."

"Well, you've done such a brilliant job of unraveling the warp thus far, tell me, why *did* I go to so much trouble to get the Rocking B in my deceitful clutches?"

She flinched as that horrid, gut-wrenching hate burned in his eyes again.

"You thought owning this ranch would be the same as owning me. Ain't gonna flatter myself with why you sighted me in. I suspicion it had a lot to do with knowing how it felt to be powerless, and wanting, just once, to hold the sword over somebody else's neck."

"You're wrong, Dan."

"I wish I was. I truly do."

Jenna strode to where her velvet reticule lay in the dusty lane. Shaking so badly its drawstrings almost defeated her, she fumbled for a sheaf of foolscap she'd tucked inside it after leaving Charley Tremain's office. Holding it out to him, she said, "Read this."

He scanned the document's first page. "You really know how to stab a man and wrick the knife, don't you? Take your goddamned deed and—"

"The attachment to the bottom sheet. *Read* it. Aloud."

Dan hurled it to the ground. "Read the sumbitch yourself."

She knelt to retrieve the papers, smoothing the creases against her thigh with the flat of her hand. The knot in her throat muted her raspy, tremulous voice. "On this, the twenty-first day of September, in the year of our Lord eighteen hundred and seventy four, upon acceptance of one dollar as legal consideration, all rights of ownership pertinent to the aforementioned property known commonly as the Rocking B Ranch are hereby transferred from Jenna Wade French and Harry Thaddeus Glasscock and assigned in their entirety . . ."

Jenna paused, raising her eyes to meet his. ". . . to Daniel Marcus Brannum."

His jaw dropped like a stone. "You and Soupbone signed the deed over to me? For a blessed damned dollar? Why?"

"Because the Rocking B is as much a part of you as your bowed legs and brown eyes. I couldn't stand by and let someone take it away from you.

"Because Soupbone yearns for a warm, peaceful place to rest his tired bones. I thought he might find that here.

"And because . . . because I do love you, you stupid, arrogant, bullheaded damned Texan, with all my heart."

Chapter Thirty-four

Jenna awakened languidly, her body nestled against Dan's like spoons in a slotted chest. Sunlight streamed through the *hacienda's* windows, dust motes capering on the beams, glinting gold, silver, and blue.

Rolling over to face him, she murmured in a sultry voice, "I'm told you're from Texas."

That beloved, lopsided grin told her he also remembered the day they met. "That's right, little lady," he drawled. "Born and raised in the San Antonio Valley, if it's particulars you're after."

With a silky touch she caressed the particulars she was most interested in. "Then, you know the cattle trade."

"Um-hmmm." He nuzzled her neck with his lips. "And I do believe you're catching on to the difference between cows and bulls."

Her laughter echoed in the spacious room, furnished only with a pallet and the lovers entwined upon it. "Think so, eh? Well, here's a promise I chose not to make last night in front of Soupbone and Josh and everyone: If you ever speak to me again the way you did yesterday afternoon, I'll show *you* the difference between a bull and a steer."

He kissed the purpled welt on her chin. "Seems to me, after the fracas died down, everything smoothed out righter'n rain, didn't it?"

"Well, not quite everything."

"You love me, don't you?"

"Yep."

"And you know I love you, don't you?"

Wondrously aroused by the boldness Dan had not only allowed but encouraged, she cackled, "No doubt about it."

"Then, what's the hitch, darlin' gal?"

She waggled an accusatory finger under his nose. "I'll have you know, Mister Brannum, you *still* haven't paid back the dollar you owe me for the deed to this place."

Pulling her tightly to his chest, he growled. "Ever heard of taking a debt out in trade . . . Missus Brannum?"

Author's Note

By early 1874, news of enormous gold strikes near Dease Lake in British Columbia had swelled the trickle of prospectors to a veritable "yellow-fevered" stampede.

Captain William Moore, a renowned Stikine riverboat owner/operator, was turning a respectable profit by ferrying gold miners and supplies between Wrangle, Alaska Territory and Glenora, British Columbia, but quickly realized that constructing a tollway trail between the river port town and the gold fields would pay for itself many times over.

When government inspectors declared Moore's trail suitable for travel, he was given permission to collect two cents a pound toll for freight, fifty cents per head for horses and cattle, and twelve and a half cents per sheep.

Between Moore's fleet of steamboats and his control of the only cleared route between Telegraph Creek and the Dease Lake area, hardly man nor beast could reach the Canadian version of El Dorado without lining Moore's pockets. The enterprising captain did not, however, hold the monopoly on profit-doubling entrepreneurship.

Another gent known only as Dooley divined that since the going rate for transporting freight from Glenora to Dease Lake was about half-again the per-pound price of fresh beef, a fortune could be made simply by using slaughter cattle as pack animals.

Consequently, Dooley lashed three hundred pounds of much needed high-priced supplies to each of his twenty-six head of beef cattle, which he'd had shipped from Puget Sound.

Although the distance between Glenora and the gold fields was only approximately a hundred and sixty miles, British Columbia's mountainous, heavily forested terrain, snowmelt swollen rivers banked by incredibly deep gorges, and lowland swamps where mosquitoes swarmed like buzzing, black blizzards had already defeated countless men and pack animals alike.

According to an excerpt from explorer Dr. Alfred Pearce Dennis's account of his travels in the region, "The gaunt and wasted carcasses of dead horses and dogs by the wayside told the story of overwork and of exhausted food supplies."

Dennis also described the natives' attitude toward the treasure-hunting invasion: "The sudden irruption [sic] into the solitudes of a far country of hundreds of swarthy men with horses, bullocks, goats, dogs, and impediments by the ton, amused the simple natives in much the same way as children are pleased at the antics of a menagerie of performing animals.

"All day long the bucks, wrapped in Hudson's Bay Company blankets, sat stolidly upon piles of lodge-poles on the bank, absorbed in the contemplation of the busy scenes on the river. They were amazed at the prodigious quantity of supplies; they marveled at the energy which had braved the snows of the river, but all shook their heads discouragingly at the prospect of taking the heavy outfits over the mountain trail into the interior."

Despite the travail Dooley surely encountered en route to Laketon, a miner's camp-cum-boomtown on the banks of Dease Lake, he accomplished what most had dismissed as impossible: the driving of a cattle herd—encumbered or not—across the Canadian wilderness.

A hundred and twenty years after the fact, reading a scant reference to Dooleys' feat inspired *Deliverance Drive*, a wholly novelized version of that historic cattle drive.

It's impossible to explain how a paragraph-long mention of Dooley's deed could evolve into the story of a con man's widow, a transplanted Texan, a she-bear-sized prostitute, and a one-eyed cook herding sixty-five steers to the same destination.

The best answer, perhaps, is one a child would give if asked how a baseball got thrown through a neighbor's living room window.

"I dunno," he'd likely reply. "It just did."

Be sure to read
Suzann Ledbetter's next book,
Colorado Reverie,
coming soon
from Signet Books.

Sam Weingarten tossed his busted straight on the table. "Dianna, I'll swan, I'd rather lose to you than win with anyone else."

She winked at the grizzled prospector as she swept the pile of coins across the table. "In that case, why not donate your poke when you come through the door and save me several hours' work?"

"Mought as well, Samuel," his partner, Enoch Blevins piped up. "Ye canna draw a hand with a pencil tonight, and that's a fact."

"Oh, yeah? And where might I ask, ol' sot, is your blinkin' fortune?"

Enoch's eyes twinkled like star sapphires. " 'Tis in Miss Dianna's reticule, a'course, where it belongs."

She laughed with the tattered reprobates whom she'd secretly dubbed her Friday Night Favorites. "If I didn't know you shared in one of Central City's richest lodes, fat tears would surely course down my cheeks."

Sam winged his arms behind his neck and

arched backward in the chair. Slat ribs corduroyed the nap of his flannel shirt. "Must be gettin' late," he moaned, "or I'm gettin' old."

"Glory, it's not yet midnight," Dianna protested, stacking the chips in neat silos. "And the vineyard's not picked clean."

Enoch's chair scraped the rough-hewn floorboards. "Ye're nowt sa greedy as to begridge us a wee libation afore the day's full spent, are ye?"

"Promise next Friday to me, and I won't."

Extending his hand to clasp hers, Sam brushed her knuckles with his lips. "We'll be here if we have to walk the miles on our knees."

Dianna smiled sincerely. "I'll be wait—"

"May I avail myself, Miss Redieu?" a familiar nasal voice inquired.

Palmer Watts laid claim to the back of the chair Enoch had vacated. Apparently, he thought his smarmy grin was veritably swoon-inducing.

"Me and Enoch's gonna tarry a spell at the bar," Sam stressed as the partners sauntered across the room.

Dianna addressed the new arrival in the iciest of tones. "Your privilege, Mister Watts."

Opening his coat by its lapel brought a handkerchief unfurling from an inner pocket. He bent at the waist and dusted the seat with comic vigor before planting his posterior upon it.

He leaned back stiffly and regarded her in an

oddly pigeon-like manner. "I find you a challenging woman, Miss Redieu, and rather handsome, after a fashion. Will you partake of a late supper with me this evening?"

"No."

He blinked in disbelief. "Is there any particular reason why not?"

"Because I'm a lady gambler, Mister Watts. I'm not, nor will I allow myself to be, nothing more than a trophy."

For an instant, his eyes dulled like one overdue for a dose of laudenum. "So be it." He placed a cowhide pouch on the table. "Do you deal as straight as you talk?"

"I pride myself on it."

"Then what a rare opportunity this shall be," he said, emptying the poke in front of him. "Most who handle the pasteboards are cheats of the first rank."

Her lips set in a grim line. She splayed her fingers the way a cat extends its claws as it yawns itself awake.

Praying for another joe or three to join them, which wasn't likely, due to Watts' reputation as Governor Gilpin's toady, she quickly glanced at the silver and gold puddle of coins corralled by his forearms.

Actions speak louder than words, she mused. A man should never gamble when he's so obviously afraid to lose. Besides, it takes all the fun out of running a bluff.

"Pure poker's the game, Mister Watts."

"I'd prefer jacks or better."

"As would I, but it's no contest for two players. If you'd be kind enough to poll the bar for others of the sporting persuasion, your will be done."

He peered over his shoulder and turned back. "No, go ahead, Miss Redieu. Pure poker, it is."

"Called hands must be shown, losers or not," she said with a sigh. "Ties split the pot, unless the queen of diamonds appears."

"I've closely observed your style, thus familiarized myself with your quaint little rules."

The haughty simper he'd adopted vanished when she replied, "Really? I hadn't noticed your frequenting the Auraria."

Matching his ante, she shuffled the cards with the aloof dexterity of a professional. The deck slapped the oak table, inviting Watts' cut.

He bobbled it, a few cards skittering off the top of the section nearest him. "Sorry," he muttered, but had the audacity to watch intently for trickery when she melded the stacks.

Beginning with Watts and alternating the pitch, as Dianna dealt, the lines and scrollwork decorating the cards' backsides blurred to solid blue.

Watts tight-fanned his five Linens, clutching them so close to his chest he had to crimp his neck to examine them.

Dianna assessed her own potential: the trey, nine, and jack of clubs; in poker parlance, a monkey flush. With a four of diamonds and six of spades completing it, her hand was nigh worthless.

The odds of drawing two clubs to fill the flush were one in twenty-four. Of being gifted by a deuce and five of any suit to stretch the three, four, and six into a straight? Approximately equal to the Auraria Club's catching fire and relieving her of Watts' company.

The option of keeping the higher valued cards, discarding the rest and getting another jack or nine, a different pair, or three-of-a-kind were one-in-five and one-in-nine, respectively.

"I'll go four bits," Watts stated. A half-dollar clinked against the ante.

"Call."

Prying discards from their supposed betters, he said, "Two, please, milady."

She complied, simultaneously weighing his prospects. By his draw, Watts either held triplets, a monkey flush, or three-to-a-straight.

Smart money presumed the best as the hand to beat, so with triplets, chances were one-in-fifteen of his landing a pair to make a full house; one-in-twenty-four of improving to four-of-a-kind.

Pairing both her jack and nine wouldn't beat his triplets. Even if she drew three-of-a-kind, his trips might well outrank hers.

"Dealer takes two," she decided. The odds of making her flush weren't good, but if she did, it'd take a full house to beat her.

An awareness of Theodosia and his woozy,

clinker-happy accompanists distracted her. Adjacent shouts of "Buck that tiger, Jed," and "Damn it all, I'm caught in hock" beckoned like shade mocks a sweat-drenched farmer.

A perfunctory look at her hand inspired a second. Five clubs, anchored by the ace and four threatened the gambler's famous, inscrutable expression.

"Four bits," her opponent challenged.

"Call, and raise back."

"You do?" The tip of his tongue lodged behind his dingy incisors. He uprooted several coins, palmed them, and meted each between thumb and index finger as a clerk dispenses change to a customer. "Call, and come back."

At this rate, I'll clean him slick in another hand, Dianna crowed to herself. "Call."

"Full house," Watts exhaled, fanning his cards. "Eights and kings."

She locked her jaw to prevent gaping at a miracle worthy of biblical mention. Alarm bells sounded in her mind. Odds be damned. For both their hands to improve to that degree required Divine Intervention and her opponent was no Moses.

"Congratulations, Mister Watts." She displayed her club flush with the dignity it deserved. "Collect your stake and the deal with it."

"God Almighty, I've got into a square game at last," he smirked. "I'd have side-bet anything you'd pull up fours, at least."

"My, what a gracious winner you are, sir."

An hour later, Dianna was down over a hundred dollars. Thanks to earlier victories against young Jimmy McNassar and his swaggering friends, the Hayden brothers, Sam, and Enoch, she was still ahead for the night overall, so it wasn't the loss that rankled her. It was the principle of it.

Watts was cheating. He was adept at it, she'd give him that, but by actual count, he'd held fourteen paired or triplet eights. Worse, with every win, he trilled, "A fellow can't lose when the game's a square one."

She seriously considered catching him in the act. As surely as she knew her name, a fistful of Linens stashed to sweeten a hand as needed would fall like autumn leaves with a smart shake of his coat.

Concern that Watts' public denouement might backfire against Jotham Huxtable gave her pause.

"You look a bit weary, Miss Redieu," Watts observed, then chuckled. "Beyond the hours spent here at the Auraria, do you devote many to practicing your, uh, skills?"

"Actually no, I—"

"Well, if this evening's any example, perhaps you should in the future."

A searing heat suffused her from heels to head. *Why, you cocky, conniving, little bastard,* she seethed. *I was seconds from declaring the* table closed and allowing you to simply totter off with your ill-gotten gains.

Raising an arm, she waved toward the bar. "Zeus," she called, her fury disguised by a melodic lilt. "Bring me a glass of cold water, would you please?"

The towering Negro's eyes flicked from Dianna to her opponent. "Glad to, Miss Dianna. Be right there."

Watts dealt and won another pot while she awaited service from the bar.

Zeus lumbered over, his expansive hand supporting a wooden tray upon which reposed a stemmed crystal goblet brimming with water. He bowed as formally as a monarch, the tray descending with the gesture.

Its edge bumped the tabletop. The top-heavy glass tipped on its base. Dianna whisked the requested "cold" deck from Zeus' concealed palm. Droplets of water splattered her rose taffeta dress.

The mixologist gasped as he righted the conveyance. "Lord have mercy, I done ruint your pretty gown, Miss Dianna."

He whipped a rag off his arm and dabbled at the specks. "I'm so sorry—"

"No need to fret." She lifted the goblet from the tray. "Thank you kindly for the refreshment."

Watts glared at the humble giant as he departed the table. From near the second floor stairway, Jotham Huxtable bellowed, "Zeus!"

Human nature being the soul of dependability meant all eyes, including Watts', averted to the white-suited Kentucky gentleman. Dianna switched the shuffled deck resting on the table with the one in her lap.

"I didn't hear you apologize to the lady, boy."

Attention reverted to Dianna. She waved a hand dismissively. "Well, he did, Colonel, most graciously. I'll thank you to tend to your own knitting."

Laughter rumbled the length of the room as patrons returned to their own pursuits.

"Clumsy nigger," Watts muttered. "Shouldn't have tried putting on airs."

Dianna pitched the pre-stacked hands in her customary fashion. As Watts picked up each pasteboard, a jaw muscle twitched spasmodically—not an unusual reaction for one blessed to receive four queens and a ten-spot.

Leaving her certain four kings and a trey kicker face-down where they fell, she took a dainty sip from the goblet. She then gasped, "Well, I *am* a dunce, Mister Watts. I must declare a misdeal."

"Wha-what?" His feral features sagged as if he were breathing his last. "I don't understand . . ."

Dianna set the glass down and tapped the table's bare center with a fingertip. "In the commotion, I failed to call for an ante."

Covering her mouth, she yawned theatrically. "Oh, pardon me." She waggled her head. "And

I am terribly tired. Rather than reshuffle, maybe it's best we just call it a night."

Her opponent appeared to be verging on apoplexy. "If you're agreeable, we might as well play this for the last hand."

"But sir, there's no ante to play for." Presenting a bovine demeanor almost brought a fit of giggles.

"It's a friendly game, isn't it, between the two of us?" he wheedled. "Let's go sky's the limit, ante and all. Have some fun before the band plays 'Good Night, Ladies.' "

"If you're positive that's the way you want it, Mister Watts."

"Absolutely. And to prove it ... what the he—devil, I'll ante up twenty-five dollars."

"Glory, you are quite the gambler. Done."

"And I'll wager another—"

"Please, Mister Watts. I haven't even glanced at my cards yet."

Allowing him to squirm a full minute, Dianna raised her eyes to his, signalling him to proceed with his bet.

"Ten dollars, Miss Redieu."

"After such a reckless ante? I'll call, and raise back twenty."

"Call. No, wait—" he peeked at his holdings—"another ten."

"Call."

Dianna noticed the hair at his temples darkening with sweat. "Will you draw or stand pat, Mister Watts?"

Again, he examined his cards intently. The pasteboard on the outside skimmed across the table. "One card."

She complied, improving his hand with an ace of spades, though any gypsy worth her salt could tell him the card represented festering evil.

"One for me, as well," she said, trading the lowly trey for a jack of hearts. To fanciers of cartomancy, its position beside a king translated as protection.

"It'll take twenty dollars to stay," Watts challenged gruffly.

Dianna matched it without hesitation. "Call, and raise back, twenty-five."

He glared at her venomously. "Are you trying to buy the pot, Miss Redieu?"

"As I recall, *you* suggested sky's-the-limit."

"You drew only one card."

"The same as you, Mister Watts."

"Calling your bet'll break me."

"Then don't. Fold your cards and leave a few dollars richer than when you arrived. The choice is yours."

Shoving his remaining coins toward the center, he all but yelled, "Call, damn you."

His four queens and an ace fluttered atop the heaping booty.

"A fine hand, Mister Watts."

"Can you best it?"

"For the first time since we began play, I do

believe I have the winner." She ruffed her four kings.

Watts knuckled the table and leaped upward from the chair. "You double-dealing bi—"

"Don't finish the expletive, sir. Don't make a move to harm me, or I'll see to it you're relieved of those hold-outs and with them, your stellar reputation. I doubt if your beloved William Gilpin wants a penny-ante cheat in his cabinet."

He blanched, the menace dissipating like steam from a kettle removed from the flame. Without a word, he stood and started for the door, then whirled to snatch a Liberty dollar from the pot.

"That's for the queen of diamonds," he snarled, and stalked away.

Dianna gathered the coins into a kerchief borrowed from a neighboring gambler. To her, Watts' money seemed tainted and dirty.

Smiling as she knotted the cloth's corners, she mused: *but won't the Widows and Orphans Benevolent Society be thrilled to find this windfall in their donation box tomorrow morning?*

Creasing the paper carefully, he tucked it into his mackintosh's pocket. Behind him, with their bellies full of fodder and good water, the herd was bedded as peacefully as suckling lambs.

General Sherman and a few of his sod-pawing lieutenants hadn't taken kindly to the jerry-rigged, pack rope corral Dan had strung, but they'd been more bellow than brawl.

He was about to stretch out under his blanket when he heard the footsteps he'd been expecting since supper. Though he knew even a loaded shotgun wouldn't slow his caller a step, he aimed a fierce scowl in that direction.

So much for the power of prayer. Just like poor old Adam, God ain't shining any mercy on me, either, he thought.

"I brought you some coffee," Jenna said, proffering a tin cup.

"Well, that's right kind of you, ma'am, considering you've been looking at me cockeyed and pickle-pussed since dawn."

Mindful of her own cup, she sat down, arranging her legs Indian-style. It appeared she was settling in for a long siege.

Dan groaned inwardly, yet couldn't help noticing the waning light's bewitching effect on her fine-boned features. The justice she did to a flannel shirt and Levi's could make a man forget three or four of the Ten Commandments.

"I've got questions, Dan, and won't take your guff for answers."

"Guff, eh? Well, it works both ways, little lady. Don't start by dishing it out."

"All right." She regarded him haughtily, like a house cat roosting on a sunny windowsill. "Why'd we have to lose a steer before you'd do any kind of night herding—if that's what dragging your bedroll out here is supposed to be."

"A couple of days ago, you didn't know a fat cow from a poor bull. How'd you get wise to night herding?"

"What differnce does it make?"

Dan struggled to keep the lid on his temper. "A big one if you and the others are joining up against me. Damned if I'll wrestle steers and the greeners driving 'em, too."

"There's hardly a mutiny afoot," she said, sneering. "I was raised on a farm, and I can read, Mister Brannum. There's a wealth of knowledge to be found in a library."

"Books? What kind of—" A notion struck him, and he didn't know whether to laugh or cuss like sixty. "Jesus God and Mary Magdelene, once upon a time you stuck your nose in a stack of dime novels and come out a cowhand."

Judging by her kicked puppy expression, he'd struck pay dirt. "I reckon if you read Ned Buntline's sea stories, you'd join up with the navy, next." He chortled, then burst out laughing.

Jenna's eyes narrowed to slits, and she planted a fist on one knee. "I'll have you know, they were true adventures. It said so right on their covers."

"Uh-huh. And most of 'em's written by Yankee toffs that's never been west of the Hudson River."

He hesitated, not really wanting to make her feel foolish, but wanting desperately to make a point. "If you don't believe me, ask Soupbone about them gold hunter's guidebooks you'll find in every tinhorn's rucksack. They're supposed to be pure fact, but there ain't a lick of truth in any of them."

"Well," she huffed, tossing her head, "I didn't come here for a literary discussion. As I recall, night herding and shooting that steer was the original subject."

Dan flipped his coffee dregs into the darkness, then leaned over to bang the empty cup down near his tormentor. He was stalling and could tell that Jenna knew it.

"With only four horses, there's no way we can guard them beeves proper," he began. "They're pretty fair mounts—Blackie especially—but they can't bear saddles all day and half the night, too."

"I understand that, only why didn't you rope the herd in before? Bad enough you had to put that steer down, but I hate how it must have suffered."

"You think I don't?" Dan replied evenly. "It was my mistake and I already owned up to it. And don't count on that line coralling them for long, either. They'll bust it easy as twine if they've a mind to."

Those gorgeous, dark sloe eyes averted to her boot tips. Fingers traced a split above one sole.

He hadn't noticed before, but by their size, those box-toed, custom-mades must have belonged to her husband. Either they were stuffed with paper, or she was wearing three pair of socks to keep them on.

That she'd had to settle for hand-me-downs irked him. He'd bet a month's pay that hooligan never once bought her a new dress, or even a hair ribbon.

"Is there a chance we'll lose them all before we get where we're going?" she asked, her voice almost a whisper.

"Sure there is. There's no guarantee us two-legged critters'll make it either."

Dan cogitated a moment, studying the anxiety he saw as clearly as the tiny mole on her cheek. "Partner, I'm no dime novel hero, but I'm as bad in need of hard coin as you are. I didn't sign on to collect forty percent of nothing when we're done."

"Why did you, then? In fact, how'd a born-and-bred Texan wind up here in British Columbia?"

None of your dad-blamed business, he wanted to say, but on second thought, he realized that soul baring might be the best way to gain her trust.

"Well, it's like this," he drawled, wishing he'd